The 1.

And in good time, a R   the nation together in peace. Male and Female alike. Each equal to the other. For the Redeemer shall be the One and the Both. Sister and Brother. Husband and Wife. Mother and Father to the coming race.

Childe Rolande

SAMANTHA LEE

Futura

AN ORBIT BOOK

Copyright © Samantha Lee 1988

First published in Great Britain in 1989 by
Futura Publications, a Division of
Macdonald & Co (Publishers) Ltd
London & Sydney

ISBN 0 7088 8323 0
Typeset, printed and bound in Great Britain by
BPCC Hazell Books Ltd
Member of BPCC Ltd
Aylesbury, Bucks, England

For David . . .
to whom I should have had the sense to hang on.

Futura Publications
A Division of
Macdonald & Co (Publishers) Ltd
66–73 Shoe Lane
London EC4P 4AB
A member of Maxwell Pergamon Publishing Corporation plc

The Prophecy

And in good time, a Redeemer shall arise to bind the nation together in peace. Male and Female alike. Each equal to the other. For the Redeemer shall be the One and the Both. Sister and Brother. Husband and Wife. Mother and Father to the coming race.

Prologue

I AM FATIGUED.

The clouds, bleak as shadows, hang over the grey hills and threaten rain.

Soon it will be time for my nap.

Time hangs heavy now that the birth draws near. I am unwieldy and uncomfortable and can no longer ride or hunt or do anything much at all.

In the morning I hear petitions of course – or the three of us do – but Morangy insists that I rest in the afternoons.

Morangy has become an old fuss-pot. I tell him I am as strong as a horse, but he watches me like a forktail all the same. I am a precedent, he says, and he cannot take the chance that something might go amiss as it did with my mother.

McCloed is busy most of the time but Ymer has been a tower of strength, massaging my back, playing the harpsichord, singing and telling me stories, taking my mind off my aching breasts and my swollen belly.

She it was who suggested that I write this history down – to pass the time – so that those who are to come might know the truth. Things aye become distorted when they are handed on by word of mouth. Writing a thing captures the moment as a fly is caught in amber.

Ymer has been a great help too in filling in the bits I didn't see, or couldn't know. Her childhood in the Inner Sanctum, for instance. Holy ground. Untrod by the likes of me.

My first nine years were spent in basic survival and complete freedom. Ymer, on the other hand, spent hers in indolent luxury, pampered and cosseted, yet trapped, secure as a bird in a golded cage. Young ladies of the Royal Household were seldom permitted to leave the confines of the Castle and Ymer says the

7

principal memory she has of childhood is the perpetual boredom. If it hadn't been for Buchan, she says, she would have gone as mad as Fergael.

I was the lucky one. The days were never long enough for me. So much to do. So much to learn. So much to see.

Poor Ymer . . . Poor Buchan.

Buchan was Ymer's plaything. She kept him on a leash and he slept on a cushion at the bottom of her bed. They were very close in age with only a moon's phase between them, but whereas Ymer's birth had been accompanied by rejoicing, Buchan's had been a source of shame to his Initiate mother.

Campbell was my mother's contemporary and, like her, Handmaiden to The Source. After the birthing she returned to her duties in the sure and certain knowledge that the Godhead had found her displeasing. Why else should she have borne a son? A useless, good for nothing man-childe? She flung herself into penance with a ferocity bordering on desperation, starving and flagellating herself, with Fergael's encouragement, until she became as thin and bitter as the High Priest herself.

All this left her scant time for Buchan – she spurned the childe as the Maxwell spurned Ymer. Natural then that they should grow over fond of one another.

Buchan doted on my sister. She was the only person in his world who showed him any mind. He followed her slavishly wherever she went, happy to let her heap him with any indignity in return for an occasional kind word.

My sister has a cruel streak to her, but she treated Buchan only as she was conditioned to treat him – like something less than human.

She was very fond of him in her own shallow, selfish way, stroking and fondling him, plaiting his hair and feeding him with her fingers. But if she was out of sorts, Buchan was the one who suffered. She would pinch and slap him and make him do without his supper and he, poor bairn, not knowing why he was being punished, would suffer agonies of rejection until he was back in her favour.

Children can be gae cruel – especially when one is set in power over the other.

Adults are no different.

I must remind myself of that should I get too big for my boots.

From the time that she could walk, Ymer was taken daily

for Instruction by the Handmaidens of the Godhead. Her training was particularly rigorous since she was to succeed Fergael.

She was taught to despise men as inferior and encouraged to observe the Initiates at their love-play. She was also taught to masturbate so that she might give herself pleasure until such time as she was old enough to take a mate.

This was not normally done until after the blood ceremony but Ymer says there were plenty, even then, anxious to insinuate themselves into the graces – and bed – of the future High Priest.

By the time she was eight years old Ymer was mistress of most love techniques, knew how to give pleasure and receive it. She always had a sense of the erotic and she took to her instruction as a duck takes to water. Her sexuality is open and honest, without inhibition.

She is still a sensual and accomplished lover, which is why, when she comes to soothe my backache and oil my oversize belly, the purely medicinal session frequently turns into something else entirely.

Intercourse between the sexes was completely taboo in those days but Ymer was never one to stick to the rules. The day that Fergael initiated her into the art of masturbation Ymer promptly went back and held her own initiation ceremony – with Buchan – under the bed. Thereafter they were inseparable and continued their love-games until the fatal day when Fergael caught them in the act.

How they got away with it for so long remains a mystery.

Ymer insists that they were very careful, never touching in front of others and always finding a safe hideaway for their experiments no matter how urgent their impulses.

Ymer learned early that the punishments for deviation were severe. Death for the boy. Clitoral circumcision and permanent disgrace for the girl.

That they defied these strictures says something for my sister's sex-drive and for the devotion of her loyal plaything who, in the end, payed the ultimate price for their pleasures.

I can understand Buchan being besotted with Ymer.

I am besotted with her myself.

She is a beautiful creature, her skin soft as whipped cream, her breasts full, her hips firm. She has hair like jet and green eyes arched by raven's wing brows and fringed in long, spider-leg lashes.

As for her mouth – it is as accomplished as it is expressive.

She has a tongue to coax an erection from a three day dead corpse. Her imagination is formidable. She has never ceased to excite me and I doubt she ever will. She is my twin, my mirror image.

Once, in a book, I read a passage where a young woman — Cathy by name — declared her undying love for a gypsy boy . . .

'I *am* Heathcliffe,' she said.

And so it is with Ymer and myself. We are one — as I am one. And both — as I am both.

She was taught early to love woman, and loved men by inclination. And so her love encompasses every facet of my sexuality.

It is not so with McCloed. But he is learning. With help he will lay those last ghosts of prejudice and learn that love has many faces.

The world must learn that if we are to escape the eternal power struggle that has dogged our history. And since Alba is now in such a state of flux, none knowing for certain which way the world will turn, I suppose I maun set down the historical facts before the past becomes overlaid by the future.

The structure of Society during our youth had been built up over many centuries since the Fall. It was rigorously guarded and jealously maintained. Man had no place in the scheme of things, being held responsible for the world's ills. Woman only was thought to be the world's salvation.

At the top of the pyramid sat the Lady Maxwell, with, one step below, Fergael the Black, titular consort to the Monarch, Representative of the Great Mother and Commandant of the dreaded Secret Police.

The Maxwell dominated all Alba and tried to rule wisely and well. That she did not always succeed was not the fault of her personality, which was kind, if inclined to melancholy, but lay in the basic lie on which the society was founded . . . inequality of the sexes.

Fergael represented everything that was evil in the concept. She controlled the minds and beliefs of all Alba from her Dark Tower and fear of her power was widespread. Her word was law in the priesthood and her displeasure punishable by death in its most hideous forms. Her natural cruelty had been kept in check during her marriage to the Queen, but after it ended, malice became her dominant trait. All Alba was terrified of her wrath and that terror permeated the Inner Sanctum like the stench of a rotting corpse.

The High Priest was attended by a retinue of Sister-Priests, each of whom had a responsibility to train a half-dozen Initiates. These, if they did not inherit a place in the Inner Circle, would eventually go forth to the hinterland to take up positions in the various outposts. Although important in maintaining the *status quo*, in that they provided the court with a vital intelligence network, still to be an 'Outlyer' was considered a fate worse than death and places in the Circle were much coveted. Should a Handmaiden falter, there was always a young Initiate eager to transplant her. The atmosphere was one of paranoia laced with an unhealthy dose of moon-mad hysteria. Fergael encouraged spying and tale-telling so that even paramours could not trust one another.

Fergael herself chose her lovers for their ability to stand pain . . . Buchan's mother was such a one. Their union lasted longer than most but when the unfortunate Campbell was eventually cast aside it was without hope of ever finding another mate. Fergael had marked her mind and body to the point where the only sentiments she excited were pity and disgust.

Is it any wonder then that my lovely sister, Ymer, sometimes sinks into black despair? When one considers the evil and the poison that she breathed during her formative years, it is a miracle that she has any faith at all in the future of the human race.

The other sections of society spearheaded from Castle Ballater were the Army, overseen by the ubiquitous Cameron (whom the Queen called Locheil) and the Medical Services – officially organized by the Medic Aurora (but in reality under the auspices of Morangy). The crack force were the Clanswomen, the Maxwell's private guard.

Elsewhere, each settlement had its own platoon of Police-force Militia overseen by a Captain who was answerable only to the Outlyer and who had the power of life and death over all civilians in her area. All major landowners were women. Men did the unpleasant, the menial, the uncomfortable jobs. Tax-collecting, garbage disposal, animal slaughter. They also kept house. The medics, surgeons, anaesthetists, were all female, orderlies and eunuchs, male. Teachers nationwide were women too, as were artists, writers, musicians, in short all the creative section of the population. Men were considered too ignorant, ignoble or insensitive for any of these professions. Occasionally

11

one would find a castrati who danced well or could weave or play the pipes but they were the exception rather than the rule.

This then was the class structure in which Ymer was raised, secure in the knowledge that she would some day stand second in the land only to the Maxwell.

She was not to know that by the time she came to such a position the world with which she was so familiar would have changed beyond all recognition. For under the evident stability brought on by generations of female supremacy, the foundations of Alba were crumbling. In the High Hills the Wildemen were massing and freaks of nature, the result of chronic in-breeding, had become almost the exception rather than the rule. More and more breed-beasts were found to be infertile. The sperm banks were running low. Corruption and moral decay were widespread. In short, Alba was ripe for revolution.

But I am getting ahead of myself . . . 'Begin at the beginning', was Ymer's advice.

Here comes Ymer now. I can hear her light footfall in the hall and the sweet sound of her voice as she hums one of my favourite airs.

I must finish this for the moment and prepare to greet her. It will be good to see her, to feel her soft hands caress my body, smell her dark hair as it falls across my face.

My sister, my love, my dove, thy breasts are like twin hearts . . .

Now where did I read that?

No matter.

Ymer is here. And perhaps it is only co-incidence but already the veil of clouds is lifting from the ridges and the sun is pushing through.

I feel better already.

If only this damn childe of ours wouldn't kick so much.

THE TRUE CHRONICLES OF THE REDEEMER

And it came to pass, in the last days of the Maxwell, when women ruled and men were counted beasts, that the Lady Ymer, paramour to the Queen, was delivered of twins. It was a virgin birth, for the Lady had not known man, and one infant was a girlchilde while the other was a magical being, a chimera haloed in light and carrying in its eyes the wisdom of all ages. And the Lady Ymer died in childbirth. And blood covered the moon.

Chapter
1

THEY HAD THE HEAVIEST FALL OF SNOW IN A LIFESPAN, THE night that I was born.

Midwinter in Alba is harsh at the best of times but this was beyond remembering. Whole herds of deer disappeared under the white blanket and ice on the river Dee backed up almost to its source.

The normal privations of the cold season were worse than ever that year. Thousands died. The old. The weak. Many children. More babies.

But I, at least, survived to tell the tale.

They say a darkness covered the moon that night, eclipsing all light from the almost day-bright northern sky. But that may just be an old gossip's tale. I have lost count of the tales old gossips have spun around me since. I try to discourage them, but there, the old aye need something to gossip about.

My mother, Ymer, did not survive the birthing. Even with the help of Morangy, the greatest Midwife-Healer that Alba has ever known, she could not hold up through the rigours of childbirth. She was so young – barely sixteen – and so slight, with hips too narrow to allow the passage of the head. Which was why Morangy had to resort to the procedure, although by the time the Lady Maxwell gave her permission to make the cut things had gone too far. My mother's system was too weakened for her body to withstand the shock of the knife. Her heart failed and she died, poor Childe, almost before she had begun to live.

I am not one of those who believe that Fergael killed my mother with the evil eye. I try to deter such thinking. It is not healthy, this belief in the supernatural and the second sight, though it was prophesied that I should come – and here I am.

But superstitions die hard and the rumour that Fergael put a hex on Ymer has persisted to the present day.

Certainly the High Priest of the Moon Goddess had plenty for which to hate the girl. My mother had transplanted Fergael in the Queen's bed. Worse, she had done what that black hag could never do – conceived a childe of the union. Or two children. For I am one of twins.

My sister Ymer was born first and her arrival was greeted with joy by the waiting court. A girlchilde, unblemished, a virgin birth and a cause for celebration.

Fergael, who had been pacing outside the birthchamber for the entire two days and nights that my mother had been in labour, took the baby in triumph to the Lady Maxwell.

But the Queen was not interested in the childe – only in the wellbeing of her paramour. When told of the death, she took to her bed.

'You said this would be the One,' she accused her High Priest. 'Merciful Heavens, how tired I am.'

'The portents were ill defined, Majesty,' countered Fergael. 'It would appear I misinterpreted them. But we must give thanks to the Source that the offspring was, at least, not a male but a fine girlchilde, an heir for the antlered throne. A cause for rejoicing.'

'Take her from me,' said the Maxwell. 'And leave me be. I hate the very sight of the bairn.'

No room in her heart, no crumb of affection, for the tiny helpless creature that had been torn from the still-warm corpse of her beloved Ymer. She gave over the baby to Fergael the Black to raise in the Priesthood and issued instructions that she should not set eyes on the Childe again until the official three-year mourning period was past.

It was hard for Ymer. The Maxwell never forgave her for killing our mother. Perhaps that was why she gave herself so freely later on, to try to regain a little of that love she was denied in childhood.

Still, for all the Queen's despair, the rest of the court delighted in Ymer's birth. The arrival of a girlchilde was always a cause for rejoicing. And this was a Royal girlchilde, her blood-mother an initiate of the Moon Goddess, her Clan-mother that Goddess's living incarnation on earth, the Lady Maxwell, Warleader, Virgin, Ruler of all the tribes of Alba.

They cleaned the baby and swaddled her and wrapped her

in the softest furs. Then they placed her in the waiting crib and gave thanks to the Goddess in an orgy of self-indulgence.

A Childe of the Blood Royal.

Not even the bitterness of the night could dampen the spirits of the Inner Circle. Nor the fact that the Queen refused to join the celebrations. Even the knowledge that my poor, dead mother lay with her life-blood drying on her mutilated body spoiled the party not one whit.

The feasting went 'til dawn.

A whole pig was roasted and there was jugged hare and venison pasties and fresh salmon from the inland lake, sugared oranges and Dundee cake and athol brose.

A great deal of whiskey was consumed and more ale (to whet the baby's head) so that by the time the sun rose over the Grampians there was hardly a person sober in the whole of Castle Ballater. Except for the Lady Maxwell, who had locked her rooms against the revelry and lay in her lonely bed weeping away her loss.

Morangy was sober too.

Out of deference and regard for my mother, whom he had birthed himself sixteen years previously, he stayed behind in the birth-chamber to clean the body and make it ready for the fire.

That was when he found me.

He was bathing my mother's face with rose-water cloths when he heard the cry. It was so faint that at first he thought it might be a distant owl-shriek, or the screech of a rabbit that had been taken by a stoat. But as he bent to wipe the encrusted blood from the sickle-shaped wound in the belly, it came again, the mewling of a kitten in a drowning-sack.

He plunged his arms elbow deep in mother's stomach, rootling round in her womb until he found me, pressed hard up against her rib-cage, a pathetic scrap of skin and bone, half the size of my sister, wrinkled and purpled as an old prune.

My eyes were closed, screwed tight against the light from the fish-oil lamp. When I opened them, Morangy says he felt a shock pierce his body like a shaft of cold steel. The eyes glowed in the lamp-light the same dull gold that they still are now, liquid amber with purple pupils and in them, he says, was the wisdoom of ages, the knowledge of all things, present, past, and future.

'I have been here before,' said the eyes, 'and am come again. Save me.'

16

And Morangy, as he never tires of telling, was powerless to resist.

But the message in my eyes was not the only shock that he suffered on that fateful night twenty years ago.

He cut the cord and placed my emaciated body in the birth-fluid, singing to me gently as he sponged away the blood and mucous, cleaned out my nostrils and soaped my hairless head. Then, as is usual, he ran his practised fingers over my person to make sure that all my parts were intact. He felt each vertebra in my spine, from the base of my skull to the tip of my prehensile tail, testing for strength and flexibility. He bent my legs at the knees and my arms at the elbows making sure that nothing was dislocated or out of joint. He uncurled my fingers, feeling the grip as they recurled to grasp his small, sure hands. Finally he checked my tiny sex organs, easing back the foreskin of the penis.

There would be no rejoicing on my account.

A male childe.

Another candidate for the cages.

He felt underneath my member for the balls that had yet to drop, then ran a forefinger along the groove connecting my testicles to my back passage. It seemed uncommonly deep.

He turned me upside down to inspect it more closely and discovered that under and behind my eggsac lay a perfectly formed vagina.

I was twin-sexed.

A hermaphrodite.

A freak.

It was at this point that someone hammered unceremoniously on the door.

Morangy says that it's a wonder I'm here today. The noise startled him so much he nearly dropped me on my head. As it was, he almost smothered me trying to keep me quiet. I had been quite content in his competent midwife's hands but the sudden commotion alerted me to the danger of my situation. As I expanded my lungs for a good old yell, Morangy clamped a tiny hand over my mouth and the sound was still-born.

'Who is it?' he shouted, moving to the door and calling through the keyhole.

'It's me – Cameron. I've brought you a dram.'

It was the Captain of the Guard. Well oiled by the sound

17

of it and strong enough to break in the door should the mood so take her.

'Bide a wee.'

Morangy wrapped me in an old tartan cloth, pushed a fake tit into my mouth and placed me in a dirty linen basket which he then hid under the bed.

After that he opened the door.

'Hold your whist,' he said, staring up at the Clanswoman. 'Have you no respect for the dead?'

Cameron drew herself up to her full height. She was wearing the dress uniform of the Royal Guard, plaid trews and a great swirl of tartan cape held in place on one shoulder by a huge cairngorm pin. An imposing sight, made the more menacing by the belligerence the drink had brought out in her. She glowered at the Midwife standing less than half her height.

'Mind your manners, wee mannie,' she said, 'or I'll drink this firewater mysel.'

'Drink it then,' said Morangy, anxious to see the back of her. 'I'll take no dram 'til I've laid this poor kwine to rest.'

'Suit yoursel,' sniffed the Guard Captain. 'If you wish to cut off your nose to spite your face that's your affair.'

She threw back her head, swallowing the sizeable measure in one gulp.

Morangy watched it disappear with a mixture of distaste and disgruntlement. He could have done with the dram to steady his nerves – and to keep the cold out of his bones. The night was bitter. The fire that he had tended so slavishly during my mother's labour now burned low in the grate and even the heavy tapestries and furlined window-drapes could not hold at bay the icy blasts that howled round the thick granite walls, insinuating their way through every nook and cranny in the masonry.

'Fergael bad me bring you to the feast,' said Cameron. 'She says it's only fitting, seeing as how you saved the Childe.'

'And lost the mother,' said Morangy, under his breath.

'Shall I tell her you'll be by?'

'Aye, tell her I'll be honoured, just as soon as I've placed the coins on Ymer's eyes.'

'Can I view her?' asked the guard, straining over the Midwife in morbid curiosity.

Morangy rested a firm palm against the woman's breastplate.

'You may not. You know better than that. The birthchamber is sacred to the mother – and the Mother Goddess. You can pay your respects the morrow like everyone else – when she's been removed to the Circle.'

'Well, well,' grumbled Cameron. 'If you must stand on cere-mony . . . We'll see you in a while, will we?'

'In a while,' nodded the Midwife.

Cameron whirled and stalked off, anxious to be back to the ceilidh. As she strode across the tiled floor of the ante-room, sparks from the brazier struck fire from her dark red hair and Morangy reflected that he would rather be Locheil's friend than her enemy. Once again he silently thanked the Goddess for the protection of the Lady Maxwell, the only thing that stood between him and the sacrificial knife.

He closed the door on the Clanswoman's retreating back, locking it with the iron key and pushing the bolts firmly in place. Then he hurried to the bed and withdrew me from my hiding-place.

He need not have worried. I was fast asleep, snuggled in my tartan wrap, sucking on the cat-gut tit.

Looking at me then, a freak like himself, Morangy knew that he could not deliver me up as an eveling but must hide me, protect me, save me from the death that was once marked out for him.

Let me explain about Morangy.

He is a midget. Perfectly formed but only half the height of a normal person.

Up until recently it has been the law that evelings, that is any male childe born deformed in mind or body, should be returned to the Godhead for remaking, which means that they had their throats cut and their bodies fed to the Holy Flame. There were rumours that Fergael ate them but I doubt the ver-acity of that. Not that she was not capable of it.

Morangy was an eveling. He should have died at birth. But Morangy was lucky. His smallness of stature did not evidence itself until his third year. By that time he had exhibited such extraordinary powers of healing, laying on of hands and a knowledge of herb-lore that it was thought ill luck to harm him. When he cured the Lady Maxwell of her persistent and debilitating falling-sickness, he secured for himself a final par-don and the unheard of honour of growing to become the first male Healer since the Fall.

Of course, they castrated him.

19

So it was natural that Morangy should feel an affinity with me – an eveling like himself. And then, there was the prophesy, though we were not to learn of that until much later.

Seeing I was so content, Morangy popped me back into my linen basket and finished dealing with my mother. When she had been arranged to his satisfaction, her rose-pale skin bathed and anointed, her long golden hair combed and dressed with silk ribbons, the cavity of her stomach filled with sweet smelling spices and stitched close with gut thread and the gold death-coins in place on her eyes. Morangy smoothed out the white gauze lying-in gown that would now double as her shroud and turned his attention to me.

Secreting me in the hide pouch that normally housed his surgical knives, he took me to the cages beneath the Castle and hid me among the great, docile breed-beasts.

No-one hindered him.

No-one was sober enough.

He bedded me down in the warm belly of a wolfhound bitch who had cast a litter the day before, and left me suckling with the rest of her pups at the animal's breast.

By that time he felt he had earned his dram.

Pausing only to caution the Chief Eunuch to keep my presence secret until his return, he made his way to the great hall and got roaring drunk.

THE TRUE CHRONICLES OF THE REDEEMER

Then the witch, Fergael, fed the Lady Ymer to the Sacred Flame. And the Maxwell took to her bed in sorrow. So the witch took the girlechilde and dedicated her to The Source and called her Ymer — in memory of her dead mother.

Chapter
2

My Mother's body was cremated the next day at the sacred circle of Standing Stones atop Ballater Brae.

As was the custom, the ceremony was performed at sunset.

I have been to many such ceremonies myself and the timing could not be bettered.

The sunsets in Alba are spectacular. The orange glow from the funeral pyre seems to be reflected in the eggshell skies shot through as they are, like a taffeta ballgown, with silken strands of crimson and purple.

It had been a lowering day, grey and dreath, the temperature never rising above freezing. The crescent moon overlooked the skeletal landscape like the wall eye of a blinded dog.

The faces huddled round the stone circle were no less grey, their lack of colour highlighted by the holly-crowns of mourning as they circumnavigated the bier, hand in hand, dragging frozen feet through the churned snow, chanting the dirge of the dead.

My mother lay surrounded by mistletoe and draped in hide blankets. A waste of warmth, for even their weight could not breathe life into her day-cold bones. The women gazed at her pale beauty and the chief mourner began to keen, a high piercing moan that ebbed and flowed like water in the wind.

Another woman took up the sound. Then another . . . and another . . . until soon the whole circle was wailing. And as the women keened, they rocked, clutching their robes around shivering bodies as though trying to stop their own troubled spirits from floating away on the night breeze. Each face bore the stamp of loss . . . and of guilt. For my mother had been well loved, not least for her sense of humour. She had been capable of making the Lady Maxwell laugh, an ability that was to be sorely missed.

Many now regretted their callousness of the previous evening – not to mention the amount of strong drink they had consumed.

The only person in the circle without a throbbing head was the Queen herself, and she looked as though she would never laugh again. She stood, red-eyed and erect, the hood of her mourning-gown shadowing features made gaunt by grief and lack of sleep. She watched the proceedings like a somnambulent, in them, but not of them.

She set the ceremonial torch to the wood as was the custom, but as the flames began to lick around Ymer's body, caressing and devouring it as the Maxwell had done so many times herself, the Warleader of Alba, whom none had ever seen flinch, shuddered and stepped backwards, covering her face with her hands. As my mother's long, golden hair ignited with a whoosh, the Queen buckled at the knees.

Fergael was at her side instantly, supporting her with strong clawed hands, but the Lady shook her away.

'Get me to Ballater,' she muttered, 'I can endure no more.'

'Your Majesty *must* remain,' hissed Fergael, 'to scatter the ashes and name the Childe.'

'The wind will scatter the ashes,' said the Queen. 'It needs no help from me.'

And as if to prove her point a sudden gust blew the hood back from her bowed head.

'Then what of the Childe?'

'The Childe may rot for all I care.'

'The Childe *must* be named. And by you. You are her Clan-mother. It is the law.'

The Lady Maxwell fixed Fergael with a stare so intense that the High Priest was forced to look away.

'I am the law,' she said icily. 'And I *will* not name the infant. She is yours. Dedicate her to The Source and keep her out of my sight.'

Fergael inclined her head.

'As my Lady pleases,' she said. 'But I do not have a name in mind.'

'Then call her Ymer,' said the Queen with a hollow laugh. 'A life for a life . . . Locheil . . . '

The Captain of the Guard hurried to where the Queen stood swaying in the icy wind.

'Your Majesty?'

'Your arm.'

23

The Guard Captain whipped off her plaid cloak, throwing it round her shivering mistress. Then, wrapping her arms around the grieving woman, she half-led, half-supported the Queen away from the sacrificial circle.

'Her Majesty is clearly unwell,' announced Fergael, at once outraged and unsettled that the Queen should allow her feelings to overcome her duty. Angry too that her moment of triumph should be thwarted. For the Lady Maxwell would not now set her seal of approval on the religious adoption by naming the childe in public.

'We will continue in her absence,' she said.

Hastily she intoned the litanies for the dead, stumbling over the incantations as she supplicated the Great Mother to take Ymer back to the body of the earth, anxious to move on as quickly as possible to the dedication of the baby. She did not even attempt to conceal the gloat in her voice as she scattered her rival's ashes to the four corners of Alba.

But if Fergael expected to return to the Lady Maxwell's favour, she was to be sorely disappointed. The Queen never took her back to her bed, never took anyone except the occasional concubine for the next twelve years . . . when she fell in love with me.

Fergael sacrificed a white dove that night, ripping its head off and splattering its life-blood on the still-smouldering fire so that the fumes should be carried upwards in the woodsmoke and incense.

Something to whet the Great Mother's appetite.

For the real sacrifice.

Abel, the great breed-beast who had been Ymer's special pet, was to be sent to the Goddess in thanksgiving for the birth of a girlchilde.

He did not die well but had to be dragged to the killing-tree, bellowing like a wounded bull, the issue of his bowels running down his tree-trunk legs as evidence of his terror. It took ten Clanswomen to raise him and lash him, feet-first, to the upturned mushroom of the radar-disc before Fergael could castrate him and cut his throat. He struggled to the end, his blood cascading onto the frozen snow, while the High Priest cursed his intransigence and attempted to trap a few spurts of the precious liquid in the ceremonial chalice. It would be needed later for the Naming.

Fergael was close to Holy Ecstasy. She had eaten nothing all day but a mess of vegetables liberally laced with magic mushrooms. Soon she would be in touch with the centre of things. The

24

Source. In it and of it. She would cry aloud with the many tongues of the spirits who infiltrated and guarded the inanimate land. The spirits of the rivers and trees, the wind, the fire and the great Standing Stones themselves. All would speak through the mouth of the High Priest.

She held the ceremonial cup out before her, a beggar supplicating for alms, and one by one the Priestesses of the Source added the magic properties that would imbue Fergael with the Power . . . Fermented tubor, ground futret bane, birth-fluid squeezed from the placenta of the unbaptised childe's dead mother. . . A potent mixture.

When all was ready Fergael raised the cup to her lips and drained a great draught of the brew.

The potion stormed its way into her veins, shaking her stick thin body with tremors of vision and light.

Fergael used to file her teeth. An affectation I always felt. But an effective one.

She must have made a fearsome sight with the blood dripping from her fangs and her drug-crazed eyes raised starwards, the wind billowing her long, black robes until they resembled nothing more than the wings of a carrion bird, her crested hair a rising cockscomb on her shaven head and her nose-rings glittering in the moonlight.

When they handed her the baby she ripped aside the fur shawls and held her aloft, displaying the tiny, naked body to the surrounding women. Raising her voice above the howling of the approaching gale, the High Priest spoke the words that would bind the infant, as she herself had been bound at birth, to the selfless service of the Great Mother.

The words have never before been written down.

Ymer dictated them to me but yesterday. Though not without consideration. Before she passed them on to me they had been handed down, by word of mouth from Mother to Daughter, guarded jealously from all ears save those of the Inner Circle.

Swinging my sister head-down over the funeral pyre, these then are the words that Fergael spoke.

'Great Mother, Source of all life, take this Childe as thine own.
May her life be pledged to the service of the Godhead.
May she be the living receptacle of the Godhead's will on Earth.
Her thoughts – the thoughts of the Godhead.

Her desires – the Godhead's desires.
Here bind I this Childe, Soul, Spirit and body, to Thy will.
May she be as pure as the first Winter snowfall. Faithful as the swan.
And should she ever falter – or betray these sacred vows.
May her body be brought in hideous agony
To the dishonour of an unmarked grave.'

The smoke rose around my sister's blue-cold body, choking her cries, mingling with the hoare-frost breath of the Initiates as they leaned forward to make the responses.

Finally, Fergael named the Royal baby . . . Ymer. As the Queen had requested. Then she anointed her and drew the crescent moon over her heart in Abel's blood.

My Mother's hair was golden – like mine.

My sister's is black. Black as the breed-beast's whose blood she now bore.

If anyone noticed this analogy they said nothing.

Probably they did not even make the connection.

In those days the Great Lie was still thought to be the Great Truth.

Re-clothing my sister at last in the warm fur shawls, Fergael laid her on the central stone slab, with only her belly exposed.

One by one the women filed past, touching the bloodied sickle and intoning her name.

Ymer. Ymer. Ymer . . .

When all had passed, Fergael the Black lifted her up and, clutching the infant to her milkless paps, led the torchlight procession down from the windblown heights and back to the warmth and sanctuary of Castle Ballater.

THE TRUE CHRONICLES OF THE REDEEMER

Then a voice spoke to the midwife, Morangy, saying 'Save the Eveling'. So he made a herb-spell, rendering the Childe invisible and took it from Castle Ballater to the Prophet Colluden who dwelt in the High Hills.

Chapter
3

THE QUEEN LOCKED HERSELF IN HER ROOMS AND REFUSED TO see anyone. Warrants were left unsigned, petitions unheard, the commerce of the court, never a speedy process at best, came to a grinding halt. People went around on tiptoe fearful of inciting the wrath of the murderous Cameron who guarded the Queen's privacy with the ferocity of a She-Devil.

Only Morangy was permitted to enter the Royal presence.

When he did, it was to find the Lady Maxwell consumed from within by a malady that sucked, vampirically, at her will to live.

The Midwife decided on a drastic solution.

He would place the Queen in a state of suspended animation, half-way between death and life, until her empty soul renewed itself and her ailing body regained its strength.

He mixed the drugs and fed them to the Maxwell himself, cajoling each silver spoonful into her mouth as though she were a sick childe.

He stayed with her while the drugs took effect, checking her blood count and monitoring her breathing while she sank through the levels of consciousness to that comatose state that in some animals is known as hibernation . . .

When he was quite sure that she had reached nirvana, he dimmed the lamps around the great antlered bed and left the chamber, locking the door firmly behind him.

He pocketed the key and informed the hovering Cameron that the Lady Maxwell was not to be disturbed under *any* circumstances until his return.

'Why, where are you off to?' demanded the Guard Captain, suspiciously.

'Her Majesty has graciously granted me leave of absence,' Morangy lied in his teeth, 'to visit an ailing relative up in the Highlands.'

'That's all very well. But what if she wakes before you get back?'

'You need have no fear of that. I've given her enough medicine to keep her sleeping for a moon-phase . . . Just mind you don't wake her is all . . . Not unless you want her death on your conscience.'

'But what if there's a crisis man?'

'I've no doubt that Fergael will be up to handling any crisis that might arise,' Morangy assured her. 'I'll just leave instructions with the medics to keep watch on the Queen. But no-one else must go in. You understand me? No-one.' And so saying he hurried off before the Guard Captain could fine another excuse to delay him.

The Healer made his way through the labyrinthine corridors of the old castle until he came to the Hospice where he briefed the chief Medic, Aurora, on what was to be done. A rotation of nurses would monitor the Lady Maxwell clock-round.

The Medic noted the top-up formula, took possession of the key and dispatched the first of the Auxilliaries, a plump cheerful eunuch with a bag of knitting, to his post by the royal bedside.

Duty done, Morangy made his way down into the cavernous bowels of the building where the cages of the breed-beasts had been built into the dirt foundations. There he retrieved me from the belly of the wolfhound, much to my chagrin so I am told, and carried me back to the cell that he occupied on the servant's floor.

As cells go, it was spacious and opulent, befitting Morangy's station as Chief Midwife to the Lady. Here he kept all his books of recipes, his shelves of apothecary jars filled with powders and potions, oils and unguents. Racks of herbs from the summer garden hung drying from the rafters, while crammed on each of the windowsills, pots of the fresh variety craned their necks to catch the feeble rays of the winter sun.

I was to sit by those windows many times in years to come, listening to Morangy expound the secrets of his art. If I raise my head now I can look out across the Dee valley at the selfsame

29

view and almost smell the distinctive aroma of his robes. Spice and formaldehyde. An evocative combination.

But all that was in the future.

The first time I entered the cell I was little more than a rag, a bone and a hank of hair, my life hanging by a thread, my miserable fate in the midget's hands.

He made his preparations swiftly, filling a wicker basket with enough food and drink for a long journey and cramming a change of clothes into his saddlebags along with some soft, linen cloths that would serve as catch-alls for me.

I woke then and he fed me, fresh goat's milk laced with honey and a mild sleeping-draught, and packed me snugly back in the apothecary bag, purring contentedly.

Finally he buckled on a hunting-bow, stuck a skean-dhu down his wool sock (for skinning anything he might shoot), flung a heavy plaid around his shoulders and called for a castrati to carry his luggage down into the yard.

The clanswoman at the gate was one of the officious sort. As Morangy cantered up on Nob, the sturdy mountain pony that he used to ride, she held up a peremptory gauntlet and insisted that the Guard Captain be called to clear his exit.

Cameron, who had just sat down to a late breakfast, arrived in a fine fury to deliver her subordinate a considerable flea in the ear.

'It's the Queen's Midwife, you daft eejit,' she thundered, 'off to the Highlands on a mission of mercy. What did you think? That he's running away to sea?'

'Maybe she'd like to search my bags?' Morangy suggested. 'In case I'm pinching the Crown Jewels?'

'We'll have less cheek from you, wee mannie,' said Cameron. 'Be off, before I change my mind.'

So Morangy clattered out across the frozen moat, heaving a considerable sigh of relief, while behind him a small jackass – loaded with tools, provisions . . . and me . . . brayed in derision and Cameron continued to castigate the unfortunate trooper.

'Do you think I've got nothing better to do than traipse up and down those blasted stairs? My neeps'll be as cold as clats by the time I get back to them . . .'

Her voice carried down into the valley as Morangy urged Nob into a trot, away from the comparative civilisation of Castle Ballater and out into the brutish world beyond.

Much time would pass and with it many strange happenings before I was to return to the place of my birthing. But for now I was content to sleep, soothed by the jolting sway of the jackass's gait and the mixture of milk and honey that coursed through my veins.

We must have presented a strange spectacle as we struggled through the snow, the midget astride his long-haired pony, the laden jackass and, bringing up the rear, a bridled she-goat, her dugs laden with my supper, her silver neck-bell tinkling in the icy air.

Morangy made his way down to the Frozen Dee. The mountain pass at Tomintoul would be well snowbound and so he had decided to follow the path of the river up to its source in the High Hills. The route might be more tortuous, but it was infinitely safer, avoiding as it did the treacherous mountain mists and the cut-throats and Ben-shi that were said to haunt them.

Morangy had only a vague idea of where he was going. He had done the journey before, but not for many cycles nor in such inclement weather. And never carrying so precious a burden.

We travelled all day without mishap, coming at dusk to a small hunter's croft near Glenshi. The building was deserted, the door blocked by a snow-drift, so that Morangy was forced to cut a tunnel through before he could lead the animals inside. Snow began to fall again, almost immediately re-sealing the entrance, a circumstance which bothered Morangy considerably. The last thing he wanted was to be snowed-in – as many a traveller had been in the past, forced to eat his rotting horse for sustenance until the spring thaw arrived – frequently too late – to melt the hard-packed ice.

He built a fire to warm the small stone steading and then he took me from my tiny tomb to change and feed me. The room was smoky and none too clean but it was shelter against the night. Nob had chosen this point to relieve himself which did nothing to improve the atmosphere, but there was no question of leaving the animals outside. Apart from the freezing temperatures there were wolves and the snow-bears to consider. Nothing as succulent as a goat could hope to prosper out of doors in such harsh terrain.

They say that before the Fall the wolves only had one head and indeed I have seen pictures of dog-like creatures in one of Euan-Noag's books. But compared to our twin-headed monsters they were a feeble looking bunch. I do not wonder that as a species they did not survive.

31

After Morangy had seen to me and to the livestock and eaten a meagre supper, he wrapped himself in his plaids and lay down by the fire to sleep.

He woke to find himself surrounded by six Wildemen.

There have always been Wildemen in legend – usually associated with High Places – the Yeti, the Bigfoot, the Old Man of Mourne.

To hear Morangy tell it, these six were like every tale-scared childe's nightmare come true. Huge. Muscular. Scarred by battle. Decorated with tattoos.

Their garments were made from animal hides rather than wool, giving them the aspect of two-legged animals themselves, a similarity increased by their extreme hairiness. Beetling brows exaggerated the piercing stare of their eyes, long matted locks hung over their ears and down their backs, melting into the bearfur capes that added bulk to their already considerable shoulders. The lower half of their faces was covered in hair too – something which Morangy – surrounded as he was by women and castrati – had never before seen.

But these were not the only areas where they were hirsute.

Hunkered down as they were, in an inquisitive circle around him, Morangy's first view was of the area between their muscular thighs. Swinging there were half a dozen sets of gonads, all surrounded by fringes of yet more hair.

Morangy was stunned.

These were real men, all of whom had, by some miracle, escaped the knife. An occasional individual did sometimes evade the collective net, although the mistake was invariably rectified, to the said individual's considerable discomfort, later on. A trauma at the birthing, danger to the mother, an absent-minded midwife. Sometimes there was an oversight.

One, he could understand.

But six?

Could they be breed-beasts which had escaped?

Morangy was more flabbergasted than frightened. He sat up, rubbing sleep and smoke from his eyes and one of the Wildemen spoke.

'It's no a bairn after all,' he said. 'It's a tiny wee mannie.'

'No a mannie,' said another, scornfully. 'It has no beard.'

'It's a wee poofter,' said a third and the rest of the company laughed derisively and began to prod him with blue-cold fingers.

One of the men, the one who had spoken first, stood up, hoisting Morangy with him, lifting him easily by the scruff of the neck and holding him in front of his face for a better look.

'What are you doing without your mammy, wee poofter?' he said. 'Do you no know it's dangerous to be out after dark?'

'Aye, the Bogeyman'll get you,' shouted one.

'The Bogeyman *has* got you,' roared another.

And they laughed again, slapping their thighs as though at some rare and witty piece of humour, until one began to chant and each took up the refrain.

'McCann, McCann – the Bogey Man.'

Morangy squirmed in McCann's great fist.

'Let me down,' he squeaked, his face turning pink as the tightening collar cut off his air. 'Let me be you great, hairy pillock."

'Well, well now – it talks,' said McCann feigning astonishment. 'Come on, wee mannie,' and he shook Morangy none too gently. 'What else can you say?'

'Mebbe he can say his prayers?' suggested one.

'Then he'd better start,'' shouted another and they laid into the chant again.

'McCann, McCann – the Bogey Man.
He'll cook your guts in his frying pan.'

'Let me go,' gasped Morangy, his eyes crossing in his head. 'You're choking me, you great long drink of bog-water.'

'Why should I let you go?' asked McCann. 'What good are you are to bairn or beast? You're no more than an eveling poofter.'

'I am a Healer,' choked Morangy.

McCann loosed his grip and set Morangy down gingerly.

'A Healer is it?' he said, grabbing one of his companions by the shoulder and dragging him into the circle of the firelight.

'Can you heal this?'

He pulled foreward the man's arm, exposing a jagged stump where once a hand had been.

'I am a Healer,' said Morangy, tartly, 'not a miracle worker.'

McCann guffawed.

'And what is a Healer doing outwith the confines of a camp?' he asked.

'Alone?' said One-hand.

'On such a night?' added a third.

'I am on my way to see Colluden,' announced Morangy.

He was gambling his trump. If it didn't work he knew he was dead. Food was too hard to come in by in these mountains in the winter. If what he heard about the Wildemen was true they weren't fussy about the source of their meat. They would keep the goat for her milk and slaughter the jackass, the pony and himself.

Not necessarily in that order.

But he need not have worried. The name of Colluden was respected even in the back of beyond. At the mention of the Hermit, the Animal-men withdrew into a corner and began to argue amongst themselves.

At last McCann spoke.

'Is the prophet expecting you?'

'Not to my knowledge.'

'Then what business do you have with him?'

Morangy says I have a wonderful sense of timing. It can't be taught, he says, either you have it, or you haven't.

Whatever . . . I chose this moment to make my presence felt.

The howl that I set up would have done justice to a wild-cat and the effect on the Animal-men was instant. As one, they formed themselves into a circle, back to back, weapons drawn against the unseen enemy.

Morangy permitted himself a small smile.

'If Colluden is as impressed, I'll be pleased,' he said and he opened his bag and brought me out, red-faced with hunger and squalling fit to bust.

McCann approached for a better look.

'What is it?' he asked. 'Is it a Moggy?'

'More like a skinned rabbit,' observed another, a black-haired giant with only one good eye.

'It's a baby,' said Morangy. 'A wee boy.'

'A boy?'

The Wildemen crowded round.

'A real wee boy?'

Morangy nodded.

'He hasn't been . . . ?'

To answer their question Morangy undid my soiled catch-all and peeled it back to expose my testicles and the penis which hid the vagina which he did not want them to see.

34

'Fegs,' said McCann, prodding my intact balls. 'It is a wee boy and all.'

The Wildemen grinned at each other and began to dance around, raising their animal skins hip-high and swinging their own male organs around in lewd display.

Morangy hastily re-wrapped me and held me close, unsure of what might happen next, but the Wildemen were clearly delighted with me, darting in and out of their raucous circle one after another to peer at my ugly squalling face.

Suddenly McCann had a thought. 'Where did you get him?' he demanded.

'I stole him,' said Morangy.

This provoked gales of mirth.

'He stole him. The wee mannie stole him.'

'Where from?'

'From Castle Ballater.'

There was a sudden, deathly silence.

'You're lying,' said McCann, flatly. 'There's no way you'd get him out past the Maxwell's guards.'

'He's one of twins,' said Morangy, hurriedly. 'The other one was a girl. They were too busy with her to notice this one . . .' He looked down at my wizened face. 'I nearly missed him myself.'

McCann looked around the assembled throng as though inviting advice.

None was forthcoming.

At last my fearsome yowling made the decision for him.

'Feed the bairn,' said McCann, gruffly. 'And let's be awa.'

'Where to?'

'To Colluden, you wally,' said McCann scornfully. 'You'll no get far on your own in this season. If the wolves don't get you then the Ben-shi will.'

THE TRUE CHRONICLES OF THE REDEEMER

With the Source's protection, they came, at last, to the cave of the Prophet. And Colluden fell down and worshipped the Childe and showed it to the Wildemen of the mountains saying 'Behold, I bring you The Redeemer.'

Chapter
4

WE MOVED THROUGH A NETWORK OF SAFE-HOUSES TRAVELLING always by darkness until, at the end of the fifth night, we came to the cave at the top of the world where the prophet Colluden lived.

The company had swelled by this time to number about twenty Wildemen. Word of our progress had spread – don't ask me how – and we had picked up stragglers, singly or in groups, at various points along the way.

The weather was even colder up in those sub-arctic ridges, the temperature never rising above freezing. The skies were pale, even at midnight, and the air so clear and thin that the strongest had to pause occasionally for breath.

We came to Colluden's lair at sunrise, set, as it was, like an eagle's eyrie high above the tree-line.

Colluden himself came to the cave mouth to greet us – a man heavy in years even then – but of imposing height and ample girth.

He had no beard – having been castrated in youth – but the hair on his head, white and silky, fell like a mountain waterfall to well below his waist. A clatter of small boys of various shapes and sizes clustered about him, the tallest standing waist height to the Prophet, the smallest not yet able to walk upright but gambolling around his feet like an unruly pup.

Colluden seemed not at all startled to find himself confronted by a small army of Wildemen, a midget, a pony, a jackass and a goat.

I suppose that – as a prophet – he must have seen our arrival ahead of time.

He fixed Morangy with a mesmeric eye and demanded with

a voice of such depth and range that it rolled around the mountain peaks like thunder, what he had done with the bairn.

This evidence of the hermit's oracular powers caused the entire visiting party to fall to their knees in the snow. As one the Wildemen bent and placed their foreheads in the cold, white carpet at Colluden's feet.

'Get up, get up,' he said, testily. 'There's no need for all that. Come inside. Warm yourselves. Eat.'

The entrance to the cave was deceptively narrow. Inside a short, low corridor led back into a much larger area with a central fire and a honeycomb of passages leading off into small sleeping cubicles.

The fire was set in a circle of stones and placed beneath a strategic hole in the roof which formed a natural chimney up through the escarpment and out to the lightening sky above.

Over the flame a three-legged pot, brimful of porridge, bubbled and frothed.

Morangy was the only one brave enough to step full into the cavern and found himself immediately surrounded by curious children, some of whom were as tall as himself.

The Wildemen huddled together near the exit, shuffling their feet uncomfortably, torn between awe for the Holy Man and the rumblings of their empty bellies.

'Sit. Sit,' ordered Colluden. 'Jamie. See to the breakfast. You, friend – (pointing to Morangy) – follow me.'

While the tallest boy fell to organizing the distribution of bowls and spoons in what was, apparently, a well-rehearsed ritual, Morangy followed the Holy Man into one of the niches that led off the main living area.

'You maun starve a bittie longer,' said Colluden. 'But first things foremost.' He held out strong work-rough hands. 'The bairn,' he demanded. 'Gie us a look at it.'

Morangy scooped me out of my sleeping bag and handed me over. The big man laid me on an outcrop of rock and began to loosen the bone pin that held the linen cloth about my loins.

'You'll be wondering about the wains,' he said matter-of-factly, and Morangy admitted that he had been.

'Boys,' explained Colluden. 'Saved from the cruelty of the knife. Not many yet . . . but soon . . . there will be enough real men to challenge the rule of the Maxwell and that black bitch, Fergael.'

39

'Where do they come from?' Morangy wanted to know. 'So many?'

'Och, sure it is not hard to take a childe in this country,' said the prophet. 'Especially a male childe. The Wildemen steal them in the night. If they are skilful, folk put it down to wolves – or the Ben-shi.'

'What if they're seen?'

The Prophet grinned at him.

'If they're seen? . . . Weel now . . . doesn't everybody know that the Wildemen eat human flesh?'

Morangy fidgeted uncomfortably.

'About this childe . . . ' he began.

'Aye, he's a fine one,' said Colluden, unfolding my nappie. 'A bit puny but we'll soon put meat on his bones.'

'It's not a he,' blurted Morangy.

'Do you say so? It looks like a he to me.'

'Feel behind the testes.'

Colluden placed a finger in the groove behind my balls. I didn't like it and let him know so. As for Colluden, his face turned white as his hair and, as he rounded on Morangy, his voice cracked.

'Is it . . .?'

Morangy nodded.

'A hermaphrodite. An eveling. Male *and* female. The one and the both.'

Colluden sat down heavily and dropped his head into his hands. Morangy used the pause to re-wrap me and put me over his shoulder where I ceased yowling and began to nuzzle his ear.

At last the old man looked up.

'I saw it in a dream,' he said. 'But I never dared hope.'

'Hope for what?'

'That the Redeemer would come in my lifespan.'

'The Redeemer?'

'Don't you know the prophecy, man?"

Morangy looked confused.

'No, I don't suppose you would,' Colluden went on. 'Stuck in Castle Ballater with a load of females. They'd never let such a blasphemy get out.'

The Prophet stood up and his touch, as he patted my head, was a good deal more reverential than it had been previously.

'And in good time,' he intoned. 'A Redeemer shall arise to bind the nation together in peace. Male and Female alike. Each equal to the other. For the Redeemer shall be the One and the Both. Sister and Brother. Husband and Wife. Mother and Father to the coming race.'

'The Redeemer?'

'The same.'

'A large title for such a small thing.'

'But he will grow.'

'You mean it will grow.'

'Dinna split hairs man . . . alright then IT will grow. And when IT does, we must make sure that IT is ready.'

'A formidable task.'

'And one too great for me to handle alone,' Colluden admitted. 'Oh, I'm a dab hand at teaching the boys porridge making or how to whittle a stave to defend themselves against the wolf, but the education of the Redeemer needs to be a muckle more sophisticated than that. The childe must go to Euan-Noag.''

'Euan-Noag?'

'A man of much wisdom and more learning, a travelling man, never in one place long enough for the law to catch up with him. He runs a freak show.'

Morangy shuddered. He had heard of such shows. Outlawed by the state, they appealed to the baser elements of human nature, exhibiting evelings who, instead of being returned to the Great Mother at birth, were sold by their natural mothers to unscrupulous dealers for the titillation of the common herd. They were kept in cages like animals, baited and gawped at, mocked and jeered. Morangy had suffered much from the cruelty of insensitive fools in his time. He knew how it could wound the spirit and damage the soul.

And Colluden wanted to hand the baby over to such a life.

'Better it should die,' he said, taking out his skean-dhu. "I'll cuts its throat myself rather than submit it to such a fate.'

Colluden stayed his hand.

'Dinna fash yersel,' he said. 'Euan-Noag is a Prince among men. He will prepare the childe for any eventuality, give him . . . I beg your pardon . . . give *it* skills and resources far beyond our comprehending. In another life Euan-Noag would *be* a Prince . . . not a vagrant skulking in byroads and hiding in ditches."

'I have never heard of this Euan-Noag.'

'No . . . But you can bet your sporran the Maxwell knows his name.'

'And you're sure he can be trusted? I have grown attached to the infant. I would not have it come to harm.'

The old man drew himself up and squared his shoulders.

'If *I* trust him, he is to be trusted. I am Colluden and I can see into any man's soul.'

Morangy looked into the Prophet's fiery eyes and saw only truth there. And so, still with some misgivings, he delivered me up to my fate, placing me gently in the small wicker basket which the Holy Man proffered him.

Colluden carried me out into the midst of the gathering then, Morangy trotting obediently behind.

The Wildemen and children ceased their chewing to look up in wonder as the great man hoisted me aloft like a pork's head on a platter.

They say that a childe does not have its first memory until well into its second year. That's as may be.

I was not above seven days old but I recall that moment in every detail. It is with me still. The feeling of being high up, exposed and yet, somehow, secure. The circle of upturned faces. The flickering of the firelight. The sound of Colluden's voice, ringing through the cavern and bouncing back from the rough-hewn walls.

I remember his tone and the content of the words he spoke, as though it were yesterday.

'Behold,' he said. 'I bring you, The Redeemer.'

42

THE TRUE CHRONICLES OF THE REDEEMER

Then they took the childe over the High Ridges and left it in the care of the Medicine-Man Euan-Noag, who came from a far country away over the water. And he named the childe Rolande and taught it many magical secrets that were known only to him.

CHAPTER
5

MORANGY RETURNED TO CASTLE BALLATER AND I WAS NOT TO see him again for many years, though he kept in touch with Colluden, to make sure that I was not being ill-used.

I was taken, by stealth, across country to the High Ridges where I joined the clandestine freak show at its winter quarters by Loch a' Ghorm-Choire under Ben Hee.

Colluden left me in the hands of the Medicine Man, Euan-Noag, who, if asked, was to say that he had taken me in when my blood relatives died of the plague.

I was named Rolande and smothered in the kind of affection that I have not known since. The evelings were so anxious that I should not suffer the deprivations that they had had to endure as children that they vied with each other to spoil me unmercifully.

This was by no means the freak show that Morangy had feared. More of a circus. No-one even travelled during the hard months of the snow-season. Instead they settled down cosily in their small outpost in the lee of the great mountain until the harsh weather had passed and the Spring come again. Plenty of time then to load up the painted caravans and set out on the road.

The winter was spent in practising and perfecting skills, repairing costumes and making new props to delight the crowd. And, as I got older, there were games too. We would have snow-ball fights or construct ice-folk – our Guardians, Euan-Noag called them – setting them out in attitudes of menace before the Big House, so that anyone overviewing the area from a distance might suppose us well protected.

Not that we had much to worry about in that direction.

The harshness of the terrain made the way into the Northern vastness almost impassable when the snow was on the ground so we had few visitors. Even in Spring ankle-twisting screes and jagged boulders made for heavy going and in late Autumn the persistent rain overflowed the lochs making what paths there were dangerously boggy. Add to that vipers the length of a bullock, thick as a man's arm and nests of scorpion rats in the heather and you can see why we were left well alone.

An occasional Wildeman would come by. Out trapping wolf-fur or civet, they would arrive ostensibly for the company or the grog but in reality to take back news of our doings to Colluden in the High Hills.

Once, I remember, a runaway castrati stumbled into camp, but he did not live long. They secreted him in a small outhouse where Blossom could tend him. I was not allowed to go in for fear, I presume, that his sorry state would upset me. The night he died, Euan-Noag emerged from the outhouse grim-faced and even though Blossom tried to restrain him, plunged out into the curtain of sleet that had been falling since dusk. By the time he came back, almost two days later, the castrati had been buried, wrapped in skins and interred beneath a stone cairn, the ground being too hard to dig a proper grave. Euan-Noag never spoke of him again. It was as though he had never existed. Better for him, poor loon, if he hadn't.

During the occasional late Autumn day when the berries had ripened and there was still some heat in the sun, Euan-Noag would take me (in a sling at first but later, when I could toddle, on foot) to collect the basic ingredients for the aromatic batches of the patent medicine which he brewed in a huge still in one of the outhouses and from which he got his name. He had brought the secret recipe with him from another land and the potion claimed to cure all manner of ills. I can still see him in his motheaten hide apron, berry stains in his greying hair, stirring and sipping and telling tales. The medicine was potent stuff which, whatever else it did, made the taker feel a lot better for the taking. In moderation of course. I once drank a whole bottle of the brew and was ill for days. Euan-Noag didn't add insult to injury scolding me. He knew I'd never do it again. He came to my room instead and tried to take my mind off the cramps by entertaining me with tricks. For he was a magician too and a fantastical conjuror. Some of his tricks were mere sleight of hand, these he taught me, but some were pure magic. Those I never learned. I did not have The Gift.

Ymer has it.

But she met Euan-Noag only briefly . . . and too late.

The first winter I was over-young to recognise the freaks as anything but faces that occasionally hovered over my cradle which dangled from the rafters of the Big House. This was the communal dwelling where the company ate together, rehearsed and told each other long stories late into the night.

It was thus that I discovered that Euan-Noag had spent his youth over the water in a far country. In this land, so Euan-Noag said, they did not castrate the males. Men and Women lived together in harmony and produced children of the union. So I knew from the beginning about the Great Lie, although it was not until I came to the Dark Tower that I found out how it was engineered.

When Euan-Noag got back, he decided to spread word of this amazing country beyond the sea, to bring hope to the downtrodden male members of the Albian society. He fell in with the freak show when the dealer who owned it threatened to sell him to the authorities.

Euan-Noag killed her in a fight.

It was the one thing in his life of which he was ashamed. So he took over the running of the show and changed the lives of the performers from a living hell to one of worth and fulfilment.

As Colluden said, Euan-Noag was a Prince among men. No ulterior motive such as greed or nosiness discoloured his genuine concern for the good of others.

I have never found it in my heart to forgive the Maxwell for his death.

He must have been in his late thirties when Colluden brought me to Loch a' Ghorm-Choire and I was to stay nine winters in his care. Some were more memorable than others but all were happy and during that time I was to grow to know and love the strange company as my only family – until lately, when I have begun to form a family of my own.

Firstly there was Blossom, Euan-Noag's wife.

Before I was five I was taller than Blossom. She was a midget, like Morangy, only prettier. A small, delicate, exquisite creature, not unlike a flower-faery, her doll face, with its round, green eyes and rosebud mouth, framed in a halo of golden hair. People used to say she was a Changeling, a faery childe left by the little people for one of the human race. Though why the little people should want to exchange Blossom for one of our lumpen kind has always been a mystery to me.

She was a high-wire walker and would tiptoe along a silken rope, in her pink spangled gown, turning somersaults and performing feats of balance to stop the heart. Blossom was my first love. She taught me to walk and later to dance.

The other female in the troupe was Cilla, the bearded lady, plump as a sugar-loaf and beloved of Sanke, the Rubber Man.

Sanke, who was seven feet tall and painfully thin, could fold himself up inside a tiny cube and shut the lid.

I have seldom seen two people as much in love as were Cilla and Sanke. He never tired of combing her whiskered face and she, in return, rubbed his elongated body with linament to keep it supple.

Then there was Jolly, the Joker in the pack.

Jolly was small too, but unlike Blossom, he was not perfectly formed. His head was much too big for his body — or rather for his legs. His torso was that of a normal. His legs were short and stumpy and his arms, hanging from wide shoulders, were strong and muscular, but only half the length that they should have been. His peculiar physical characteristics made him the perfect acrobat and clown and he would have the crowd in stitches with his mummery and pratfalls. But although he courted the laughter, he was hurt by it too. He could be morose betimes and when the black moods were on him he would lock himself away for days on end.

He was secretly in love with Blossom, but although she was never unkind to him, she did not return his affections.

Her fidelity to Euan-Noag was absolute.

The situation often caused friction, especially during the winter break when we were all thrown so close together. It was hard for Jolly, torn as he was between love for the tightrope walker and loyalty to his best friend.

Everyone loved Euan-Noag. Including me, though in my first winter I was to recognize him only as a rough shoulder, a bearded face, a warm lap.

For it was Euan-Noag who tended me, fed and bathed me, changed my soiled linen . . . and talked.

He talked constantly, in his soft sing-song island accent, filling my head with facts and philosophies which I did not understand but which somehow penetrated my understanding.

47

And when he wasn't talking, he was singing, songs with history in them, songs from before the Fall. My favourite, I remember, was one called Norwegian Wood and began . . .

'I once had a girl . . . or should I say . . . she once had me . . .'

Euan-Noag offered no concession to my infancy, never spoke baby language to me, never talked down. From my earliest understanding I recall him treating me like an equal – trusting me with his knowledge. And I responded in kind, devouring information like a starving drone with a plate of eel-stew.

When I was three, he taught me to read – a feat known only to a privileged few in the Priesthood.

In the years to come, I intend that all the people of Alba should become literate. Education is death to superstition and there can surely be no greater pleasure than reading a good book. Euan-Noag had a fund of them, had put it out that he would accept them as payment for his medicine. One by one they had started arriving, dug out of attics and trunks where they had mouldered unread for centuries.

Many's the dark night I would lie, huddled under my blankets, reading clandestinely by candle-light, transported in my imagination far from frozen reality to lands where the sun always shone, where pirates raided, or wild animals rampaged, where men, not women, did deeds of derring-do and led armies to victory.

There was one poem in particular that I read and read and read again. It is still one of my favourites. As a matter of fact it was written by one of the Gordon clan who came from around the Aberdoon area. It began . . .

'The Assyrian came down like a wolf on the fold . . .'

I had no notion what an Assyrian was, still haven't, but I could just imagine them, twin-headed and ferocious, sweeping downhill on their enemies, bearing all before them.

It's lucky I didn't burn the house down. At the time I felt I was being daring and wicked, did not realize until much later that Euan-Noag knew of my midnight reading sessions – and secretly approved.

He disapproved of very little to tell truth. The negative things used to get his goat. Fear. Greed. Jealousy. Lies. Lack of faith in oneself or others. He refused to believe that there was anything which one could not achieve – if one wanted to achieve it badly enough.

48

Euan-Noag was the provider – the hunter too. He hunted out places for us to perform and made sure that we were always fed and watered. He treated all his charges equally, giving of himself without stint and expecting nothing but the joy of seeing us grow in knowledge and self-worth.

A great man . . . a model.

Unique.

The world shall never see his like again.

And it was I who killed him.

THE TRUE CHRONICLES OF THE REDEEMER

And many thought Euan-Noag to be The One. But he disabused them saying . . . 'Another, greater, comes after me. I am the One who goes before. The One but not the Both.'

Chapter
6

EUAN-NOAG WAS THE FIRST CHILDE THAT COLLUDEN EVER STOLE. That's the truth of the matter. Many things are said of him. That he came from a far country. That he was a Ben-shi in human guise. Nonsense all of it. Nor was he disfigured, as many believe. That rumour began out of the skull-mask which he wore when we were on tour. It served a dual purpose, to disguise his identity when he spread the word about the Great Lie and to give him a legitimate place amongst the freaks in the show. The mask was the reason too for why some say he came from the Poison-lands to the South. The most outlandish tale without a doubt is that he fell from the sky.

In reality he was the son of a wealthy family of the Clan McCloed who farmed areas of land on the Isle of Skye just off the West Coast.

It was in trying to get back there that he was caught in the great storm and would have drowned had not a group of fisher-folk from Tir Na Nog rescued him and taken him back to their own land.

Here in Alba we have no knowledge of things maritime. It is an oversight which I intend to rectify once the exchequer will stand some boat-building. Our only indigenous craft is the coast-hugging coracle which local fishers use to trawl inshore for crab and flatfish. Among Euan-Noag's manuscripts is one on ship-building and I intend to order a sturdy craft and send it, with a mixed crew, to search for Tir Na Nog. We have been a solitary nation too long. I would dearly love to head the expedition myself but someone has to guide the country through its present upheaval. Besides McCloed has already expressed a wish to Captain the vessel and who, more than he, has the right?

Somewhere in that green land of legend he has a step-mother, twin brothers and a sister.

Ymer will stay with me. I need one of them by my side during these trying times. We have decided to name the ship after the coming bairn and construction will begin as soon as the birthing is – fingers crossed – safely over.

But I am diverging from my narrative of Colluden and the stealing of Euan-Noag.

The old man was a Seer even then, had been since youth. Yet when a boychilde was born into the relatively wealthy household where he held the comfortable post of weather-predictor, something in the infant's future prompted him to take the law into his own hands and abandon his well-established position.

'I didnae care to, ye ken. It was a cushy number I had compared to most castrati. Foretelling the rains and reading the tea-leaves when the Mistress had a mind. Not that I wasnae good at it. The wealth of the family could be traced in no small measure to perspicacious planting based on my information. Still and all, when Euan-Noag put in an appearance I had this sudden, overwhelming conviction that here was one that couldnae be left to the knife. This was a wain, I thought, wi' more important things to do with this life than muck out the McCloed byre.'

It was a spur of the moment thing. The Midwife was washing her hands, preparatory to doing the gelding and the rest of the family were trying to console the mother, telling her there was always another time, she was young yet and all the usual blather. The bairn was on the kitchen table, awaiting his fate and Colluden simply went in there and scooped him up and left.

He stole a coracle and rowed, not without difficulties since they're awkward things to handle, to the mainland where good luck, more than good guidance, brought him eventually to the High Hills. It was Summertime and he worked his way across country, hiding Euan-Noag in the heather while he read fortunes in exchange for milk and meal. The knock of a wandering Seer was an unexpected treat in the hum-drum lives of isolated crofters and Colluden used to speak of the journey, fraught with danger though it undoubtedly was, with great nostalgia.

'The McCloeds never came looking for us. Glad to be shot of the bairn most like. I heard later they put it out the childe was a lassie but stillborn. No stigma on the name that way.'

53

After the pair of them were settled and Euan-Noag was a bit grown, Colluden got the notion that if he could lift one bairn he could lift others. In his role as 'The Prophet' as he came to be known, he could keep an eye on imminent births and return around delivery time to spirit the infant away should it turn out to be an unwanted loon. It was Colluden who invented the whole legend of the Ben-shi. He would tell of how he had often met them, emerging like wraithes from the mists on the High Hills. He described them to his wide-eyed audience in gory detail. Twice the height of a normal, fanged, clawed, covered in grey fur. He claimed immunity from their carniverous appetites by dint of a mysterious charm which hung round his neck. It was no more than an uncut Cairngorm strung on a hide thong but he put it about that it came directly from The Source. The story enhanced his already considerable reputation so that his pronouncements came to be taken as pure gospel by the gullible country folk. It got to the point where male children were set out in a basket, naked, on their birthnights in sacrifice to the Ben-shi. Colluden poached many of them this way. Those he missed, because he didn't know about them or because they were born out of their time, were taken back in the following morning castrated and brought up to be the drones which they would have been anyway. No harm done, you might say. But he managed to 'save' quite a few.

And so the Wildemen came into being.

When they, in turn, grew to Manhood, with the normal needs of the normal male, they perpetuated the Ben-shi myth by dressing in grey skins and swooping down in occasional raids on outlying steadings where they would steal young women. The families of these females gave them up for lost, assuming them eaten by the legendary monsters. In fact they were playing their part in increasing the growing tribe of Wildemen in outlying pockets of the High Hills by interbreeding with them. Curiously enough not many of the women tried to escape.

When Euan-Noag reached puberty nothing would do him but that he should travel west in search of his birthplace. Colluden knew it was in his stars and so he let him go, albeit reluctantly, secure in the knowledge that at least he was well versed in the art of survival.

Euan-Noag journeyed towards the setting sun until he came to the Straits which separated Skye from the mainland. As Colluden had before him, he 'borrowed' a boat and made for the opposing shoreline. But the winds were against him. A great storm blew up from the West and, as I have already mentioned, he was only saved from a watery grave by the timely intervention of some fishers from Tir Na Nog. Even after the storm had abated, they refused to land him on Alba, having a superstitious horror of the place, declaring it to be ruled by a Dragon who, in woman's guise, lured unsuspecting sailors to their death. They took him instead back to their own land where Euan-Noag found himself in a country beyond his imagination. Here men and women were treated as equals and lived together in harmony, each appreciated for their own particular talents regardless of sex.

The Reesh, as he called them, taught Euan-Noag many things. Practical things such as fish-catching, creel-mending, boat maintenance and swimming. Mystical things such as reading and cyphering, conjuring and sleight of hand. They also gave him the recipe and showed him how to brew up the cure-all which he used to such advantage later on.

In time he took a wife, Maeve by name, a tall black-haired beauty with amethyst eyes. He would tell me about her often – though not when Blossom was about – and his own eyes would glaze in remembrance of the happy times they had spent together and the three children that she bore him. Twin boys, Finn and Fergus, and Finulla, his little girl.

Euan-Noag would have been happy to stay with the Reesh for good and all, but the Fates decreed otherwise. On a fishing trip much like the one where he had first met his friends, the boat was engulfed by a huge tidal wave and smashed onto the rocks of mainland Alba with the loss of all lives excepting his own.

For months he waited by the shore, squatting in a lean-to hut and keeping a constant fire going in the hopes that a rescue party might turn up. He even tried his hand at building a makeshift raft of driftwood. But no party came and the raft sank and so, when the Winter snows began to fall, he acknowledged that he was stranded and made his reluctant way back to Colluden.

But Euan-Noag was no longer content to skulk in the High Hills. Bursting with knowledge and truth, he determined to spread the word to as many of the male members of society as he could reach or die in the attempt.

Travelling was actively discouraged in those days and a pass was needed, signed by the local Guard-Captain, to move outwith communities. It was one way that the Maxwell had of containing information and keeping an eye on the populace – that and the birth registers overseen by Fergael's Outlyers. Anyone found on the road without such a pass was summarily executed (if male) or (if female) faced a stiff fine and a term of imprisonment.

Euan-Noag hit on the idea of joining a Freak Show and, with the help of Colluden, constructed the hideous mask which was to turn him into the 'Screaming Skull'.

It was the perfect solution and stood both him – and me – in good stead for the future.

As a member of the circus I travelled more, in my first few years, than most inhabitants of Alba would hope to in many lifetimes. Even the Militia patrolled only their own small areas. Few knew, as we travellers did, the topography of the whole region, from the lush fertile Lowlands to the harsh heather-covered moors or saw its beauty as we did, the moon-dark tarns crouched among the mountain snows, the clear streams feeding blue-green lochs full of fish and fisher-birds. The golden white strands of the Outer Reaches, the soaring pinnacles of the High Hills, all these we knew and loved. For Alba, once seen, becomes part of the heart. A place worth fighting and dying for.

Apart from that, the maps which Euan-Noag drew and left to me have been invaluable in the planning of my military strategies.

Euan-Noag's first few phases with the travelling show fuelled his already intense hatred of the regime. The woman in charge, Gargantua, a pervert of huge girth and huger appetites was cruel as only a stupid person can be. Her depravity was legend and she treated her 'turns' with a harshness bordering on sadism. Not long after Euan-Noag joined the troupe, she beat one unfortunate to death leaving the circus short of a wire-walker.

It was because of this that Euan-Noag met Blossom and that McCloed came to be born. He is their natural son, though he was taken to Colluden, for safe-keeping, not long after his birth. This, I suppose, was why Blossom took so to me, as a substitute for her firstborn whom she still calls by his baby-name, Jamie.

To find a replacement then, the Freak Show travelled North to the most notorious of the internment camps at Sinclair. It was the first time Euan-Noag had seen such a place and it was as much of a shock to him as it was to me when I visited the self-same hole later in life.

Most of the population never saw the camps, knew of them naturally, but dismissed them as being part of the system. The law decreed that no female, animal or human, could be put to death. Female evelings then were not returned to the Source, like their luckier male counterparts, but shipped instead to the camps where they could die a slower, more miserable death. These hell-holes were all situate at the very edge of civilisation. Out of sight. Out of mind. Conditions were appalling. At Sinclair for instance there was snow for three quarters of the year. The rest of the time it rained. Disease was rife, as was hunger, the posts being overseen by the dregs of the Militia, types who would sell their mother for a dram and so saw no harm in disposing of supplies meant for the inmates on the black market, pocketing the proceeds and allowing their malformed charges to starve.

One of the first things I did after the wedding was to clear the camps. Wherever possible evelings have been returned to the bosom of their families. We must have a responsibility to the weak as well as the strong if we are to grow as a nation. If that makes me sound po-faced I care not one jot. Those whose blood relatives could not be traced are housed here, at Ballater, in the accommodation orginally reserved for breed-beasts. They are free to come and go as they please, but should they not please then they are not forced to emerge from the privacy of their own quarters. They are warm and well fed. It is not perfect, but it is a start.

At Sinclair the inmates subsisted on grubbed roots and scraps – and each other, for many resorted to cannibalising the dead bodies of their erstwhile friends in order to survive. The only way out of the camps – apart from death – was to be chosen as a pet for a normal's birthday gift or to become part of one of the Freak Shows. The more outlandish of the inhabitants had little hope of either. Some deformities are simply too hideous to give amusement.

It was children such as Blossom – different only in stature from a normal – who had most chance of rescue. That she had taken the eye of the Camp Commandant on her arrival was her misfortune for when Euan-Noag first saw her she had been in the camp for ten long years and was almost fourteen. Gargantua recognized her worth even through the layers of grime. That and her obvious strength. Not many lived so long under such conditions without succumbing to plague or pestilence. She was good stock then. Hardy. As well as being pretty. Which was the main reason Gargatua bought her, making the Camp Commandant, who was loathe to let the midget go even then, an offer she couldnae refuse.

And Euan-Noag, whose life had been empty without Maeve and his bairns, fell for her frail beauty, though it has to be said that, at first, Blossom did not reciprocate his feelings. She had seen too much of deformity and it wasn't until he removed the skull mask to reveal his true face that she found it in her heart to love him back.

As luck would have it, that self-same night Gargantua, in search of a little light diversion, chose to pay her respects to the new recruit.

Caught with more than his trousers down, Euan-Noag had no recourse but to kill the woman which he did by holding the self-same trews over her head and afterwards giving it out that her heart had failed under the weight of her gross body.

Not that anyone mourned Gargantua.

They buried her in a bog the next night and Euan-Noag assumed ownership of the Circus. He still wore his skull for his dissident preaching. But it was as Euan-Noag, the Medicine Man, that he dealt with the local dignitaries and gained our permissions of performance.

Little did those dignitaries guess that behind their back this mild-mannered castrati (for so they thought) was fomenting enough discontent to one day fuel the Redeemer's revolution.

THE TRUE CHRONICLES OF THE REDEEMER

And Rolande grew strong and prospered, gaining great skills and greater knowledge and possessing the voice of the nightingale and the beauty of the evening star. And all who beheld The Redeemer fell under an enchantment. But when an evil man coveted the Childe, a malicious dwarf came as an instrument of destruction. And the man died.

Chapter
7

WHEN I WAS SIX, MY EDUCATION TOOK A MORE PRACTICAL TURN.
'Enough of this book-learning,' is how Euan-Noag put it.
'Now you must be taught to fend for yourself.'

And so he taught me – sleight of hand, juggling and acrobatics, so that I should no longer be a bystander, but a performer, earning my keep like the rest of the company.

That Spring – after a Winter of rehearsal – I took my place in the circus with all the others.

If I may say so myself, I was a becoming childe, with none of the defects of malnutrition so common at the time. Thanks to Euan-Noag's vigilance I was free of rickets or scurvy or dental caries. My limbs were sturdy, my teeth strong and my hair, which had grown in thick and golden, lay like a shiny cap over ears that sat flat to my head. I had a good singing voice and my co-ordination was excellent. Also I was a natural show-off. I loved the crowd, the adulation, the applause.

What childe wouldn't?

Except for the colour of my eyes, Blossom and I could have been twins and Euan-Noag encouraged this notion by dressing us both in parti-coloured costumes and having us lead the parade into the ring.

I think it was this that finally caused the trouble.

Until then, Jolly had alway led the way and felt himself displaced, not only in his performance, but in Blossom's regard . . . the culprit in both cases being myself.

He never showed me any resentment to my face, but it must have been boiling up inside him all the while, festering in the dark recesses of his soul – until he was driven to do what he did.

We had come to a small outpost west of Aboyne, and had

camped in the woods for safety, while Euan-Noag went into town to spread the word that there would be a performance that eve.

There was no question of us entering the settlement. Freakshows were strictly outwith the law and although most outpost Captains were content to turn a blind eye – grateful in many cases, for the diversion that we afforded the citizenry – taking their minds, for once, off the hardness of their lot – we could not rub their noses in it by appearing on their very doorstep.

In some areas strictures were lax enough to allow the Captain and her militia to sneak in and stand at the back – naturally we didn't charge them – but in general, if anyone in authority came, it was only the Captain herself, with perhaps her paramour, both in heavy disguise for propriety's sake. Outlyers never came.

It must have been when we were setting up that Jolly sneaked away.

Certainly he wasn't there to help with the unloading of the blocks that would mark out the circle. I remember Sanke grumbling about it and Cilla soothing him, saying that Jolly was probably in one of his black humours and Sanke saying it was more likely sheer damn laziness or some such.

We were to learn to our cost later that neither was right.

At that very moment, Jolly was taking a dram with the local Tax Collector, one Corbie, a loathsome individual, well suited to his trade, who had a reputation locally for being able to milk blood out of a stone.

Corbie was much feared in the neighbourhood, having an eye and an appetite for young boys. When he came calling, male children would hide in the barn out of his sight. It was not unknown for the more unscrupulous or impecunious of the farm-women to barter their boy's bottoms in return for respite from their usual stipend.

It was to this creature that Jolly went with his tale of the new addition to the show. He painted a glowing picture of my attributes, the softness of my skin, the lightness of my hair, until the old libertine was fairly drooling. He also promised to help the Tax Collector abduct me – for a small fee – later that night.

The dwarf eventually staggered back, very drunk and with some tale of having run up against an old acquaintance and losing all sense of time. He was clearly in no condition to perform and the whole show had to be reorganised at a moment's notice, with Euan-Noag playing the clown, a part he was not well suited for.

This, and Jolly's lack of responsibility, made him very angry. I had never seen him so and the transformation upset me to start with.

He was to be even angrier before the night was out . . . and I even more upset.

There was a full moon that evening and the smell of coming Summer hung on the twilight like honey.

The copse in which we had chosen to give our display filled up fast with folk excited by the atmosphere and eager to be entertained. The clandestine aspect of the circus seemed to add to its appeal so that wherever we went we were guaranteed a full house. But tonight was even fuller than usual, the copse fairly thronging with individuals of all shapes and sizes.

I saw Corbie the moment I came onstage.

I knew little of sex then – unlike my sister who was already an adept – but something in the way he looked at me made me draw back into myself. Instinctively I knew that here was something nasty – and infinitely dangerous.

I got through my juggling with difficulty, my eyes frequently straying from my painted batons to the leering face in the front row. When I ran off, to appreciative applause, I was shaking with unaccustomed agitation.

Because of the alteration in routine I had no time to enter the main caravan but ran behind it to where my clothes had been laid on the grass for a quick change.

There was no-one around but me. Euan-Noag was in the central caravan, counting the take, Jolly was sleeping it off under an adjacent tree and Sanke and Cilla were busy fixing the rope for Blossom to perform on.

I had just dropped my breeches when a hand clasped over my mouth and I heard a voice in my ear, hoarse and sybillant as a striking snake.

'Hello, my pretty,' hissed the voice. 'And what are you doing out in the woods without your breeks on?'

A sweaty hand caressed my bare buttocks and, before I could flinch, a rough forefinger was thrust inside my anus.

The pain was excruciating.

I struggled to be free but the finger went on probing, in and out, while the voice continued pouring unimaginable filth into my unbelieving ears.

'You'll learn to like it soon enough,' said the voice hoarsely, 'That, and all the other things we will do together.'

The finger was withdrawn — none too gently — and the hand, groping between my legs, came into contact with my balls.

My violator gasped, loosened his grip involuntarily on my mouth. I used the opportunity to bite down hard, screaming at the top of my voice as soon as the hand was removed by its cursing owner.

Euan-Noag was out of the van in an instant, clattering down the stairs and demanding to know what was amiss. Taking the situation in at a glance, he grasped the repulsive Corbie by the scruff of the neck and punched him full in the face, scattering teeth in all directions.

Alerted by the commotion, Sanke and Cilla came to his aid and, while Blossom continued to beguile the audience with her singing and balancing, they gagged and bound the obese barrel of lard and bundled him into an adjoining thicket.

Thereafter the show continued as normal with Euan-Noag insisting that I wipe my eyes, change my costume and get out to do my acrobatics.

I could scarcely believe that he could be so harsh but clearly he was right. Self-pity was the last thing I needed at that point. While I changed he rushed into the arena to reduce the audience to hysterics with some made-up tale of a recalcitrant horse and a collapsing feed bucket which explained the commotion away.

By the time the show was over and the last of the revellers had filtered away into the night, Jolly had sobered up enough to be confronted by his infamy. Corbie, unearthed from the thicket and with his gag and bonds removed, blurted out the whole story.

'I paid for that wain,' he wheezed, 'and I intend to have him — balls and all.'

Euan-Noag ignored him, turning on Jolly a face which put the fear of Death into the dwarf.

'Well?' he thundered. 'Explain yourself. Explain how you, who has been closer than brother to me, could do such a monstrous thing to a mere childe?'

But Jolly could offer no excuse. Hungover and riddled with remorse, he could only cringe and weep, begging forgiveness of me, of Euan-Noag, of us all.

'And what are we to do with this wretch?' demanded Euan-Noag.

'Nae problem there,' wheedled the Tax Collector. 'My lips are sealed if . . . you let me take the boy. We can do each other a favour don't you see? You'll go free – no harm done – and I'll have a real man for my pleasure.'

Euan-Noag's face turned livid.

'You'll touch that boy again over my dead body,' he said.

'Oh . . . I see . . .' sneered Corbie. 'He's yours, is he?'

Euan-Noag slapped him across the face then, loosening whatever teeth the unfortunate man had left.

'He's nobody's, you pervert,' he said. 'Can you not get that into your fat head? He's just a boy. And while I live, no harm will come to him.'

The Tax Collector narrowed his eyes. Evil eyes, full of depravity and spite.

'You've just signed his death warrant, Medicine Man,' he spat. 'And your own. I'll tell the Captain, don't think I won't. You've an uncastrated boy with you. It's agin the law. She's a hard one that Captain McJarret. She'll no let you away wi' it. She'll hound you 'till she catches you and when she does . . .' He drew his finger acoss his neck and rolled his eyes with relish at the thought of our coming fate . . . 'It's the radar dishes for you.'

Blossom began to whimper.

The sound seemed to madden Jolly.

Before anyone could stop him he had sprung to the side of the hapless Corgie. Slick as quicksilver he slipped the skean-dhu from his sock.'

'You'll tell naebody naething,' he squealed, clamping his thumb and forefinger over the Tax Collector's nose to cut off his air.

As Corbie opened his mouth to draw breath, Jolly grasped his tongue and, yanking it foreward, sliced it off at the root.

The Eunuchs at Castle Ballater have all had their tongues cut out, so that they might never divulge the secrets of the breeding cages, but I have never seen such an operation performed before or since.

I trust the Medics were more merciful than Jolly.

Corbie thrashed around in his agony, emitting a high-pitched shriek like a stuck porker, blood pouring from his gaping mouth and running down over his beer-gut. He flopped around, swallowing, coughing and shrieking by turns until he choked on his own vomit. His eyes rolled heavenwards, silently supplicating the Great Mother to help him, but his crimes had evidently been too many and varied for her to take notice. He expired in a welter of his own excrement while the rest of us stood, in a horrified circle, unable to raise a hand to help.

The body juddered even after death, a reflex action like the terminal flight of a beheaded capon, and I found my body juddering in sympathy. I shook uncontrollably, my teeth threatening to chatter themselves out of my head while all around the silence of death threw a pall over the moonlit woods.

When, at last, Corbie's body lay still, Euan-Noag turned to Jolly. His voice, when he spoke, carried the finality of the death that lay before us.

'Collect your things,' he said, flat and low. 'And get out of my sight.'

Jolly fell to his knees, reaching up towards the Medicine Man. Corbie's tongue, which he was still gripping in his left hand, slithered from his grip and fell, like a fat pink slug, onto the damp grass. The sight of the disembodied thing was too much for me. I hurled myself at Euan-Noag, howling and sobbing as though my heart would burst.

He scooped me up into his strong arms and held me tight, while the dwarf scrabbled at his legs and tried to out-do my bellowing with his own.

'Don't, Euan-Noag,' he begged. 'Don't send me away. Where would I go? I'd die for certain. I am an eveling. Nobody would take me in.'

'You should have thought of that before you betrayed us,' said Euan-Noag.

'But . . . but it's alright now,' stammered Jolly. 'He's dead. Nobody need ever know.'

'Fool,' roared Euan-Noag. 'You think you can right one evil with another?'

Jolly cringed away.

'Please,' he pleaded. 'I'll do anything . . . anything . . only don't make me go.'

'You must go.' Euan-Noag was intractable. 'You have blood on your hands.'

'The blood of a Tax Collector,' said Jolly, and he spat.

'The blood of a human being.'

'And what of my blood?' screamed the dwarf. 'If you cast me out, that'll be on your hands.'

'I allow you to go in peace.'

'You condemn me to death.'

'You have the same chance you had as when I found you . . . no more . . . no less.'

'You send me to my doom . . .' moaned Jolly. 'I am an eveling . . . the defiled.'

'There are other freak shows,' said Euan-Noag. 'Other circuses.'

'Worse than death,' wept Jolly, turning to the midget for help. 'Blossom,' he begged, 'make him let me stay. I only did it for you . . . because I love you.'

But Blossom merely shrugged him away and ran to put her arms around my dangling legs.

The gesture defeated Jolly entirely. He stumbled to one of the vans to collect his few paltry scraps of personal belongings and wrap them in a napkin.

I shall never forget him there, defeated and forlorn as we drove away into the night. He stood silently by the freshly turned grave of the man he had murdered, his face a mask of resentment, and tears of abandonment oozing from his eyes.

Poor Jolly, he was not the first, nor the last, to be betrayed by the intensity of his emotions. Another lesson I learned that day. Love brings pain.

'What if he tells?' grumbled Sanke, as the caravans clunked round a corner and the dwarf was lost to sight among the trees.

'How can he?' Euan-Noag reassured him. 'He cannot betray us without he betrays himself.'

He looked down at me, sitting beside him on the driver's ledge, and his bearded face clouded with concern.

'All the same,' he said. 'The further we get away from here the better, and I think, young Rolande, it might be time for you to become a girl.'

THE TRUE CHRONICLES OF THE REDEEMER

Now Ymer, blood-sister to Rolande, had the gift of prophesy and the second sight. In a vision she saw the coming of The Redeemer. And her Clan-Mother, the Maxwell, and all the Women of Castle Ballater were sore afraid.

Chapter
8

AT ABOUT THE TIME THAT I WAS RELINQUISHING ONE PERSONA for another, it was discovered that my sister had The Sight.

The first visitation came without warning, like a bolt from the robin's egg sky of an Autumn afternoon awash with sunlight.

An old crone had lately arrived at the gate trailing a giant Snow-Bear which she avowed could dance and wrestle as well as any human alive. A display had been arranged and the whole Castle was ahum with excitement.

The animal, chained to a whipping-post in the central keep, was as fierce as its mistress was feeble, but there was no doubt as to who was in charge. The hag carried a knotted whip and a wand with a heated tip which, should the animal misbehave, she would ram up against its soft underparts, making it bellow with fear. The bear was big enough to flatten her with one swipe but it was clear that she had had it since a cub and the poor thing had never overcome the terror instilled while it was still weak and helpless.

Such is the conditioning we receive in youth. It stays with us for life.

The beast was light on its feet for such a bulky creature. It did somersaults, turned arse-over-tip and danced its shambling way around the inner courtyard, all at the crone's bidding. She prodded and baited it, cackling her toothless orders and bending the great dumb animal to her will.

The whole of Castle Ballater turned out to see this sorry spectacle. The Maxwell was there with her entire Guard. Fergael and Campbell, already slightly demented and mumbling to herself as she picked absently at the scab on her latest self-inflicted wound. Ymer – now seven and re-admitted to the Royal presence – came leading Buchan, apeing the bear, on a thonged collar and chain. Morangy had turned out too, along with the entire Hospice staff plus the complete conglomeration of the Inner Circle barring one unfortunate who had been confined to bed with severe toothache.

Even the breed-beasts had been brought up for the occasion although they were kept tethered and well away from the women, hard up against the end of the yard where stood the row of machines on which every tri-day and under strict supervision of the Barracks-Master, they were used to exercise their bodies. Strange, ominous contraptions these machines were, of weights and levers and studded harnesses, not at all unlike the torture instruments that lined the walls of the punishment cells.

The breed-beasts of Ballater were unique, being reputedly the only males who had not been castrated in the whole of Alba. They were only released from the cages for tournaments, training or to be used as cannon fodder. On the infrequent occasions when the Maxwell was called on to take the field against the interlopers from the Poison Lands to the south, they were used as a human shield, taking the van in any engagement.

These were the proud sons of the Inner Circle, permitted to keep their manhood intact only because their balls contained the courage to lend them bravery in battle.

Not that they were braver than the Clanswomen.

No-one was braver than they.

But a breed-beast had more muscle power – and being male, they were more expendable.

While they lived, they lived in some style. Eunuchs were provided for their pleasure and they were fed fresh eggs and raw liver to keep up their strength.

They were exercised and oiled and pampered like the finest bred war-stags.

All they lacked was their freedom.

Still, thanks to regular infusions of tranquillising herbs, the breed-beasts were, in general, a docile lot.

Occasionally a rogue male would kick against the system, try to foment unrest or make a half-hearted attempt at escape. One such made his bid during my first year back at Castle Ballater. His name was Fingus, a great red-headed brute he was, a half brother to Cameron and just as mean. And yet, before he died I saw him reduced to a blubbering mass of writhing flesh, crying like a babby for the Great Mother to put him out of his misery.

69

There was usually no more than one escape attempt per generation. And I'm not surprised. Anyone who watched The Punishment was unlikely to count an abstract concept such as Freedom worthy of such a risk.

The death had been devised by the first Fergael, directly after The Fall, and had been strictly adhered to, because of its efficacy, ever since.

The unfortunate renegade was force-fed Backshi berries and then nature was simply left to take its course.

After several days when the worm in the berry was thought to have emerged, the victim was brought out to the centre of the Inner Courtyard and strapped to a wooden bench. His eyelids were then removed, so that he was forced to watch, as well as feel, the incubated worms as they burrowed their way out through his gut to erupt from his stomach in a writhing mass of putrefaction.

The process took a long time.

Several days at least before the eggs, nestling in the warmth of the intestines, hatched. Long, endless hours of anticipation, horror and living death as the mind cringed away from the inevitability of what was to come. If the victim was lucky, he went mad during those first days.

If he did not, then he was fully *compos-mentis* as his belly began to heave, like that of a pregnant sow whose piglets, impatient to be born, turn urgently in the womb. Unable to turn his mutilated eyes away, he could only stare, as his navel inverted, swelled and eventually burst, allowing the wriggling mess to push its way out to temporary freedom.

Temporary because, when they finally emerged, the parasites were doused with pitch and set alight.

This was the moment for which the breed-beast prayed, the agony of the fire, as flesh roasted and hair singed, coming as a blessed relief after the unbelievable torture of being consumed alive from within.

All the court was forced to watch the execution.

Nobody was exempt.

Just as no-one was excused the sight of the great Snow-Bear that afternoon, as its sadistic keeper prodded it forward to the foot of the Royal Dais to make obeisance to the Lady Maxwell.

She, with her usual air of aloof disinterest, gave her permission for the demonstration to begin and, after the customary preliminaries of tricks and tumblings, the crone threw down the challenge for which all had been waiting.

Who would wrestle with the great animal?

After some deliberation, Tor, the Maxwell's pet breed-beast, was led forward.

Tor was a giant of a man, a mere hand height shorter than the Snow-Bear, and his entrance into the arena, flanked by two Eunuchs, brought much appreciative applause from the royal household.

The combatants circled each other warily. The animal, its yellow fangs dripping saliva, facing the prospect of the first decent meal it had had in days. The man, naked but for a box covering his soft private parts, oiled muscles rippling in the warm Autumn air, facing his own private fear as he weighed up his adversary's strengths and weaknesses. Brain versus brawn. Not that the crowd, clamouring for blood, credited Tor with any more brain than the bear.

He was a man – a breed-beast – an even match for the creature whom he fought.

They cheered him on of course, not because he was human, but because he was the Lady's Champion. They urged him to fight, willing him to do the Castle and his patrons proud.

With the roar of the crowd in his ears Tor closed with the beast, felt its hairy arms encircle him. He must have known in an instant that he had made the ultimate mistake; that the brute's strength was far superior to his own; that he had lost before he had even begun; that he was a dead man.

In the breath-held silence of the afternoon was heard the sickening sound of ribs cracking.

It was at this point that Ymer had her vision.

She has tried to explain the experience to me many times since and I can do no better than to put it in her own words.

'They fascinated me,' she admits. 'The beast and the man-beast, grappling for supremacy. Faced with their brute strength, the smell of them, the fear, I felt my insides soften and begin to liquefy. The spectacle stimulated my innermost cravings and I could feel the soft flesh of my inside thighs dampen beneath my smock. I shifted in my chair and Buchan, recognizing the expression in my eyes, began to rub his forehead against my knee. I was forced to slap him, hard, across the face to stop him from giving the game away. But when I looked around I realized that I was not the only one aroused by the tournament. All about, women were wriggling in their seats and their faces had taken on that high, sharp colour that signifies sexual excitement.

71

The assailants were writhing on the ground now, the Snow-Bear atop Tor, its great haunches heaving while it tried to throttle the life out of him. Tor struggled feebly and attempted to kick his adversary where it would hurt most. Blood was beginning to pour from a wound in his side. The scent of it, warm and acrid, mingled with smoke from the Autumn bonfires down in the valley.

'The familiar pulse between my legs was becoming too urgent to ignore. I moved around on my stool, feeling for a protrusion, an irregularity, anything against which I could rub myself to produce the desired effect.

'Close by me, Fergael gave a hoarse cry. "Kill," she wheezed.

'And the entire audience echoed . . . "Kill, Kill, Kill."

'That was when I came, a great rushing sensation, convulsing my body, soaking my underclothes and spattering the ground at my feet.

And in that instant, the world began to turn. Tor disappeared in a wave of blood and the great white Snow-Beast rose on its hind quarters and advanced towards me. And suddenly it was a beast no longer but a male figure, naked to the waist, with a woman's bare breasts. This apparition was crowned by an opaque head-piece that covered the face from view. Curious characters, which I could not decipher, were etched across the visor.

'Then I was in the midst of a battle. Women and men fighting hand to hand, a great lizard breathing smoke and a flag with a raven fluttering over all. The Clanswomen were there in force, in the full dress regalia of the Maxwell, but the men, great, hairy things, faces bristling with fungus, huge two-edged swords swirling around their wild heads, were clad only in animal skins. Unthinkably, the men seemed to be winning, beating the Clanswomen back.

'And ever among them, darting from skirmish to skirmish, urging them on, ran the mysterious helmeted figure.

'I tried to make myself invisible, hoping that no-one would notice me there, but the very thought seemed to attract the figure's attention. It turned in my direction, golden eyes probing the mist, seeking me out.

'The figure came towards me, willing me still, pinning me as a butterfly is pinned on a display-board. And then slowly, deliberately, the figure began to unbuckle the headpiece.

I did not want to look. I tried to turn my head away but was powerless to do so. The helmet came off. And the face revealed was my own face, crowned with hair, gold as a gorse-bush flower. An avenging angel of death. My destiny and my salvation.

'And a name entered by head unbidden.

' "The Redeemer!" I screamed.

'And then I fainted . . . dead away.'

Morangy was sitting behind Ymer when the incident occurred. He recalls it as the rest of the crowd must have witnessed it. I give you his version, though he has an overblown sense of the dramatic and I have no doubt but the tale has become somewhat embellished in the telling.

'The beast had just despatched Tor,' he says, 'ripping his face away with one bloody swipe. It rose and beat its chest, turning its head this way and that as if in search of new victims. Its reddened eye fell on the Queen's torque glinting in a shaft of sunlight.

'Nothing its trainer could do seemed to deflect it from its purpose. She screeched and prodded it with the heat-stick, thrusting it up between the animal's legs. But blood-lust is stronger than pain. The bear continued to advance. The crone began to whip her charge, laying into it until the blood darkened the white pelt.

'The bear never halted in its stride. Like a cow flicking away a fly, it gave her a back-handed clout that snapped her scrawny neck. She flew against the barriers and slid down the cobbles, limp as a rag-doll, dead as a door-nail.

'And still the beast came on.

'People were beginning to rise from their seats now, trampling on each other's toes and pushing each other in their haste to get away out of the stands. The Maxwell stood up and Cameron stepped in front of her, unsheathing her battle-axe, preparing to give her life, if necessary, in defence of the Monarch.

'That was when Ymer screamed.

'She was a small childe still but the scream was that of a Ben-shi, forced from her frail lungs in an earsplitting howl that halted both the bear and the audience in its tracks.

'She stood, straight as a ramrod, her body shuddering, her eyes rolling in her head and foam flecking the corners of her mouth.

'The world held its breath.

'Ymer held out her hands, pushing with her palms as

73

though to keep some frightful apparition at bay, and she screamed again so that the hair on everyone in the courtyard stood on end at the sound. Then she shouted one word, something that made the Maxwell blanch as she had not blanched at the approach of the Snow-Bear. And that word was shouted in a voice that bore no relation to the childe's own. It rumbled up from the depths of the Clan's unconscious, its tone harsh and bitter as the newly turned sod on a suicide's grave.

' "The Redeemer!" she screamed.

'And then she collapsed.'

The delinquent bear was all but forgotten in the confusion following Ymer's pronouncement.

She was scooped up and taken back to the Dark Tower to be tended and fussed over until she came round.

It was left to Cameron to dispatch the Snow-Bear, which she did with a blow from her battle-axe that split its skull from crown to nape.

As for my sister . . . Ever the opportunist, she revelled in her new-found infamy.

Emerging from her trance to find herself overlooked not only by the most senior members of the household but also by the beloved mother who had hitherto ignored her, she realized that her talent was something she could use to good advantage.

Ymer has The Sight in truth.

But that is not to say that she has not faked a visitation on occasion. And for that, I suppose, I should be thankful.

Had my sister been more scrupulous, I might not be here today.

74

THE TRUE CHRONICLES OF THE REDEEMER

Then Rolande, who had the power, assumed the form of a woman in order to go safely in a land dominated by women.

Chapter
9

THE LOSS OF JOLLY LEFT US WITH A SEVERE GAP IN OUR COMPANY. One less pair of hands to shift scenery and lift props.

And . . . most important . . . no clown.

Magic and acrobatics are all very well, but best of all, an audience likes to laugh.

Euan-Noag stepped into the breach temporarily by turning our show into a spectacle of magic and hypnotism. Billed as 'The Great Sorprendo', he would enter the arena in scarlet cloak and mask, call for volunteers and then charm them to sleep by swinging a silver talisman in front of their eyes. I have the bauble beside me now, a tiny five-pointed star slung on a leather thong. No-one could resist the power of the thing and when they were under its influence, Euan-Noag could persuade them that they were dogs or donkeys and they would cavort around the arena making animal noises. The crowd loved it, laughing uproariously at the antics of otherwise sober members of the community. But it was a cruel sort of humour and Euan-Noag was never totally at ease with it.

And then, several seasons after Jolly departed, we came across Isla, in an isolated outpost on the wastes of Culloden Moor. There can surely be no bleaker place. Night drops like a stone from leaden skies and the ever present wind cuts through the bones like a scythe.

Isla, like Jolly, was a dwarf, the sole survivor of a rival freak show which had fallen victim to an attack of blackwater sickness. She came to us courtesy of her ne'er do well mother into whose ale-house she had staggered begging shelter. The woman had sold the poor wretch once already and, seeing the opportunity to make a double profit out of her daughter's affliction, kept her in the hop-barn, feeding her sparsely on bran-mash, until our show made its annual visit in the early Spring.

Euan-Noag paid two month's takings for the dwarf and the woman, having driven an outrageous bargain, went away well satisfied.

For a while it looked as though he might have wasted his money altogether.

Isla was a walking skeleton, her rib cage etched in stark relief against paper thin skin. It was touch and go whether she would live at all.

But live she did . . . more thanks to the quality of her spirit than anything else. A quarter year of rest, good feeding and liberal doses of Euan-Noag's magic medicine made a new woman of her. She filled out until she was almost buxom, the triple dots that had marked her boney chest swelling into handsome breasts. They were to make a voluptuous display in the Indian Temple dance which Blossom devised for her. Not that three breasts were so unusual in an eveling, but one was generally set below the original, giving a lop-sided look to the physique. It was seldom one got them so aesthetically placed – in a straight line across the chest.

Isla was nowhere near as fetching as Blossom, having broad shoulders, crinkly red hair and an abundance of freckles, but her disposition was such that she appeared a good deal prettier than she was. She was forever happy, forever smiling. Considering the way she'd been treated, it's a wonder she could smile at all, but there was no situation, however dire, to which she could not see the funny side. Her face seemed creased in a permanent grin, her eyes constantly twinkled as if at the remembrance of some untold joke. Truly, she made the room light with her presence.

Her optimism was infectious. She made the rest of us smile just to see her. And her ability to touch the audience was phenomenal. Her warmth flowed out over the footlights so that they forget for a moment the harshness of their lives . . . and they loved her for it.

Blossom loved her too. Cilla had always been totally wrapped up in Sanke (sometimes literally since he would wind himself round her like a snake) and in Isla, Blossom found the companionship which she craved from one of her own sex and her own size. Isla would hang on her every word and Blossom, in turn, refused to leave her friend's side, to the point where Euan-Noag threatened to bill them as 'The Siamese Twins'.

They were like a pair of children, gossiping and giggling in corners together over shared secrets and their closeness threw Euan-Noag and I more and more together.

He spent every daylight hour teaching me Science, History, Astrology, Folklore and the Humanities.

After the Corbie incident, Blossom had taught me to strap up my penis and had begun to dress me as a girl. My hair now hung to my waist and on stage I wore rouge and face paint just like the other women. But I hunted and wrestled and got into trouble like any boy. The ambiguity bothered me not at all. I had yet to reach the age of puberty with all the conflicting sexual doubts that it brings.

It would have been unthinkable for a normal woman to be part of a circus, so, to reinforce my disguise Euan-Noag pretended that I was a fully grown midget, just like Blossom. The previous winter she and I had developed a 'sister' act incorporating my juggling and her wire-walking and culminating in a song-and-dance routine during which members of the audience were brought up to perform reels with us. The contrast between the great hulks we danced with and our neatness made the whole concept a great success.

And then, it must have been a few moon-phases after Isla joined us, Blossom began to put on weight. Her belly started to swell alarmingly and her normally bird-like appetite underwent a drastic change. She seemed to be always hungry. What's more, her choice of nourishment can only be termed bizarre. At the time I could not understand it. In the last few months I have come to regard it as utterly normal. She would devour quail's eggs laced with buttermilk, sliced onions smothered in goose grease or apple turnovers doused in pickling vinegar.

I waited for someone to mention this wierd behaviour but no-one seemed to remark it but me. Except for the fact that Euan-Noag seemed more besotted with her the fatter she became, everyone seemed to regard Blossom's quirks as totally normal.

At last, convinced that she was under some evil influence, I took my fears in secret to the Medicine Man.

'She must be bewitched,' I said, 'To behave so perversely and allow herself to become so grotesque. She's as fat as a butter-ball already. If she doesn't stop eating she'll explode.'

But Euan-Noag only laughed.

'She's eating for two,' he said – and when I asked him to

explain he added gently, 'She is with childe, Rolande. Blossom is going to have a baby.'

'She has been visited by the Goddess, then?' I said.

'And by me,' said Euan-Noag with a grin.

'And what have you to do with it all? To have a childe one must be touched by the Goddess. Everyone knows that. Has Blossom been so touched? When?'

Euan-Noag's answer was to get down his book-box and select from it a huge tome entitled 'Grey's Anatomy'. It was a volume that I had not seen before and proved to be a fascinating cornucopia of information concerning the human body and all its functions. It was liberally laced with illustrations and by the end of the afternoon I knew how Blossom's baby had been conceived and how it would come into this world of pain.

I took some persuading, mind you.

Up until then my only sex education had been doled out behind hayricks by the odd childe daring enough to defy its mother and keep company with a freak. They must have thought me mighty innocent for a full grown midget. But from these clandestine conversations I had learned that it was in the power of women only to perpetuate the human race. Men had no part in the reproductive process and it was this that made them so much inferior to their female counterparts.

What I read in Euan-Noag's book gave the lie to this philosophy.

When I said as much to my teacher he stroked his beard and looked thoughtful.

'I know,' he said. 'It doesn't make sense, and yet it is so. Something must have altered in Alba after The Fall. Some mutation allowing the women to re-produce themselves.' He grinned. 'More efficient but less fun.'

'The process is fun?' I must have looked dubious. 'It sounds revolting to me.'

'You wait', Euan-Noag promised me. 'You'll change your mind one of these days.'

'And will I have a baby one of these days?' I was curious.

But Euan-Noag said he didn't know, I'd just have to wait and see.

'Which am I then?' I demanded. 'The male or the female?'

'You are unique, Rolande. You are the both.'

'I don't want to be unique,' I protested, quite alarmed by the whole thing. 'Surely in Alba it is better to be a girl?'

'I cannot deny it.'

'Then how could you be so cruel?' I protested. 'Why did you not let them castrate me at birth. That way I would be normal, living like a normal person. Not skulking around the country with a bunch of freaks.'

Euan-Noag put one hand on my shoulder and, with the other, he tipped my chin up so that I was staring directly into his eyes. I could not bear the expression of reproach that I saw there and tried to turn my head away, but he held my gaze until I blushed with shame and stammered out some kind of inadequate apology.

'Never think of them as that,' said Euan-Noag. 'As I never think it of you.'

'But I am not a freak,' I said. 'I am almost normal.'

'You will *never* be normal. Nor should you wish to be. The future holds great things for you. You are a very special human being.'

I felt the skin on the back of my neck prickle as the hairs rose.

'The destiny of Alba is in your hands, childe.'

Euan-Noag looked at me solemnly, his eyes dark and deep as a mountain tarn.

'How so?' I stammered.

'There is a prophecy,' he said. 'Dating from the time of The Fall. It tells how one day a Redeemer will rise in Alba. A twin-sexed being who will overthrow the reign of the Maxwells and lead the land into an age of enlightenment. That Redeemer is you, Rolande. Of that I am convinced. You are the One who is destined to free Alba from the female yoke.'

'But I am female,' I said.

'And male.'

'I cannot be true to both.'

'You must try. It is the race's only hope.'

'I will try,' I promised.

Which is why, despite everything, I am trying still.

THE TRUE CHRONICLES OF THE REDEEMER

And the witch, Fergael, drank human blood and coupled with Daemons and great was her wickedness. Under her auspices the Initiates of the Goddess lay down together, possessing each other carnally. But the Lady Ymer broke the laws of the Mother and lay with her pet, the malechilde Buchan. And Fergael enclosed Ymer in a dark place and struck the boy dead.

Chapter
10

YMER, MEANWHILE WAS GROWING SLOWLY TOWARDS WOMAN-
hood.

She walked ever in Fergael's shadow and learned to fear
and admire the Madwoman in equal measure. Fergael taught
her to harness her talent for prophesy and to induce visions by a
combination of fasting, sexual stimulation and the use of certain
drugs.

The results, Ymer tells me, were dubious, and although she
payed lip service to the veracity of her nightmarish and terrifying
dreams, she never set much store by them. Only by the ones that
came unbidden. Those she heeded – as well she might. And then
– in the winter of her eleventh year – her bleeding began.

She had anticipated it but, when it came, it came in the dark
hour before the dawn and with such ferocity that it saturated
the bed-linen and soaked her from waist to heel. The flood was
accompanied by racking spasms of pain.

Nobody had told her to expect pain.

She panicked and rushed to Morangy for reassurance that
she was not about to die.

The Midwife persuaded her that all was 'as normal as might
be', bathing her bloodied limbs and staunching the flow with
linen pads. He showed her how to bind herself and made a
posset to ease away the cramps.

'You are become a woman,' he told her. 'You must be glad.
Now you can bear a childe of your own.'

'She will never bear a childe, Midget.'

It was Fergael.

She had divined that Ymer's menses had begun and had

arrived to collect the soiled clothes to burn as an offering to the Great Mother.

'Childbirth is not in her destiny,' she went on. 'Which is as well since she is as frail as her mother was before her.'

Her eyes glittered in the rays of the rising sun as she stared pointedly at my sister's swelling breasts. 'But you are right, Midwife,' she said. 'Ymer *is* become a woman. At Imbolc she may bear witness to The Coupling.'

And so it was that on the day of the Spring Equinox, three moon-cycles after her bleeding had begun, Ymer made her first entrance into the Dark Tower.

The Tower was a fearsome place, set alone and apart from the Castle, a bleak, phallic finger rising from the side of Ballater Brae. It sprang from the earth like a narwaal's tusk, black as basalt yet constructed not from stone but from some magic metal whose elements have long since been lost to humankind. A precarious-looking edifice, the bulbous upper story perched incongruously atop the stalk-like base, it stands there still, despite all my efforts to tear it down, a salutory reminder of all that is worst in us — the human race.

It was Fergael's Holy of Holies and she used it for those religious ceremonies that were too secret to be held in open forum. Also because its windowless walls allowed no cry to escape. Thus could the hapless victims of her more gory rituals be dispatched at leisure, their desperate screams unheard by the world without.

Ymer says she felt like a victim that chill February morning as the two Initiates, Scawthatch and Ailil, led her barefoot across the cobbles and up the stony path to the Dark Tower. Even though she had done no wrong, the place evoked in her a feeling of terror, as though, like so many who had trod this path before, she was travelling to her doom, a vision of the future which she thrust away from her by biting down hard on her tongue 'til the blood came warm into her dry mouth.

No door showed in the sheer face of the odalisque, but the Initiate Ailil inserted a small green card into a slit in the metal and a hatch slid back to allow them to enter.

It closed directly behind them, shutting out light and air and my sister, who has never been good in confined spaces, was overcome by the choking feeling of one who has been buried alive.

Ailil lit a taper and held it high to light them up the narrow, spiral staircase. This, too, was metal, painted grey, the paint peeling so that it scourged the soles of their feet as they ascended. They climbed it single file, Ailil first, Ymer shivering behind, and Scawthatch bringing up the rear, pinching my sister spitefully if she showed any signs of slowing down.

Ymer counted three hundred and ninety-nine steps before they emerged through a trap-door into the body of the tower itself, a single, vast circular room, dark, claustrophobic, dimly lit by guttering lamps, the air blue with smoke rising from the votive fire.

There was an overpowering stench of burning blood and singeing hair. The acrid smell made Ymer want to gag. She found herself shaking and knew it was not from cold. To one side of the living flame, which Ailil whispered was never allowed to go out, a Handmaiden sat, continually feeding the fire with a pile of soiled napkins that lay before her on a metal dish. To the other side, another handmaiden clutching the drum barron which she beat with a human bone, set up a thrumming that picked up the heart-beat and pulsed through the blood.

Scawthatch, a nasty girl who took inordinate delight in being as unpleasant as possible, informed Ymer that the drum-skin was made from human skin flayed from the bones of an Initiate who had betrayed her vocation and had been found in the company of a man.

Ailil told her to 'Hold her whist.'

The room was dominated by a lifesize statue of the Mother Goddess, bare breasted and holding aloft two coiled pythons.

The figure was frighteningly lifelike, having been coloured in the tints of the human body. The eyes, staring golden in the half-light, seemed to bore into the soul. The skin-tone was darker than usual and the hair, golden as the eyes, lay looped over the head in an elaborate arrangement of waves and whorls. It was real human hair, shaved or torn from some unfortunate's scalp. The nipples, erect on the pendulous breasts, were golden too, as were the long spiked fingernails and the torque that encircled the slender column of neck. Below the nipped in waist, the statue was clad in a belled skirt, held away from the body in a series of hoops. Bright blue in colour, to match the sapphire set in the centre of her forehead, it was painted in circular patterns of snakes, shells and coupling animals.

Ymer's eye was drawn to a strange contraption affixed to the ceiling above the figure's head. It was a pulley affair and consisted of a pair of looped chains, each one ending in a hook. Some instrument of torture she supposed. The shelf of grinning deaths-heads that peeped at her from behind an adjacent pillar did nothing to change her mind.

At the farthest end of her room, diametrically opposite the great idol, hung a set of heavy, blood-coloured drapes. From behind them Ymer could hear the murmur of human voices and guessed that the High Priest and her lesser acolytes were preparing themselves there. A glass case, the height and breadth of a coffin, stood upright nearby with, beside it, a huge brass cauldron set on three legs.

The only other objects in the tower were the great cavern altar, set between the Goddess and the sacrificial flame and a series of thirteen footstools, each embroidered with a zodiacal sign, which circumscribed the room.

The rhythm of the barron suddenly increased in urgency and, as if this were some kind of signal, the drapes parted to reveal a quorum of thirteen Priests, each bearing a ritual object. One a chalice, one a dagger, a box of ointment, a jar of oil, a phial of blood and so on.

Chanting a medit they filed into the room and took their respective places, settling themselves on the footstools and resting their trophies before them in their laps. The chanting ceased but the thirteen mouths continued to move in rhythmic motion, sacred cows each chewing a cud of futret bane.

Ailil handed a pellet to Ymer, but she shook her head, preferring, for some perverse reason, to face her destiny in cold blood.

Finally, the High Priest made her entrance, flanked by her two permanent Bodyservants, Doal and Machan. Behind her, shuffling, head down, came Campbell, Buchan's crazy mother.

Fergael was in another dimension, her pupils pinpoints in heavy lidded eyes, her mouth slack, her breathing shallow, her neck weighted down by a brass collar through the central loop of which a long, circular length of chain ran to connecting rings in her manacles and leg-irons. She wore the traditional bride-gown of yellow muslin, transparent enough to expose the angular contours of her body. The colour of the garment seemed reflected in the jaundiced tint of her liver-diseased skin.

She stopped as she spied Ymer, jerking tight the silk lead-reins held by her assistants. Campbell collided with her rump and started back, arms raised to ward off the expected blow.

But Fergael ignored her.

'Bring the kwine to me,' she said.

So Ymer was nudged forward until the High Priest could lift a weighted finger to draw the sign of the inverted cross in the air above her forehead.

'Regard well what follows here, Childe,' she mumbled. 'This is your future. When others of your generation are initiated into their Bloodrite, you will not join their games. The hymen of the High Priest must be penetrated only by The Source of all Creation.'

She turned towards the idol and genuflected and all the other priests followed suit while Ymer was ushered back into the shadows and forced to her knees on the hard floor.

Fergael dropped on all fours for her final approach to the high altar. There her robes were stripped from her and a harness of leather straps criss-crossed over her torso leaving breasts and genitalia exposed. The strange garment, with its huge epaulets each with a single iron ring set over the point of the shoulder, gave the High Priest a mishapen, hunchbacked appearance.

When all had been adjusted to their satisfaction, Doal and Machan lifted their emaciated mistress and spreadeagled her on the cold altar slab.

One by one the Acolytes rose and stepped forward to prepare the bride for the coupling. Blood from the phial was mixed with the contents of the chalice (which Ymer later found out contained semen from the King Stag) and given to Fergael to drink. Her hair was plastered with pomade and polished with silken cloths 'til the spikes sparkled like metal. Rouge was applied from little ivory paintpots, not only to contour the face but to emphasise navel, nipples and the shaven genital area. The Handmaiden who carried the knife applied the point under Fergael's left breast, pricking the skin to draw a drop of blood which was then transferred to the forehead.

Finally the perfumed oil was used to anoint the body, massaged into the skin by the Priest Mide who began at the toes and worked upwards in smooth rythmic strokes to the hollow of the High Priest's neck.

When all was done, the two who had led Fergael to the altar, and who were now stationed at its base and head respectively, leant forward to pinion her wrists and ankles. Doal hoisted her arms up and back bringing her elbows level with her ears. Machan pushed the legs wide so that the body was held vice-like, in the shape of an X.

Then it was Campbell's turn.

Pulling off the loose smock that was her only clothing, she climbed up onto the altar and straddled the captive woman.

A sigh of anticipation hissed around the room.

Campbell began to caress Fergael's armpits, running her thumbs into the hollows, smoothing her palms down and across the breasts until the nipples stood up taut and hard. Holding the tiny stalks between thumb and forefinger, she nuzzled them alternately like a greedy piglet desperate for milk.

Fergael moaned, writhing against her human clamps, arching her back upwards.

Campbell slid back and down, tongue tracing a path to the navel and then lower, to the painted genitalia. Prolonging the agony, she chose to bypass labia and clitoris, concentrating instead on the inside of Fergael's spread thighs, nibbling the slick flesh with sharp, white teeth. Her breasts hung like ripe melons in the area between her lover's knees. Her hands continued to manipulate the stiff brown nipples.

A creamy liquid began to trickle from between Fergael's legs. She was panting now and had begun to shiver involuntarily.

Campbell stopped her teasing at last, bringing her fingers down to hold her labia wide and allow her probing tongue to hone in on the engorged clitoris.

Ymer, wet with her own juices, waited for the scream which she knew, from experience, would herald the climax.

Instead, the High Priest opened her eyes and cried hoarsely. 'Enough!'

Campbell's head snapped up and back. She scrambled from the altar and crawled away into the shadows to transfer her attentions and her fingers to her own breasts, her own thighs.

All around, women had begun to writhe and moan, hoisting their robes waist high, stroking and massaging themselves and each other.

The sound of the barron was one long, continuous hammering roar now, the smell of sweat and sex mingling with the burning cloths was almost overpowering.

Ymer felt her thighs wet from groin to knee. Beside her, Ailil was making small mewling sounds in her excitement.

Doal began coupling the hooks from the ceiling to the iron eyes on Fergael's black harness. Machan meanwhile, climbed

87

the stairs to the foot of the idol, grasped the blue skirt and tore it aside.

Ymer's heart jumped in her breast as all around her women began screaming and sobbing. For underneath the woman's trappings the Source stood straddle legged. And wonder of wonders, beneath the rounded female belly, the tiny waist and the heavy breasts, a huge male member rose rampant from a bush of curling hair.

'Hurry,' cried Fergael. 'Now. I am ready now.'

Using the pulley mechanism, Doal began to winch the High Priest off the ground. The leather thongs tightened, biting into her body as she dangled from the padded epaulets like a huge mishapen trout fly. When she was high enough, Machan grasped her swinging legs and guided her, slowly but surely, towards the Source's erectile penis.

Ymer had a sudden insane desire to laugh. One look at the two faces beside her was enough to change her mind. In this mood they would gladly tear any detractor limb from limb – and probably eat the pieces. As she looked back, Machan let down the incredible contraption, impaling Fergael on the giant phallus.

The High Priest gave a squeal that persuaded Ymer that she had been split from stem to stern. But clearly the passion overrode the pain. Grasping the idol by its naked breast, Fergael began to writhe on the penis, raising and lowering her buttocks to manipulate herself to orgasm.

She came almost immediately with a shriek that drowned out the barron and brought the cacophony of mass hysteria to an immediate and unnerving halt.

Ymer, drymouthed, pondered on what Fergael had told her, that in this spectacle of degradation and lust, lay a vision of her own future.

She was at once repulsed and exhilarated, rejected the idea yet could not resist it, longed to take the shaft of cold marble within her, while dreading it above all else.

How did it feel, this penetration, this giving up of one's body? Was there any way she could anticipate the coming event? Buchan! She had never before considered such a deviation . . . should not think of it . . . dare not . . . and yet . . . who would know? The women of the Inner Sanctum were involved in their own pursuits. She looked around at the pile of entwined bodies, missed Scawthatch and Ailil, spotted them at last in a huddle by the stairwell.

Doal and Machan were consoling one another on the high altar while Fergael, satiated and half senseless, clung to her lifeless mate as though her own life depended on it.

By the eternal flame, the barron player laid down her drum to administer to the firefeeder.

Ymer, safe in the knowledge that no-one would miss her, slipped silently down the skeletal steps and out of the Dark Tower. Sure and certain that the rest of the Inner Circle would sleep clock round, she scurried back to her cell in search of Buchan.

Her body ached for him. She had been sworn to silence, on pain of direct torture, as to the content of the coupling ceremony. Still she longed to imitate the sensation that had reduced the normally cold and calculating High Priest to a helpless frenzy.

But Buchan was not in his cell . . . was nowhere to be found.

At last, in desperation, she called on Morangy, asking whether he had seen her plaything.

'He is gone,' said the Midwife.

'Gone? What do you mean, gone?' Ymer stamped her foot. 'Tell me where he is immediately or the Maxwell shall know of it.'

'The Maxwell already knows,' said Morangy, patiently. 'It was she who ordered it. Just as you are a woman now — so Buchan is a man. He has been removed to the cages.'

'No!'

'It was his time, kwine. Tomorrow he will begin his training as a breed-beast.'

Ymer began to scream with temper, hurling herself against the wall again and again until Morangy had to call two Medics to help him restrain her.

He strapped her into the cot used to confine those who had overdosed on the magic mushrooms, then gave her a tonic to calm her nerves and help her to sleep.

'Buchan was upset too,' the Midwife told her. 'You might pay some mind to his feelings. He begged they let him wait to say "Goodbye" but Cameron insisted it was better this way. She was probably right.'

'What do you know of right, eveling?' hissed Ymer, between clenched teeth.

'No need to be rude,' said Morangy, unperturbed. 'I take it then, you don't want the message that he left wi' me?'

'What? What?' begged Ymer, tears of self-pity and frustration running down her cheeks.

'He bade me to say he will always love you – no matter what.'

'Is that all?' said Ymer. 'I knew that already.'

'Ungrateful vratch,' Morangy was scandalised. 'Do you think love is so easy to come by? Sleep now – and think yourself lucky that there is one in this Castle who values your welfare above all else.'

But Ymer did not sleep.

She dozed fitfully, keeping one eye open, waiting – for an excuse to escape from her bindings – and to relieve the Midwife of the bunch of keys which she knew held one that led down into the depths of the Castle where Buchan would now be languishing amongst the breed-beasts.

Although her first concern was for herself, she felt some sympathy for Buchan too, though she would have been loath to admit it. She knew he would be miserable away from her – and she feared she would miss him also. Who else would take her moods and her abuse and love her still? And what would she do without their love sessions to keep the nightmares away?

She lay for many hours, her arms and legs a mass of pins and needles, until her chance came.

Morangy, who had been looking in on her from time to time during the day, sent instead a young auxiliary whom she had little difficulty in persuading to loosen her bonds. Then all she had to do was wait for the Castle to retire for the night.

In the wee small hours, when the last sounds of activity had finally died away, Ymer slipped from her cot and made her stealthy way to Morangy's sleeping cell.

Morangy had always liked his dram . . . does still, and, as luck would have it, he had partaken over liberally of the aqua-vitae that evening. He lay on his back, snoring heavily, with the belt carrying the coveted keyring curled like a snake on the mat beside his bed, where he had dropped it before flopping down, fully clothed, to sleep it off.

90

Carefully, Ymer slid off the great brass key which she knew opened the gateway to the forbidden vaults below. Many's the time she had accompanied Morangy on his tour of duty around the Castle, administering potions and pills, dressing burns and soothing scalds. But those tours had always ended when he extracted the great key to go 'Down There.'

'This is as far as you maun go, kwine,' he would say and Ymer, despite all her arguments and protestations, would find herself with the heavy door closed in her face.

Well, tonight she would get her own back.

Tonight she would delve into the secrets of what lay below stairs . . . and find and bring her Buchan home.

Deep down into the dimmest, darkest reaches of the ancient building she crept to where the air was stale and fetid, warm and welcoming as a cowbyre on a winter's afternoon. Past small cells where groups of Eunuchs lay snoring gently in each other's arms she hurried, coming eventually to the great, vaulted hall where the breed-beasts were housed.

Ymer was overawed by the size of the place and by the sheer number of cages which bordered its walls, each holding either a beast or, if they were catamites, a duplet.

In the centre of the room, a middle-aged Eunuch of awesome girth lay fast asleep, head down at his watch-table in a pool of stale beer. He would later live to regret his sloth. But not for long. They hung him at cock-crow.

Ymer, however, paid him no mind — would not have done even had she been privy to his fate — so intent was she on accomplishing her own plans, fulfilling her own desires.

She found Buchan in the last cage but one. He was fast asleep but came with her gladly when she unfastened the simple bolt latch that kept the drugged animal men in situ. He had been tranquillized too and staggered a little as she led him away upstairs. But the effects of the sleep-potion were cumulative and, since this had been his first dose, soon passed off.

They entered Ymer's sleep-cell by stealth, stripped hastily and crept into bed together, hugging and giggling with delight and relief.

'We must not sleep,' warned Ymer. 'I maun have you back before daylight.'

She proceeded to recount the ceremony of the coupling to Buchan, much as I have recounted it to you. Before she had finished, the youth was as hard as the statue had been and Ymer was ready to receive him.

'Now,' she said. 'Will you do that for me?'

'Like animals you mean?'

'Just like animals,' Ymer was delighted with the notion.

'But if they catch us . . .'

'Cissy,' Ymer's voice lashed him, scornfully. 'Maybe you *can't* do it.'

Her castigation had the very opposite effect to the one for which she had hoped. Buchan wilted visibly and had to be coaxed back to attention. When she eventually pulled him over on top of her, spreading her legs to receive him, he could no longer resist.

It was at the precise moment when he was about to enter her that Fergael strode into the cell.

Her anger was horrible to see. She flung the boy across the room with the strength of a Daemon, screaming to rouse the Castle for the guards to take him away.

Then she turned to Ymer.

My sister knew that she was as near becoming a drumskin as she had ever been in her life and with an ingenuity born of desperation she flung herself on the High Priest as if on a Saviour.

'Fergael,' she wept. 'Lady. You came just in time. He . . . Buchan wanted to . . . to do terrible things . . . I told him "No!" . . . I said it was a sin . . . I was promised to The Source . . . If you had been a moment later . . .'

'You would have been deflowered . . . and I would have seen you dead!' she spat, kicking my sister in the ribs.

Ymer howled and curled herself up into a ball.

'Mercy. Mercy, Holiness,' she pleaded. 'It wasn't my fault. It was him. He was gae strong for me.'

'Gae strong, eh?' snarled the High Priest, cockscomb quivering with rage. 'And how did he get up here? Somebody must have let him out. Or did he walk through walls?'

'I fetched him . . . I confess it . . .' sobbed Ymer. 'But I only wanted a cuddle. I was cold . . . and afraid of the Bogle . . . I never thought . . .'

Her pleas were interrupted by the arrival of the Maxwell, bleary eyed with sleep and trailed by the faithful Cameron.

On being told of the reason for the commotion, she hauled

Buchan to his feet fixing him with a stare that had Death written all over it.

'What have you to say for yourself, breed-beast?' she enquired, her voice icy calm with menace.

'What she said . . . ' began Buchan.

Fergael slapped him across the mouth with all the force of her fury. The boy's head snapped back with a painful crack and his lip started to bleed where his front teeth had cut through the tender skin.

'She?' she howled. 'She? You dare to speak of the Lady Ymer as "She"? You ingrate. You animal.'

Buchan began to cry.

The sound froze Ymer's heart.

'Do not hurt him,' she begged. 'He could not help himself. A breed-beast is not responsible . . . one cannot expect it to be.'

'Enough!' The Maxwell halted her hysterical flow.

'Take him to the hospice,' she ordered.

'And the Lady Ymer?' enquired the High Priest.

'The future Fergael,' said the Queen coldly, 'is your responsibility.'

So Ymer was locked away in the dark for half a moon's-phase in a box only a few inches deeper than her own body size, without food and with only a cup of water per day to keep her parched lips wet.

When the lid was removed she could not bear the light. The soles of her feet were rotten from standing in her own urine and she had wasted away to half her weight.

In this condition she was taken to see Buchan being gelded.

As a final act of malice, Fergael had decreed that the operation be carried out, not by the skilful Morangy but by the boy's feeble-minded mother.

As a result, Buchan bled to death in terror and pain.

And Morangy let him.

'Why not?' he said to me later. 'The poor loon had no future but the Backshi berries. I spared him that, at least.'

Buchan never betrayed Ymer, even at the hour of his death, and she has suffered the tortures of the damned ever since. The heart she had shrivelled in her breast the day he died and the only emotion that consoled her from then on was her hate. In that there is some parallel between us. We of the royal blood hate well.

93

She soon recovered from her physical deprivations, but the wounds to her mind have never quite healed. She still suffers from fits when the black moods are on her. In her prison-box she saw many visions and dreamed many dreams. They drove her mad and kept her sane at one and the same time. For most of them had a recurring theme and this she held on to as she held on to life. Her dreams were of the destruction of the witch-woman who had brought her to such a pass, the black hag in whose footsteps she must follow as the next Fergael. And Ymer gloried in every mutilating detail, embroidered and embellished and refined them until they were honed to a point glistening as a blinding-needle.

She knew she would live then because each dream told her the same thing, that she would kill Fergael with her own hand. And that the revenge would be sweet.

THE TRUE CHRONICLES OF THE REDEEMER

Soon after Rolande in woman-form came to Invernyess to sing before the Queen. And the Lady Maxwell, mesmerised by the magic of the song, fell in love with Rolande and brought her to the Summer Palace to be companion to her daughter Ymer. And the children, ignorant of the fact that they were twins, became lovers.

Chapter
11

IN THE SUMMER OF MY TWELFTH YEAR I WAS TAKEN TO PERFORM at the Beltane Feast.

It seemed the whole of Alba had gathered at Invernyess that May morning and the sun that shone bright from the cloudless sky had the first warmth of the year in it.

Invernyess is set on a wide river which flows, through fields, green and yellow with rape, into the great loch to the South West. It can be a cold, unwelcoming place in the dark months but, come the Spring, with the sun glinting off the granite of the turreted buildings, it has a special magic about it, clear and bright as crystal.

Here the Maxwells had chosen to build their Summer Palace, well away from the damp vapours and midges which plagued Ballater in June and July.

Euan-Noag and I went alone, leaving the rest of the disappointed troupe outwith the city. The Queen and the entire court were to be at the fair and Euan-Noag could not so openly defy the regime as to bring his freaks into public view. I, as the only normal, was to perform in the public arena and it was hoped that I would make enough money that day to feed the rest of the company for a half-year at least.

If crowds were anything to go by there was no doubt that I would. The world and his wife had come to the northern capital for the celebrations and everywhere one heard the jingle of coins as people, who had been saving all year for the event, squandered their hard-earned cash on fripperies and furbelows.

The atmosphere was infectious and exuberant.

Ale-stalls had been set up around the town square and there

were hawkers everywhere, selling everything from candy-apples to chaffinches in wicker-wire cages.

There seemed to be a tumbler or a fire eater on every corner and, over by the duckpond, a swarthy romany with a gold ear-ring in her nose had pitched her tent and was telling people's fortunes by inspecting the palms of their hands.

I begged Euan-Noag to allow me to see my future and he indulged me in this – though it would have been better if he hadn't.

One look at my palm was enough to turn the gipsy grey beneath her tan and she virtually threw the money back at Euan-Noag with the imprecation that we should 'Get awa oot of it,' which we did.

The incident upset me at the time, but Euan-Noag treated me to a sweetmeat and, in the way of most children, I soon forgot, my attention distracted not only by the confection but by the group of itinerant wains playing 'tig' around the green.

I would dearly have loved to have joined them but Euan-Noag hurried me on, past the pit where potatoes lay baking in hot embers and the spits where whole beeves were roasting, to the tents and flags of the arena where the entertainments were to be held.

Already the stalls were filling up with folk anxious to see the caber-tossing (the Clanswomen's speciality) or to cheer their village team on in the tug-o-war.

Outside the enclosure itself, on the rising ground, clumps of people jostled for position, laying out small encampments of blankets and cushions, unpacking picnics and settling them-selves for the day, in enclaves whose boundaries soon melded into a seething mass of humanity.

Every few footfalls I found something new to gawp at, until an exasperated Euan-Noag was forced to take me by the hand and half-lead, half-drag me to our destination.

This was a tent, distaff to the main enclosure, striped in green and white and bearing the Royal Standard of a horned horse and a great golden cat.

Inside, chaos reigned as pipers tuned their instruments and dancers and contortionists fought for space to practise steps or limber up. The heat from the morning sun was intense, mingling the smell of fresh trampled grass with the sweet, pungent scent of human body odours. In every available corner putative per-formers had set up stools and benches. Costumes of every hue hung from make-shift pegs and in the multiple mirrors that reflected one another, the more dramatic agonized over coifs and make-up.

Euan-Noag presented me at the trestle table at the centre of events, behind which sat an imposing woman of middle years, magnificent in cloth of gold with crystal stars spangling her purple hair.

This was Finnibair, Master of Ceremonies and Pageant Planner to The Maxwell.

She raised a magenta eyebrow as we approached, then lowered it again, apparently unimpressed by what she saw.

'Well?' she enquired – and Euan-Noag explained that he had brought me to perform for the delectation of The Lady and to the glory of The Goddess.

'What does she do?' enquired the Pageant Master.

'Sings like the cherubim and performs magic to delight the most jaundiced eye,' Eaun-Noag assured her, with more confidence than I was feeling.

'Show me,' said Finnibair.

And I was obliged to sing a few notes and do several simple sleights of hand to prove, I suppose, that I was not some bumbling amateur.

The tricks seemed to please her well enough for she nodded peremptorily and indicated a tiny area at the far side of the tent where we might prepare ourselves.

'The show is already overlong,' she warned. 'And we might not even get to you. It depends on how soon the Lady Maxwell becomes fatigued. Your fee is five gold bits. No performance, no pay.'

She clapped her hands.

'First turns at the ready,' she called. 'The Lady should be here at any moment.'

And, as if on cue, the skirl of bagpipes at the opposite end of the arena announced the approach of the royal party.

There was a sudden stampede for the tent flap as the performers rushed to catch a glimpse of their Queen. I was as anxious as any to see her but Euan-Noag led me away instead to our changing area to prepare me for the performance.

'You'll see her soon enough,' he told me as he began to plait beads into my hair. 'And more important – she will see you.'

For the first time in my life I felt stage-fright. My heart

fluttered like one of the caged chaffinches and my knees turned to water.

'I can't do it,' I squeaked. 'I want to go home.'

But Euan-Noag merely tutted and continued to plait.

'You were well prepared,' he assured me. 'You have nothing to fear.'

Easy for him to say. And yet, I knew he spoke true. I had been practising my tricks and songs for almost a sixmonth. If I did not know them now, I never would.

I tried to recall the sequence of my act and was horrified to discover that my mind had gone a complete blank.

I abandoned myself to despair, scarcely hearing the applause, polite or thunderous, that greeted the various acts, staring miserably into the chipped mirror while Euan-Nog transformed my face into a painted mask and decorated my arms with twining snakes and writhing vines. By the time he had dropped the muslin gown over my head and placed the last mayflower behind my ear, I was almost catatonic with fright.

'She is difficult to please today,' muttered a fat juggler, staggering back into the tent to desultory applause. 'I almost cut my hand off perfecting that sword-twirling trick and she hardly even looked at it.'

Finnibair raised the tent flap and peered out.

'That's it,' she announced. 'Show's over. The Maxwell is leaving.'

A collective groan rose from the remaining artistes, who had not yet performed and thus would not get paid.

'Better luck next time,' said Finnibair. 'To the losers, a free meal – courtesy of the management.'

Euan-Noag placed the guitar in my hand and prodded me in the small of the back.

'Go,' he said, shoving me towards the stage entrance.

'But . . .'

'Go,' he insisted . . . and I went, darting past the astounded Finnibair to fling myself out into the ring.

In the royal enclosure, the Maxwell had already risen and was preparing to depart. My sudden unheralded entrance did nothing to dissuade her, for though the buzz of the crowd stilled in anticipation, the Lady continued to turn away as though I held no more interest for her then a beetle crawling across her boot.

I stood stock still, unsure of what to do next. A wit in the audience began to sing 'Why are we waiting?'

That was when Ymer spoke up.

I did not know it was Ymer then, of course. All I saw was a girlchilde of about my own age, with jet black hair and a face painted even more outlandishly than my own, reach up to tug the Maxwell's sleeve.

'Look Majesty,' she said. 'It is a wain. Should we not watch it afore we go?'

The Queen stopped and looked over her shoulder at me. Even from that distance I could feel the sadness emanating from her . . and the power.

The audience began a slow hand clap.

The Maxwell smiled tightly and removed the little girl's hand from her arm.

'Why not?' she said and the childe gave a war-whoop and waved delightedly at me.

During the ensuing flurry, while the ladies of the court re-arranged themselves in their places, Finnabair strode from the tent to grasp my arm tightly and hiss in my ear.

'You young tyke. Do you want to get us all hung and drawn? What's your name, anyway?'

'Rolande,' I winced.

The furious face was instantly transformed into a mask ablaze with bonhomie as the Master of Ceremonies wheeled towards the Royal stand and projected my introduction with a theatrical flourish.

'Your Majesty . . . Ladies . . . Allow me to present . . . Childe Rolande.'

Then she left me to it.

I allowed the audience to settle as I had been taught, then began with my simplest tricks, pulling coloured handkerchieves from my sleeves and golden coins from my mouth. I then gradu-ated to the more difficult items until – as a climax – I produced a live dove from the folds of my gown.

The crowd loved it, especially the part where I sent the bird winging to the dais to perch on Ymer's outstretched arm.

Then I sang to them, songs of love and death, plucking the strings of my little guitar as Euan-Noag had showed me so that the round notes floated out into the air to capture the listeners with their beauty and strength. By the time I reached my final ballad I had completely forgotten my former fear and held the audience in my hand as closely as I had held the dove.

The song was 'She Moves Through the Fair', a tale of love unrequited that ends in tragedy and untimely death. As the last note died away, I could swear there was not a dry eye in the stadium and even The Lady wept openly.

A moment of silence ensued before the applause erupted, tearing the eardrums in its vibrations.

Accustomed though I was to public adulation, I had never heard anything like it. I looked around, dazed and uncertain of what to do next, searching in vain for a glimpse of Euan-Noag. But my friend and mentor was nowhere to be seen. Instead Finnibair, bustling from the tent, solved my dilemma by taking my hand and leading me forward to be presented to the Maxwell herself.

I went reluctantly, half-enchanted, half-repulsed by what I saw.

From a distance, the Ladies of the Court were splendid in their finery, peacocks in jewelled plaids and feathered bonnets. On closer inspection, their painted faces held more than a hint of depravity and a few, whose make-up stopped in an orange line around their chins, looked positively debauched.

My eye was drawn particularly to the tall, gaunt woman by the Maxwell's side, with her cockscomb hair and her glittering nose-jewels. Fergael. Never had I seen such an evil countenance. Her black eyes bored into me as I approached, until I felt certain that she could read the very secrets of my innermost soul.

Beside her sat Ymer and, next to her, what I at first assumed to be another childe but which, as I got nearer, proved to be an eveling. The midget, Morangy.

The Queen smiled her sad smile at me, inclining her great, leonine head in my direction.

I was struck dumb by the proximity of the Warlord of the Clans – as well I might have been.

The Maxwell was a magnificent specimen. Nearly two meters tall, clad all in green hunting tartan, her red-gold hair a burnished halo around a face that almost flamed with an inner light.

'What is your name childe?' she asked, gently. 'I fear I have forgotten it already.'

'Rolande,' I whispered.

'Speak up childe,' said Finnibair, prodding me.

101

'Rolande,' I said, louder this time.

'You have done well, Rolande,' said the Maxwell. 'You may choose a gift . . . a reward for your excellence.'

She looked deep into my eyes and a strange, half-fearful expression flitted momentarily across her features as though she had almost been reminded of something but could not quite remember what.

She shook the look away.

'What would you like?' she asked. 'Gold perhaps? Or land to build a croft? Or a horse of the best pedigree?'

'I don't know.'

Finnibair prodded me again.

'Say m'Lady, when you address the Queen,' she said.

'I don't know m'Lady,' I said, and curtsied, to be on the safe side.

'I know what I want,' interrupted the dark-haired girl excitedly. 'Please, Mother, may *I* not have a reward too? After all it was me who brought the wain to your notice.'

The Queen turned her head and smiled the same tight smile she had smiled at the childe before. There was no warmth in it, no affection.

'Very well, Ymer,' she said. 'You too may have a gift. But something small. Ask while Rolande is making up her mind.'

'I choose her,' said my sister.

There was a puzzled silence.

'I choose the girlchilde,' said Ymer. 'To stay with me and be my plaything. I have not had a plaything since Bu . ..'

The cockscombed woman's hand snaked out to smack Ymer across the face. She reddened but did not cry.

'I have not had a plaything in a long time,' she corrected herself. 'I am gae lonely. She is of no consequence. She would be company for me.'

'Ymer,' chided the Queen. 'A woman is always of consequence. You know too well that they may never be designated as a "plaything". That is for males and cast-outs.'

'Then let her be my Bodyservant,' pouted the childe. 'My companion.'

'Companion?' the gaunt woman was outraged. 'You are a Princess of the Blood – the next Fergael. We don't even know this guttersnipe's origins.'

'What is her pedigree?' the Queen appealed to Finnibair. 'Does she have a mother with her?'

Finnibair looked embarrassed.

'No, Majesty. She came with a man.'

The Maxwell looked none too pleased.

'Bring him forth,' she commanded.

And so Euan-Noag was led out and quizzed about my beginnings. To his avowal that he had taken me in out of the kindness of his heart when my family had died of the plague, she showed little mind. Her only concern seemed to be that I was in his charge.

'The childe will soon reach puberty,' she said. 'It is not seemly that she should be in your company. I propose to adopt her — as companion. Bodyservant to my daughter. (Here Ymer squealed with delight and the black woman snorted). 'I take it you have no objection?'

Euan-Noag regarded me sadly while I desperately tried, through look and gesture, to convey to him that I did not want to stay at the Palace.

'Your Majesty is very kind,' he said at last. 'I could not ask for more.'

'Noooooooo,' I cried, flinging myself at him and holding on tight.

Needless to say they prised me away, and just before they frog-marched Euan-Noag from the arena, I saw a look pass between him and the midget in the stalls. Fergael caught it too and turned to stare at the mannikin but his bland face betrayed nothing untoward and she looked back to me with narrowed eyes.

The Queen rose.

'Convey the childe to the Summer Camp,' she ordered Finnibair and then, to me, 'Do not be greet, Rolande. Ymer will see to you. Later I shall come and give you your reward.'

And so I was taken to the Summer Quarters with Ymer dancing alongside, fed and stroked and cleansed of my make-up.

I submitted to it all like a dead thing. Who knows but that I might not have flung myself from the window and dashed myself to death had not Morangy bustled in and shooed every one of them, including Ymer, from the room.

'Shame on you,' he scolded. 'Scaring the bairn half to death. Can you no see she's half wild? Leave her to me. I'll see she's bathed. I have to inspect her for lice and scabies anyway. Shoo! Begone. I'll call you when it's done.'

When at last the door was safely locked behind them and we were alone, the Midget proceeded to coax me from my hiding-place and still my fears. By that time I *was* like a wild thing and it took some time to persuade me that he was a friend of Euan-Noag, knew my origins and my 'problem' and that my secret was safe in his eveling hands.

He undressed and bathed me, restrapping my penis and re-dressing me in fresh linen. And all the while he soothed me with a running commentary.

'I will ask that they apprentice you to me. That way you'll be out of harm's way while Ymer is in training with Fergael. It will no be easy, concealing such a secret here in the Palace. Folk will wonder why you do not go naked like the rest of the bairns do betimes. But your puberty will be here soon so we maun do our best 'til then . . . if the prophesy is to be fulfilled.'

There was a knock on the door, followed by Ymer's voice.

'Let me in,' she demanded. 'The Maxwell will be here soon. Rolande and I must decide on her reward.'

So Morangy admitted her, assuring me, under his breath, that he would convey word of my safety to Euan-Noag.

'Let the childe decide herself what she wants,' he said to Ymer. 'And don't bully her. She's gae shy. She need coaxing out of herself, not traipsing on.'

But Ymer's method of 'coaxing me out of myself' was hardly what Morangy had in mind.

No sooner was the Midwife out the door then she was demanding to know whether I had been taught to 'pleasure myself' out in the wild.

When I looked blank she offered to demonstrate.

I'm afraid the spectacle was too much for me. I found myself with my first erection. And Ymer found it too, exploding with laughter as she lowered my breeches to be confronted by my shame.

'You are not a girl after all,' she whooped.

'I am both,' I confessed . . . and burst into tears.

I had not been in the Palace above a quarter day and already two people knew my secret. The strain was too much. I was convinced that only a whisper separated me from my death. But far from being disconcerted, my new friend seemed to be entranced at my revelation. She insisted on exploring my private parts herself to satisfy herself as to the truth of my assertion. Having done so, she was quick to recognize the advantages in the conjugations of my dual sexuality. And Ymer, being Ymer, she was anxious not to miss any of its myriad possibilities. She assured me that the last thing she wanted was for anyone else to find out what she knew.

'They would skin us alive,' she assured me and then, at my renewed burst of weeping, she turned on me the scorn that I was to know many times since. 'Get into your breeks,' she instructed. 'The Queen will be here soon. Dry your silly eyes – you big soft boy . . . and stop worrying . . . I'll think of something.'

And, of course, she did.

When the Maxwell arrived, flanked by four of her Clanswomen and followed by the usual gaggle of hangers-on, Ymer was ready for her.

'Rolande wants a torque,' she piped up. 'A silver torque, shaped like a snake, with emerald eyes and a ruby tongue.'

'Indeed?' the Maxwell was amused, despite herself. 'And where is the demander of such largess?'

Ymer darted behind the curtain and led me from my place of concealment. My face had been cleansed of make-up and my long blonde hair undressed to hang loosely to the embroidered girdle at my waist.

The Queen stared at me hard, her face draining of all colour.

I lowered my eyes, fearing that Ymer's demand had displeased her or that, somehow, she had learned my guilty secret.

But whatever affected her, it was not anger.

'Who does she remind you of, Locheil?' said the Queen, addressing the red-headed Guard Captain who stood at her elbow. 'Raise your eyes childe.'

'The Lady Ymer,' said the woman, without hesitation. 'Both the Ladies Ymer. Why, if it wasn't for the hair, the kwines might be twins.'

Ymer and I looked at each other then, both recognising our own features in the face that stared back.

'This alters the complexion of things,' said the Queen, softly.

'What things?' demanded Ymer.

'All things,' said the Maxwell, stiffly. 'Where is Morangy?'

'Here, Majesty.'

The midget stepped from the shadow of a pillar which had been concealing him.

'You have examined the childe?'

'I have.'

'And what is your opinion?'

'She is well nourished. Good teeth. Without blemish.'

'Undress her,' ordered the Maxwell.

Morangy's eyes popped wide with alarm.

'But . . why, Majesty?'

'I have my reasons.'

'May I know them?'

'There is no reason why you should. None that you shouldn't either. I intend to take the girl as my own Bodyservant. Before I do, I must assure myself that what you say is true.'

'Not fair,' shouted Ymer, stamping her foot in rage. 'You cannot have her. You promised her to me.'

The Queen ignored her.

'Undress the childe,' she repeated.

Two of the Clanswomen advanced on me and I fled, shrieking, to the opposite side of the room, where I climbed onto the windowsill, perching precariously over the cobbled yard below.

Ymer flung herself on The Lady.

'She is shy,' she howled. 'Ask Morangy. She does not want you to see her private parts. It is thought shame in the wilds.'

'Nonsense,' snapped the Queen. 'If Rolande is clean, I intend to take her as bride when she is old enough. I *must* inspect her before I take that step.'

The Clanswoman drew closer, circling warily as I tottered on the edge of the ledge.

'Don't touch me,' I threatened. 'I'll jump!'

And I would have done too – had not Ymer gone into her 'act'.

She drew herself up to her full height so that her very hair seemed to stand on end. Flinging her arms wide and rolling her eyes up in her head, she drew her lips back from her teeth . . . and screamed.

The sound echoed and re-echoed around the room, it's force almost propelling me from the window. Groggily, I grasped the window-sashes and lowered myself to the floor.

I could have escaped then – run from the building and no-one would have said me nae. All eyes were riveted on Ymer as she began to turn, slowly at first, and then faster, until she was whirling like a spinning jennie, her tongue lolling from her mouth as the scream went on forever without her seeming to feel the need to even draw breath.

Then quite suddenly, she stopped, and pointed at me.

'You may not see her, Maxwell,' she announced in a strange, dry voice. 'The shame would be her undoing. She has been defiled.'

'Defiled?' The Queen was horrified. 'By whom?'

'By the man. The man she came with. He has not been gelded. He has violated her.'

'Defiled' and 'Violated' were words unknown to me . . but from the Maxwell's reaction I could tell they were something pretty bad. The Lady's next words proved that I had not been mistaken.

'Bring the man, Euan-Noag,' she demanded. 'Throw him into the deepest hole in the compound. Prepare him to meet his death.'

THE TRUE CHRONICLES OF THE REDEEMER

And Ymer told that Euan-Noag had carnally used the Childe Rolande. And the Maxwell was much angered, ordering the Medicine Man's death. So became Euan-Noag the first martyr of the Redeemer's Revolution.

Chapter
12

It fell to me – as the defiled – to despatch Euan-Noag.

Violation was such an unheard of crime that they had to look up the punishment in the Book of Law.

The Maxwell explained to me that this method had been devised by an eminent psychiatrist in Pre-History. The theory was, that by killing her attacker, the victim would lay forever the ghost of guilt often associated with such a crime, wherein the person felt that she might have perhaps, somehow, 'invited' the act. The ritual death was designed to expunge all such feelings, to give the defiled back a sense of her own worth, show her that she controlled her own destiny.

I was to castrate my friend, cut his throat and catch his life-blood in a votive chalice.

'Some you will drink,' the Maxwell told me. 'The rest, Fergael will offer as sacrifice to The Goddess.'

Euan-Noag's body would be quartered and fed to the hogs. His head would be spiked and left to the vagaries of the elements, a warning to others that such deviations would not be tolerated.

I was not permitted to see Euan-Noag or given the option to waive my rights.

'It is the law,' I was told – then locked in my lonely cell to prepare myself for the great moment.

That night was the longest and most bitter that I have ever lived through. Being so young and unused to the cruelties of the court made it even harder to bear. I could not believe such a nightmare was happening to me, but felt sure that I would soon wake, safe in the Big House in the shadow of Ben Hee.

I lay in blackness, my mind full of blood, living and re-living the only death I had ever known, that of the Tax Collector,

Corbie. I must have dozed fitfully, for in dreams the fat deviate became Euan-Noag and I was Jolly, slicing off his tongue and watching him choke in his own gore.

I woke in a cold sweat, wanting to scream, knowing it to be useless. I was caught like a fly in the great web of fate. Nothing could now release me from my appointed destiny.

Shortly before dawn Ymer slipped in to comfort me. She found me empty, tearless, my dead eyes more those of the condemned than the executioner.

She wanted to 'play' but she found me an unwilling subject. I slapped her hands away and she retreated, pouting.

'Why are you so fatched?' she said. 'He is only a man – and of little consequence.'

I rounded on her then.

'It's your fault,' I said. 'You condemned him . . . I hate you for it.'

'Nor do I regret it,' Ymer tossed her head. 'It was either him or you.'

'I wish it was me,' I said. 'Instead I have to kill the man who has been my father and my friend.'

Ymer was shocked rigid.

'Do not utter such blasphemies. If anyone should hear, you would die for certain.'

'Do you think I care?'

Ymer stroked my face.

'It will soon be over,' she told me. 'Try not to think of it.'

'I can think of nothing else. Will think of nothing else until the day I die.'

And indeed my words were prophetic. I have re-lived Euan-Noag's death a hundred-thousand times in the intervening years and the memory never becomes any easier. I cannot rightly explain how it feels. All I hope is that such feelings never fall to you for, once planted, they sprout like an evil seed that rises to throttle us in those dark hours that herald the dawn.

I had thought myself drained of feeling, but somehow, in that moment of black despair, my body dredged up a last, cleansing flow of tears.

Ymer put her arms around me and began to stroke my hair. It was the first of many times that she has comforted me so – she does it still.

'I cannot kill him,' I sobbed.

'You must. At least he will die quick and clean.'

She told me the alternative – of the Backshi death that Euan-Noag would suffer should I fail in my duty – and I realised, finally, that I had no choice. I must do what was expected of me. I must kill this man that I loved.

The cell-door creaked in the darkness.

It was Morangy – come to take me to make my farewells.

They had chained Euan-Noag to the wall in some rat-infested pit in the cellars. He was a big man, as McCloed is big, but somehow he looked as though he had shrunk overnight. His clothes hung in shreds over a body that was massed in bruises. One eye was completely closed and his face was lacerated where they had lashed him with knotted whips.

I told him what I had to do, wailing it out in hiccupping phrases, pressing my face tight to his battered chest.

'Hush, hush, childe,' was all he said. 'It was meant to be.'

'When I have done it, I will turn the knife on myself,' I vowed . . and was surprised to find the man pushing me away angrily.

'And so I will have died for naught,' he rasped. 'Rolande, Rolande, have you learned nothing from me?'

'I have learnt love. I would not live in a world that has none.'

'Then change it.'

'I cannot.'

'You can, and you will. That is what you are here for. That is why I must die.'

'What good can it do?'

'It is my fate . . . and yours . . . I know it now . . . I knew it when I was cast back on to these dismal shores. Otherwise I would have drowned with the rest of those unfortunates. I was kept alive to nurture you. And now my task is done. I have been living on borrowed time.'

'But what good can be served by your death?'

'The greatest good for the greatest number. I die that you may live – and change the world – for a hundred thousand others.'

'But where is the justice?'

'Do not expect justice until you can mete it out yourself, Rolande. And when you are in that position, never forget that justice and truth . . . and love . . . are the three most important things in life.'

If there is anything I want to do in the time left to me it is to improve the image of those three most sullied words. In this I have tried to be true to the memory of a man who knew the real meaning of them all.

'When the time comes,' he told me, 'you may feel that you cannot do it. You must look at the amulet then and I will help you.' And he took the small talisman from within his shirt and swung it gently before my eyes as I had seen him do so many times on the unsuspecting subjects of his hypnotic experiments. It brought me back to the warm, close moments I had known at the circus, to my innocence, and to the happy time that would never come again. And I shed the last tear that I have ever shed from that moment to this.

'Take care of Blossom for me,' was all he said. 'And remember the amulet.'

And that is how I got through it. When they led me out to confront him next morning, my heart failed me – as he knew it would. They had lashed him to a cruciform and he hung, naked and defenceless, while the eager crowd pelted him with excrement and imprecations.

There was a gasp and then silence as I made my appearance in virgin white, flanked by two Initiates, one carrying the sickle knife, the other the chalice to collect the blood.

I wanted to turn and run, but Euan-Noag raised his head to look at me and in the look I found the strength I needed to approach him.

In my parallax vision I was conscious of Fergael, hovering like a vulture on the periphery of the tableau.

The last thing I remember is Euan-Noag's smile and the current of love flowing from him to me as he bade me look at the talisman.

I focused on the tiny star, staring, concentrating . . . and it seemed as though the world was dissolving, imploding and I falling into its centre, whirling, turning in a sea of light that became a sea of blood. And in the midst of the whirlwind's thunder I heard a great despairing cry, whether his or mine I shall never know.

When I came to myself, Euan-Noag was dead.

His body hung limp from the cross. His eyes were closed and his throat had been slit from ear to ear.

In my right hand I held the chalice, now filled with blood, in my lefft, the dead man's testicles.

I turned and handed both to the waiting Fergael.

It was over.

I had killed Euan-Noag.

But I could not bring myself to drink the blood.

When the chalice was proffered I deliberately dropped it, to Fergael's immediate and immense displeasure. She might have made more of it had not the Maxwell come to my aid, saying that I was overwrought.

She kissed me on the forehead and commended me to Morangy's care for the healing of both my body and my mind.

I have never been able to fathom whether Ymer's vision that day at the Summer Palace was real – or whether she read my mind.

How could she know, otherwise, that in my imagination Euan-Noag had been guilty of the crime of which they accused him?

What I had fantasised us doing together on the long winter nights of our last year had never seemed like violation to me.

Nor does it now.

Love is Love – wherever one finds it.

THE TRUE CHRONICLES OF THE REDEEMER

Then the Prophet Colluden summoned Rolande to the High Hills. And Rolande came in Manform. And Colluden presented him with the Sword Enfidion and the Helmet Suzuki and the Gae Bolga beloved of Cuchullain. And Rolande became The Redeemer in truth and great was the rejoicing among the Wilde mountain men.

Chapter
13

SO I WAS ATTACHED TO MORANGY AS AN APPRENTICE HEALER, and, for a world's turning, he taught me the secrets of herb lore and the paths of the life force. From him I learned to massage away a stomach pain or ease a fever by manipulating the soles of the feet wherein lie the root of most problems. The feet, our contact with the forces of nature in mother earth, are the conductors of energies — both good and bad. Look after the feet, they say, and the body will look after itself.

Morangy also — in his role as Chief Shrink — managed to keep at bay the advances of the Lady Maxwell, which daily became more amorous.

Because he had cured her of her 'falling sickness' she held his opinion in great regard and so he was able to bamboozle her with the most flagrant psychiatric jargon, warning her of the dangers to my Id should she force her attentions on me before I was ready to receive them. Not only had my body been violate, he told her, but my mind had been almost permanently damaged by my 'experience' with Euan-Noag. The balance of my sanity was a finely tautened wire which, once tripped, might never be restrung. Approached too soon, before my rehabilitation was complete, I would descend into utter madness and be of no further use to anyone.

And so the Maxwell had to content herself with petting and stroking me — which she did, frequently — and with looking forward to the day of my recovery — and our projected Marriage.

'What will we do then?' I would ask, anxiously, more and more often as the time appointed for the nuptials grew nearer. 'We cannot keep my condition a secret forever.'

'We'll cross that bridge when we come to it,' was all the Midwife would say and I had to content myself with that.

That, and the constant administrations of Ymer, with whom I shared a cell – and a bed.

Ostensibly, Ymer was the only one I would trust and in company we were careful to make the greatest show of firm friendship and the utmost propriety, while in private she debauched me utterly, teaching me in a few short months the tricks it had taken her years to acquire, leading me into the paths of licentiousness and daily introducing me to new delights.

With Ymer I could be all things. One day the protagonist, the next the receptacle, for she had various devices and phallic objects (smuggled secretly from the Dark Tower) which she took great delight in demonstrating – to me and on me.

Each evening, when I had finished poring over my recipes and Ymer had been dismissed her duties by the dreaded Fergael, we would console each other in the only way we knew how and from one night to the next I could never anticipate who was to do what, with what, to whom.

So life was far from dull.

Ymer kept our love-games always exciting, always new. She still does. And I am pleased to say that I proved an eager and willing student, with a proclivity for her more bizarre excesses which astounded even her.

But she could be tender as well as passionate, my sister, my love. When the bleeding began, she was the first to reassure me, explaining the cycle of the moon and its influence over the life force. And I, in turn, told her of the duality of the human race. But of course she didn't believe me, being still a slave to the Great Lie. So I left off my lecturing and abandoned myself to her ministrations.

When my breasts began to swell and the hairs to sprout on my private places and under my arms, Ymer taught me how to oil my nipples to make then pliable for when I should have a childe – if I *could* have a childe . . . at this point even Morangy was doubtful – and to shave the hairs away with an ivory scraper, for it was considered unsightly to be hirsute anywhere except the head. I also began to grow hair on my face, which would have proved awkward had it not been very fair and fine and so easily removed with the self-same scraper that I used to denude my other areas.

All in all, I enjoyed my learning time.

117

I found I had an aptitude — not only for making love — but also for my chosen profession — healing. Morangy insisted that the one was synonymous with the other. No-one, he told me, who does not carry within him a surfeit of love for his kind, can be a true Healer. For without love there is no genuine concern for those afflicted. In the laying on of hands especially, it is pure love which penetrates the diseased parts and soothes away the badness. It is love which takes the real physician into the eye of the epidemic and which brings him out unscathed.

I witnessed my first epidemic that season.

It was the cholera and it threatened to engulf the entire Cawdor area. It also gave us an excuse to make a sortie into the outside world. It is an ill wind that blows no-one good, I suppose.

The Maxwell was reluctant to let me go — to expose her favourite to danger — and I must admit to being not overly keen myself. I knew we would be away for several weeks and I was loathe to forego my nightly exertions with Ymer.

But Morangy was adamant.

'It will immunise the kwine,' he told his Queen. 'She would be a poor sort of Healer if the plague descended on Castle Ballater and she was afeared to go among it. Besides, it's time for me to renew my stock of special herbs. I maun take her into the High Hills and show her where they grow.'

So the Maxwell was eventually persuaded, though there was a further delay while Morangy argued against her sending a troop of Clanswomen along to protect us from the attention of the Ben-shi. I could not imagine why he was so determined that we should go alone until he confided in me that the epidemic and the herb-gathering were mere smokescreens and that the real reason for our journey was to renew our acquaintance with Colluden.

'I canna very well arrive at his door with a troop of the Maxwell's best in tow, now can I?' he said with a grin. 'I fear but the man would be a bittie put out by that.'

He got his way in the end, persuading the Maxwell that it would be of no benefit to anyone if her troops contracted cholera and landed us with extra work in their healing.

With all this arguing and arranging it was Lugnasa already, the first day of the sun's month, when we set out on the same journey we had undertaken last when I was a baby, hidden in Morangy's apothecary bag. It was a boiling hot day, humid, with storm clouds lowering away to the west. The whole Castle came to wave us off and this time there was no guard to halt us at the gate. The Maxwell kissed me full on the lips in view of all, sealing the contract of our coming betrothal to the delight of almost everyone, except Ymer. When I turned to her to make my goodbyes, she glared furiously at me, gave me a perfunctory peck on the cheek and flounced off.

She didn't even wait to wave me farewell and this saddened me greatly for I knew I would miss her over the coming days, and I also knew that, when she came to herself, she would be riddled with remorse at her malhumour and would punish herself for it until my return.

We cantered down to the banks of the Dee, Morangy and I, me looking over my shoulder, he staring straight ahead, remembering the route that we had rode before. But what a change in circumstance. No snow now, the going easy as we picked our way along by the river, swift-flowing with recent rain. The sun, hot on our heads, sparkled off water where brown trout leapt, locked in a dance of death with the multihued Dragon-flies. The only blot on a perfect day came with the clouds of Clegs. The giant horse-flies tormented our mounts, buzzing around us in droves when we traversed the more swampy areas and forcing us to pull our hoods up around our heads to stop being stung about the face. For a Cleg-bite near the eye will swell alarmingly, rendering the victim blind for several cycles and the accompanying itch is well-nigh unbearable. Dock-leaves and spittle are a good antidote. Best though to avoid the bite in the first place.

Morangy led on Nob who, although he had thickened in girth since the previous outing, was still a sturdy mount, and I followed behind on the bay mare that had been a farewell gift from My Lady. I named her Starflower for she was bright as the former and delicate as the latter. Although I ride the King Stag into battle (when I am not pregnant, that is), Starflower is still the animal that I choose to ride for pleasure.

We turned distaff at Tor na Coil, heading straight up into the centre of the plague, stopping en route at the various outposts and villages where the cholera had taken its deadly hold, administering help to the ill and succour to the dying. Craigevar and Frazerburr were the places most affected and the trip was a salutory experience for me. I had not realized until then how much Euan-Noag had shielded me from the more unsavoury

119

realities of life in Alba. People received treatment, not according to the severity of their affliction but strictly in order of rank. Firstly the Outlyer, after her the Mayoress/Captain and her troop, then the female civilian population. And finally, if any supplies and/or energy were left, the male drones.

I was appalled at the conditions that these poor wretches lived, and died in. In outhouses, stables, some by the roadside, expiring in their own filth, they were left to rot where they lay without benefit of burial or even a cairn to mark their passing – food for wolves and the midden-dwelling jackrat with its centipede legs and serrated teeth.

Furious and frustrated, I had to be restrained by Morangy from showing too much concern, 'Lest it be remarked and reported back to the Maxwell.'

'There is no justification for it,' I remember exploding to him one evening, after a small boychilde, belly bloated with wind, had died bloodily in my arms. 'These are human beings. It is unthinkable that they should be treated with less regard than one of the Maxwell's lap-cats.'

'You will have your chance to do something about it,' Morangy soothed me.

'When?'

'Soon. That is provided you dinna spoil the whole thing by blowing your cover in advance.'

And so I was obliged to keep my tongue in my teeth, to do the best I could, which was little enough, to salve my conscience and to nurture that first trickle of resentment against the female half of my race that was to swell into a damned flood by the time I had a chance to rectify some of the wrongs that I saw perpetrated on that trip – and on subsequent others.

It got to the point where I could hardly look the wretches in the eye so ashamed was I of being female. By the time we got to Colluden's cave I was fit for nothing. Overworked, overwrought, unslept and exhausted.

Colluden greeted us by himself this time, holding a bairn, of three or four Summers, by the hand.

'Come awa' in, Rolande,' he said, speaking as though he'd seen me but the day previous. 'The men are out on the hunt. We maun make you presentable for them afore they return.'

He led me away into a back recess where he bade me remove my soiled clothes and make use of the steaming tub that had been prepared for my coming. Touching to know that the second sight can have its practical uses.

'I will send someone to take care of you and bring you food,' he said. 'The wee mannie and me will have a dram meanwhile, and a bite while you prepare.'

I had barely time to fling my filthy gown from me and immerse myself in the scalding water when who should come dancing out of the shadows but Blossom.

She was overjoyed to see me – and I her.

She told me how the troupe had been left high and dry when neither Euan-Noag nor myself had returned the day of the Summer Fair. They were without money and, since Euan-Noag always made the arrangements, totally without a sense of direction. If it hadn't been for Morangy, she said, who had arranged that they be spirited away to the High Hills and had made provision for them to stay with Colluden and the Wildemen, they would have all perished for sure. They hadn't seen Euan-Noag's death, just heard of it, and apparently didn't know that he had met it at my hands. I did not enlighten her, nor tell her that it was I, fulfilling my promise to Euan-Noag, who had arranged for Morangy to take care of the Circus performers.

'The boychilde is mine,' confided Blossom. 'The one Colluden was minding when you arrived. I named him Euan – after the father he will never see. I have a suitor here,' she continued, while she washed and rinsed my matted hair, easing out the tangles as she always used to do, with a bone comb. 'A kind man, Hamish, and loving.' She halted in her ministrations and her face clouded. 'But no Euan-Noag.'

'There will never be another Euan-Noag,' I said. 'And I am glad that you are happy.'

'What is happy?' she said, with a shake of her blonde curls, then, changing the subject, 'The women and the wains will be back soon. Isla has taken them out bird-watching if you please. Colluden wanted the place empty for your arrival. I am the only one who knows The Redeemer is here. So now we'd better make you decent.'

By the time the Clan arrived back from their various expeditions, I had been bathed and anointed and made ready for the ceremony that would introduce me to my putative 'army'.

I had been dressed as a man, in leather battle armour that bared my female breasts and emphasised my masculinity by the addition of a heavily padded codpiece. My hair had been braided

121

into a golden rope and twisted up on top of my head in a coiled knot. My eyes had been emphasised with gold paint and my nipples gilded to match.

The reaction to my presence was startling. Though taken by surprise, each one there clearly knew who I was, had been prepared for my arrival by years of promises and predictions from their much-loved prophet.

'This is the One of whom I spoke,' he said. 'The Redeemer. He is one among you at last.'

And the Wildemen, as hairy and unsavoury a bunch as I had ever encountered, fell to their knees and bowed their shaggy foreheads to the floor.

The original troop were there in force, McCann the Bogeyman, One-arm, One-eye and the rest (though more grizzled, according to Morangy, than the first time we met), but their numbers had swelled considerably. Many of the then children had grown into fully fledged warriors and extra infants had been spirited away to replenish the ranks so that the company now numbered about fifty in all. Added to that were a few normal women and several female freaks, mates to the Wildemen, mothers of their natural children. Though not part of my army they nonetheless crowded the cave mouth to watch the fun.

Colluden called them to attention.

'Form the ceremonial circle,' he ordered. 'The Redeemer has come for the symbols of his leadership. (This was news to me.) Stand up like men so we may deliver what we ha' been guarding all this while.'

There followed much shuffling and jostling for space as the Wildemen scrambled upright and formed themselves into a rough ring around me.

Then a young man entered from one of the darkened passageways, bearing a shield covered in a plaid cloth.

The youth was about six summers older than I, tall and well set up, with russet hair and green eyes. I was to learn later, from Morangy, that he was that same boy Jamie, who on our first visit had doled out porridge to our famished crew. From the pride in Blossom's eyes and the striking resemblance he bore to his father, it was not difficult to work out that this was McCloed, Euan-Noag's first-born. He was well grown now and a Captain of his own 'Clutch', battle hardened and bronzed by the clean highland sun.

I found the masculinity of him, with his matted chest hair

122

and his curled whiskers, fascinating and somewhat forgot myself – and my role in the gathering – by staring at him in open and obvious admiration. McCloed looked away, clearly embarrassed at my boldness, turning to offer the shield to Colluden.

With a flourish, the old man lifted away the cover to expose what lay beneath.

A gasp rose from the collective throats of the Wildemen at the wonders there revealed.

A fine, strong broadsword in a rune-worked scabbard lay upon the dark leather of the shield alongside a spear with a strange, fluted tip and a black helmet of an unknown substance, which covered the head from nape to crown leaving a dark area over the eyes through which one could see but not be seen. Across the forehead of this wondrous object was written the magical word, 'Suzuki.'

Clearly all four items, including the shield, were of great value and antiquity.

Colluden nodded to McCloed who raised the great sword and handed it to me, hilt first.

'Take this,' said the Prophet, 'The Sword Enfidion. May it be your strong right arm. Use it only in the cause of good and it will never fail you.'

The heaviness of the weapon almost unmanned me. Beads of sweat stood on my brow as I lowered the tip gently to the ground and buckled the scabbard round my waist, thankful to transfer the weight away from my weak woman's arms.

McCloed gave me the spear next. It was a coldblooded instrument of death with a central point which entered the body clean, only to explode into a score of barbed spikes which could be removed from the flesh only by cutting them away. A wound from such a weapon taken in the centre of the body would pierce every one of the victim's vital organs to ensure an agonising demise.

'The Gae Bolga,' announced Colluden. 'Once weapon of the great Celtic Hero, Cuchullain, The Hound of Ulster. With it he slew his only son, Connla, in mortal combat.'

I, who had killed my own 'father', considered it a fitting gift.

Finally Colluden placed the Mask of the Redeemer, the Suzuki, on my head and handed me the round metal shield, etched in sacred symbols (one of them said 'Che Lives') and studded with seven huge Cairngorm stones.

McCloed buckled the helmet on, his fingers twitching nervously as he fumbled with the straps.

I placed my hand on his lower arm and thanked him but he pulled away as though my touch was scalding. He was to tell me later that he was appalled at himself, at the feelings that he found in himself for me.

Poor McCloed, a lovely man, but on bad days he will still refer to himself as a poofter. However, we are working on that, Ymer and I. One day soon he will understand the nature of human sexuality, recognise that no love, truly given, can ever be branded deviate or unnatural.

Perhaps the childe will be a breakthrough. It is his, after all, as much as it is mine and Ymer's.

He turned from me then, to shoulder through the silent crowd and return with his brother, young Euan, whom he handed tenderly to Colluden.

The old man held the childe aloft.

'I dedicate this bairn to the services of The Redeemer,' he said. 'To be his arms-bearer and the keeper of his War-Dogs when he is grown. Show him the mark of your approval, Redeemer. His life is yours now.'

'I show it gladly,' I said, placing a hand on the boy's head.

I was much moved. No-one had ever been dedicated to me before and I felt the responsibility for the small life greatly, vowing no harm would come to this tiny warrior if I could help it. Many have been dedicated to me since and I have tried to feel the same about each one, but I must admit that young Euan still holds a special place in my affections.

'You must name him,' said Colluden.

'But is he not already named?'

'He has his given name, yes. Euan. In honour of his sire. But you must give him a battle name – for strength – one that he may carry onto the field.'

'Then I name him Cuchullain,' I said, smiling at his tiny mother, huddled with McCloed on the edge of the throng. 'A Watchdog for my War-Dogs. May he be as fierce as them and as brave as him whose name he now bears.'

There was a huge cheer at this and the War-Dogs were led in, a dozen of them, straining at their leashes, terrifying creatures, two-headed demi-wolves, cross-bred with domestic bitches to produce barely trainable monsters with red eyes and slavering jaws.

'I don't know about the enemy,' I said. 'But they certainly scare the hell out of me.'

It was something I had read in a book once and it had the desired effect.

Another cheer arose at this and then everybody began laughing and shouting, slapping each other on the backs and giving great war-whoops until the cave rang with the echoes and young Euan-Cuchullain began to howl and had to be rescued by his mother.

Afterwards there was a celebration, with me seated between Colluden and McCloed, where everyone, including myself, got polluted on home-brew and swallowed too much half-cooked deer meat.

We all felt like living death the next day, but that elixir of hope, so far from the effete revelries of Castle Ballater, the belief in the future that permeated the evening, the certainty that our celebrations heralded the beginning of the end for female tyranny, made any kind of hangover worthwhile.

THE TRUE CHRONICLES OF THE REDEEMER

Now at that time women conceived and bore children without the aid of man. And for this man was considered a worthless chattel, lower in importance than the beasts of the field.

CHAPTER
14

THE TIME HAS COME TO EXPLAIN ABOUT THE GREAT LIE.

At approximately twelve Summers, with the onset of menstruation, the female children of Alba made their first, and in some cases their only, pilgrimage to the Dark Tower.

They came to be initiated into The Mysteries.

Some of them had never left those outposts where they had been born and bred. Many had never been separated from the reassuring warmth of the company of aunts, mothers, sisters and cousins that made up the Albian family unit. The trip to Castle Ballater, anticipated and planned since their birth, was an awe-inspiring adventure. There were those brave souls who pretended to look forward to it but most, it must be admitted, viewed the whole thing with a trepidation bordering on dread.

On their arrival, they were abandoned by tearful relatives to be herded by unsympathetic Clanswomen into collective dormitories where they ate, slept and worried until next dark of the moon. Under cover of stygian night they were led, like lambs to the slaughter, into the confines of that Tower whose black shadow had hung over them since their arrival.

At this, the most vulnerable period of their young lives, homesick and afraid, displaced, disturbed and almost certainly terrified out of their wits, they were stripped naked, made to swear dark oaths written in blood, half drugged and finally admitted to the presence of the great, phallic statue known as the The Source.

For many it ended there. Some fell into fits, others were seized by catatonic shock and had to be weeded out and sent home.

The strong ones, the survivors, were subjected over a period of several cycles to a regime of mental disorientation and physical discomfort.

Forced to lie face down on cold stone floors, scourged, starved, sluiced with icy water, subjected to the verbal rantings of Fergael, overwhelmed by the smell of sacrificial blood and the soul-stirring sounds of the barron, they were kept without sleep and liberally dosed with ceremonial wine to the point where reality and fantasy merged into one.

Finally they were led, each to a small individual cell, and left alone in the dark with their thoughts.

The chosen few, they were told, would be visited sometime during the next moon phase, by the living incarnation of the idol before whom they had prostrated their naked flesh in obeissance. If they were lucky, that flesh would be made one with the God.

And so they lay in befuddled terror, afraid of being chosen, more afraid of being rejected. Now there was no more food. Only wine and drugs. Each lay, isolated in their terror until the moment which Fergael had divined was their fertile time. Then a breed-beast was released into their cell. Some, whose cycles were appropriate, were lucky enough to be visited the first night. Others waited up to a half-moon phase for their own personal 'manifestations.' None was allowed to speak of the experience afterwards. It was one of the Mysteries, sacred to the Source of all Life.

The great dumb creatures that were the breed-beasts had been fed only aphrodisiacs for the duration of the ceremonies and were thus more than ready to perform the function mapped out for them. Gowned and gilded in the manner of the great idol, they were let loose on the childe-women in the cells.

Imagine yourself, naked and afraid, lying in the dark on your solitary cot. You are little more than a childe, hardly outgrown the nightmares of youth. Suddenly the door swings open and in the half-light from the corridor is revealed momentarily a tall, golden figure, padded under concealing drapery to represent a creature half man, half woman, wholly fantastical.

And then the door swings closed and you are no longer alone.

Can you blame those innocents, some of whom fainted and afterwards remembered nothing, if they believed that they had been personally honoured by the Godhead?

It was so beautifully orchestrated. So wonderfully staged.

And it was foolproof.

Though forbidden to discuss the Experience, nothing would ever after dissuade those women that they had not been blessed, were not exceptional, privileged human beings.

And nothing that happened to them, ever after, could compare with the supreme moment when childe became woman at the behest of the living Source.

Afterwards they went back to their farms and outposts, had their lesbian love affairs, carried on with their humdrum lives. But nothing could ever erase the memory of that supreme moment when they had been one with the supreme being.

They might love. Deeply. Passionately. But what they lived through in the Dark Tower was ecstasy, combining the best of the religious and the carnal in one.

Many conceived of the union and, since each was convinced that she had been personally deflowered by the Deity, any subsequent issue was considered sacred.

Any subsequent female issue, that is.

A male childe was taken as proof that the recipient of the Holy Seed had been somehow found wanting.

Few women recovered from the shame. As a result most of them hated the unfortunate living sign of their humiliation. A male childe was considered a disgrace to mother and family alike.

Better far to have an eveling, a deformed or handicapped childe. It, at least, would be returned to the Source immediately by the attending midwife or, if it were female, be smuggled away to the 'camps' never to be seen again.

An eveling was merely a mistake.

A boychilde was an insult.

For the Great Lie was a double edged sword, and as it deified women, so it reviled men.

Over the centuries, the females of Alba thrived and prospered (while the men grew ever weaker), secure in the knowledge that their opposite numbers were mere chattels with no place or part in the survival of the species.

It was an elaborate deception, nurtured by those privileged few who had most to lose from its discovery.

The Maxwell, Fergael and the Inner Circle of the Priesthood passed their knowledge on from Mother to Daughter carrying the secret with them to their deathbed.

Any evil was considered justifiable provided it perpetuated

the myth of female supremacy. And here the end was abominated by the means. For women, the bearers and nurturers of life, found themselves defiled by those acts formerly considered the province of the marauding male. Death, destruction, deception and despair.

To this end generations of eunuchs had their tongues cut out so as not to reveal the secrets of the cages. Breed-beasts were kept caged from puberty till death, closeted in the bowels of the Castle, brought out only for the occasional exercise period, living like well-cosseted animals but always under the threat of the obscene Backshi death, invented so that none would dare try to escape.

Not that their blasphemy would have been believed had they all stood on the highest hilltop and shouted the truth to the massed tribes of Alba.

So convincing was the Great Lie, so much part of folklore and history that even I, who had been instructed in the true state of affairs by Euan-Noag, became convinced during my stay at Castle Ballater that the coupling of men and women was some primitive form of the sex-act that had been somehow transcended by the women of Alba to the point where self-perpetuation was indeed a reality.

If the Maxwell had not passed the knowledge on to me at her death, I might be still so convinced.

As it is, the woman in me often wonders whether, in attempting to spread the more mundane truths about the origin of life, I have not forever taken something mystical from the process of birth.

It is a hard and thankless task, spawning a childe. I have assisted many children into the world and I look forward to my own approaching labour with something less than alacrity.

Perhaps the remembrance of that mystic conception, that feeling of one-ness with the Godhead which those generations of Albian women possessed, went some way to raise the procedure out of the mire and onto some spiritual level that was beyond blood and pain.

Did I do right to tread on their dreams?

THE TRUE CHRONICLES OF THE REDEEMER

Then the Maxwell took Rolande to wife. But the Childe, not wishing to couple with the Queen, sent instead a mirror-image. And this Succubus took Rolande's place in the Lady's bed.

Chapter 15

NEITHER YMER NOR I WERE SUBJECTED TO THE BLOOD CERE-
mony of course. Ymer because she was dedicated to The Source.
I, because I was earmarked for the Maxwell's pleasure.

And at last the time came when the Warlord of all the Clans
would no longer take no for an answer.

'We must take the chance,' she thundered, sweeping aside
Morangy's frenzied protestations that my sanity might not withstand a wedding ceremony which included, at its culmination,
the Maxwell donning a huge phallus and deflowering me in full
view of the court. 'If she is not ready to receive me now, she
never will be.'

So my fate was sealed.

And the date of the ceremony was set to coincide with my
fifteenth birthday, an occasion, I may say, that I did not expect
to survive.

Preparations for the nuptial feast began at once and plum-
meted me into the deepest gloom. I was set to sewing bedlinen,
a task I detested, and each new influx of pastrycooks and floral
arrangers plunged me into fresh paroxysms of despair.

For some months my bleeding had been sporadic and
Morangy had been dosing me with pregnant mare's urine to
regulate my hormones.

One of the side effects – apart from extreme nausea (have
you ever tried drinking pregnant mare's urine?) – was the onset
of melancholia and Morangy tried to cheer me now by assuring
me that my malaise was purely clinical.

But I knew better.

I was suffering from pure terror – and a feeling of having
completely lost control of my life. I suddenly realised I had been

living in a fool's paradise, pretending that the evil day would never come. Now it was here and I had no idea how to cope with it. I despised myself for my weakness, but still I was powerless to act.

While Morangy hurtled around from pillar to post trying to engineer an escape plan, I fell into a nervous collapse which immobilised me and left me unable to rise from my bed.

The Maxwell visited me in my sickroom, to pet and prod me while Morangy clucked and tutted and 'I told you so'd.'

But the Queen was not to be deflected. Though sympathetic, she was adamant. She would have me on my fifteenth birthday, whether I liked it or no.

'But Majesty,' I wailed. 'All those people. Watching. How can I bear it?'

'With dignity I hope,' she said, stiffly. 'As is your duty. I trust you will not find my embrace repulsive. And tradition demands that the court witness the deflowering of the Queen's paramour.'

'But I have already been deflowered.'

'A technicality,' the Queen frowned. 'And one of which I would prefer not to be reminded.'

And she rose and stalked from the room, leaving me more unhinged than ever.

Looking back I can almost find it in my heart to pity her. She did not mean to be unkind. It was simply that she was used to getting her own way. And, to be fair, she had shown me more patience than an absolute monarch had need to show. She may have felt her authority was being undermined by her apparent indulgence of me. Certainly the court was beginning to gossip and giggle behind her back. Fergael (was it always Fergael) brought this to her notice and told her straight out that if she did not wish to become a laughing stock then she would have to take me as bride with or without my consent.

Was she Queen, or was she not, the High Priest asked, with just the right amount of sarcasm that left the Maxwell no retreat.

So the die was cast. Die being the operative word. That was one of the options open to me. The other was to flee to the hills to be with Colluden.

Neither choice appealed.

Naturally I did not relish the thought of death – and of the kind of death that I knew awaited me should my dreadful secret be revealed, but on the other hand my Wildemen were not yet ready for insurrection and, I must admit, neither was I. Being the Redeemer still seemed no more than a game to me.

Castle Ballater was my reality. I had been spoiled and mollycoddled. I had enjoyed my privileged time at court with all the creature comforts it offered. I was in love with Ymer. I was loathe to give everything up for a cave in the hills and the company of a bunch of unsophisticated hobbledehoys.

The reluctant champion?

I could say so – but I would be deluding myself. I was nothing more than a self-seeking brat. Show me the fifteen year old who is not. I dreaded the going. I dreaded the staying. With all my heart I wished that things could remain as they were. But of course they couldn't.

And each day the nuptials grew nearer.

And each day my dilemma and my depression grew worse.

It was Ymer who eventually came to my rescue. Ymer, the strong one. The woman. For women, I have found, stick together in times of trouble, much more so than do men. My sister, then, came to my aid.

Of course, at this time, you must realise, I still had no idea that she was my sister, thought our close resemblance was a pure freak of nature. Nor did I know that the first Ymer, whom the Maxwell saw mirrored in me, had been my mother. That, I simply considered bad luck. Morangy, who doubtless had his reasons, remained close mouthed about my origins until much later.

The whole thing was resolved through a childish game of let's pretend.

Ymer was constantly looking for ways to entertain me, to brighten up my life, particularly now that I was in the doldrums. It was not that she was indifferent to our predicament, she knew perfectly well that if Morangy and I were discovered then so, as the only other party privy to the deception, was she. But after her experiences in the box, death held few fears for Ymer. She lived life to the hilt, good or bad.

'There's no earthly point in worrying about it any more,' she said one morning when the three of us had spent yet another fitful night. 'Today we are going to put the whole thing out of our minds. Today we are going to have some fun.'

Now, at this time, each member of the court had her own personalised make-up. It was designed – rather as clown's faces are designed – by the royal Maquilleause and no-one was permitted to use another's visage.

One becomes very expert at applying one's own face and so, to ensure they were authentic, we applied each other's. It was a strange feeling, working on one's own features without benefit of a mirror.

When it was done, we called Morangy through to view our handiwork.

'You're like two halves of each other. Rolande's face with Ymer's hair and vice versa.'

'Not good enough,' said Ymer, and she grabbed a length of silk and wound it round my head, turban fashion, so that the hair was totally obscured.

'Don't forget the eyes,' said Morangy, and entering into the spirit of the thing he rootled in a cupboard, producing a bottle of coloured liquid which, when he applied a few drops, turned Ymer's grass-green orbs gold as my own.

She flung another cloth-length around her own dark head then, tucking in any stray dark hairs around the edges. And suddenly, miraculously, Ymer was me and I was her.

'We must try it out on someone,' cried Ymer, laughing and clapping her hands. 'Someone who knows us well. Who shall we choose?'

But the choice was made for us.

I had just stepped behind the dressing-screen to retrieve a dropped earring when Cameron came bounding in to summon me to audience with the Queen. She addressed herself to Ymer, calling her Rolande and telling her she'd better get a move on since the Maxwell was 'a wee bittie sharp' this morning.

I was about to disaffect her of her mistake but Ymer spoke up before I could emerge.

'I'll be along directly,' she said. 'Can Ymer come too?'

'The Lady doesnae wish to be bothered with Ymer,' said Cameron. 'Just you.'

So Ymer swept out, with a wicked grin, leaving Morangy and I to pace the room and bite our nails for what seemed like half the forenoon.

We expected her back, bursting with glee, full of herself and the joke she'd played, or else to see her frogmarched in – in disgrace, having been discovered by the Lady who, when she was 'a wee bittie sharp', could be very sharp indeed.

Neither happened.

137

The Ymer who returned was strangely subdued.

'Did you fool her?' I urged. 'What happened? Did it work?'

Ymer looked at me, tilt-eyed.

'Och, it worked fine,' she said. 'That's the bother of it.'

'Explain.' Morangy was losing patience with Ymer's prank.

My sister sat down, folding her hands in her lap, twisting her fingers as I'd often seen her do when something had upset her and she was trying not to cry.

'She was so nice to me,' she said. 'For the first time in my life I didn't have to fight for her attention. She listened to me. She smiled. She touched me even. Normally she cannot bear to touch me.'

My heart went out to her, sitting there so vulnerable, pathetic even. I sat down beside her, folding her to me, holding her tight.

'I love you, Ymer,' I said.

She pushed me away.

'I know, silly, but it's not the same.'

Love is a strange and bitter pill to swallow. What a triangle we were. Me, cut to the heart by Ymer's thoughtless remark, and her not even knowing she had hurt me because her thoughts were all on the Maxwell whom she loved and who loved me.

If love is not blind, as they say, then it's gae short-sighted. The Lady only loved me because I reminded her of her lost love and only hated Ymer because she had been the cause of that love's death. Not much sense in that. Certainly no fairness.

And yet I despised the Maxwell because she was instrumental in the death of Euan-Noag. So who am I to judge?

'I have an idea,' said Ymer, looking up into my eyes, 'that could get us all out of trouble.'

'Speak out,' said Morangy. 'I'd like to hear it.'

'I will take Rolande's place at the ceremony,' announced Ymer, solemnly. 'And in the Queen's bed.'

'Talk sense,' I told her. 'You can't do that.'

Strange how we view everything from our own standpoint. The thought of being bedded by the Maxwell was abhorrent to me. In my arrogance I assumed that Ymer would feel exactly the same about it.

But she didn't.

'What makes you think I can't?' she demanded.

'I didn't mean you can't,' I said. 'I'm sure you could. I think you could do anything you set your mind to.'

'Well then . . . '

'Well then . . . it's just that . . . I can't expect you to make such a sacrifice for me,' I finished, lamely.

Ymer began to laugh.

'Oh, Rolande,' she giggled, her turban unwinding itself and falling in loose folds over her shoulders. 'Don't be so po-faced. It's no sacrifice. Can't you see? I want to do it.'

I rose and walked to the window.

Down in the great courtyard snowdrops were pushing through the cracks in the paving stones, heralding an early spring.

I did not want to leave this Castle that had become my home. Neither did I want to expose Ymer to more danger. But there was another complication. I was jealous. And jealousy is a powerful passion. I fear it swayed me then.

'I cannot let you do it,' I said. 'It's too much of a risk.'

'Think again Rolande.' It was Morangy's voice, close by my elbow. 'Colluden is ill-prepared to receive you yet. He would be glad of a reprieve. So would we all.'

'What of the hair?' I shouted, rounding on him. You don't expect her to make love to the Lady in a turban?'

' 'Tsk,' said Ymer. 'That's easily settled. I shall wear a blonde wig.'

I pursed my lips and turned back to the window.

'Please yourself,' I snarled.

Morangy coughed.

'There's just one other complication,' he said, breaking the awkward silence. 'It's a clinical one.'

We both looked at him and he turned away, embarrassed.

'Roland is supposed to have been violated,' he said. 'I had intended to break the hymen surgically before the ceremony. You are chaste. What happens when the Queen deflowers the bride, Ymer? If she breaks the hymen there will be blood.'

'I doubt that,' grinned Ymer. 'Ask Rolande.'

Morangy was shocked speechless. He looked at me and I nodded my head briefly, confirming his worst fears.

And so, with that final technicality laid to rest it was agreed.

Ymer took my place in the Queen's bed. Not only during the betrothal ceremony, which she acted out with relish, but for many years afterwards.

She played her part to perfection. For the Maxwell never knew. Even though it was I who sat beside her in the council chamber and accompanied her at ceremonials, she never seemed aware of the changeover thet took place after sunset.

People see what they want to see, I suppose. So everyone was satisfied. Or almost everyone.

There were times when I noticed Fergael studying me or my sister with more than a little suspicion and I am not entirely convinced that she did not entertain some doubts. But she must have dismissed them as being too fantastic altogether.

Which, of course, they were.

Which is why we got away with it.

As for me – I greatly missed Ymer's company a'nights – but I got used to it. And we still had the occasional 'fling' on evenings when the Queen had her bleeding and wanted to be alone.

But the times were not often. As you can imagine, the Maxwell was loathe to relinquish her new-found pleasures – and having know Ymer's propensity to please – I can't say I blame her.

The whole Castle atmosphere lightened in the wake of the wedding. The Lady, everyone avowed, was a new person, and it was all due to me.

So Ymer not only saved my skin – especially my foreskin – She did my reputation a power of good as well.

Thanks to her, I lived to fight another day.

THE TRUE CHRONICLES OF THE REDEEMER

From that time forward Rolande became ever more precious in the Maxwell's sight. And the witch, Fergael, grew jealous and sought to steal the soul of the Queen's favourite. And a mighty battle was enjoined in the land of the spirits but the good that was Childe Rolande triumphed over the evil of the witch. And the black hag was vanquished.

Chapter
16

THERE FOLLOWED FOUR YEARS OF RELATIVE CALM DURING which my hold over the Maxwell grew steadily stronger.

She rarely made a decision now without asking my opinion and in my defence I must say that I tried to use my newfound power to influence her for the good. I took every chance I could to lighten the load of my downtrodden brothers and even managed to instigate, with much support from Morangy, a better system of health-care, persuading the Lady that, in the cause of productivity, it was mere common sense to keep the workforce in the best possible condition.

Each Lugnasa Morangy and I would make our annual progress through the Hinterland – ostensibly to see that the new Health Laws were being implemented – but also so that I might spend some days with Colluden.

I became quite celebrated during these pilgrimages, hailed as something of a saviour by the male section of the communities visited. But there were mutterings too, from the reactionaries: the military – naturally – and the landowners, who still believed that the only good man was a dead man. So, although things were changing for the better, in some of the more conservative districts the changes were so slight as to be almost imperceptible.

Which is why the clash became inevitable.

I am firmly convinced, being half woman myself, that in time the women would have seen sense; accepted the equality of their male counterparts through reasoned argument; but the process would have been gae slow. I doubt it would have been achieved in my lifetime – or the lifetime of my progeny, had I survived to produce any.

So this was only the calm before the storm.

For in the High Hills the Wildemen were becoming increasingly impatient as their strength grew. They were admitting Castrati to their ranks now. Men who, thanks to my health programme, had the newfound energy and will to break from their prisoned life and make a bid for freedom.

The military hunted down such refugees ruthlessly and must have known, from the confessions they wrung from those recaptured, that there was a pocket of resistance building up somewhere in the mountains.

But the general populace was blissfully unaware of the approaching holocaust. Those escapees who fell back into the arms of the authorities never lived to tell their tale to any save their inquisitors. Information extracted was suppressed by direct order of the Maxwell. Runaways had their throats cut and their bodies hung, as an example to others, from the inverted discs of the radar dishes. There they swung, like rotting fruit in the Northerly breezes, until the over-ripe flesh dropped from their bones.

Truly, in desperation one finds nobility, for whatever torments these slave-men suffered, none, as far as I know, ever revealed the whereabouts of Colluden's cave.

Each time I visited now, I found the old man frailer. He was beginning to suffer greatly with pains in his joints and had grown cantankerous as a result. But his spirit remained undaunted and his fiery sermons as rousing as ever. As his flesh grew weaker he took to issuing directives through McCloed. He called him 'My General' and confided to me that I must use him as my strong right arm when the time came.

I took him at his word, selecting McCloed to instruct me in the art of guerrilla warfare so that, if the worst came to the worst (and I was still hopeful that it wouldn't), I should not be betrayed by a body soft from court excesses.

On the annual excursion I would hunt with the Wildemen in the mountains, travelling long distances on foot over difficult terrain. These outings exhilarated me, sharpening my eye, and improving my aim 'til I could easily spot and fell a deer in the next valley.

These weaponry skills I could practise with impunity on my return to Ballater. Cameron fairly marvelled at my expertise with a bow – telling me I was coming on 'like a house on fire'. It then only took a little well-aimed flattery to persuade her to teach me the broadsword, for which she was justly famous.

We would stage mock fights on the battlements, much to the amusement of the Clanswomen, who were more used to the class of Royal favourite who languished among silk bedspreads eating sweetmeats.

I must have been a persuasive creature altogether for I even managed to wheedle permission from the Maxwell to work out on the breed-beasts machines, an unheard of innovation, my excuse being that I needed to be able to defend myself on my trips outwith the Court. I had some difficulty with this until I discovered that Fergael had been pouring poison into my Lady's ear, suggesting that I might have my sights on the antlered throne. She was only trying to make bad blood between us. Little did she know how close she was to the mark.

Again I appealed to Cameron who had grown fond of me in her brusque way. She assured the Queen that my intentions were honourable.

'The kwine's just trying to keep herself in trim,' was how she put it. 'And if you'll pardon my saying so Ma'am, you're a bittie out of condition yersel' '.

So the Warlord of the Clans took to training alongside me and we would compete as to who could pump the most iron, working our muscles against the weights and pulleys until the sweat ran into our eyes. The Maxwell was taller and broader in the shoulder than me so she had an upper body advantage but she was also older so it wasn't long until I could almost match her. Working out became all the rage at the Palace and the Court ladies would stand in line for ages waiting their turn at the Nautilus, though most of them negated the effect by filling their painted faces with dumplings as soon as they were done.

Ymer I had to drive to the exercise. Her character tends to sloth and I fear her figure will suffer for it in later years. She hated her work-outs like poison but I had to insist. Having more male hormones than the other women, my muscles were becoming obvious and, had Ymer not managed to work up some definition at least, then the Queen would soon have seen through the difference in our body tone.

For myself I couldn't get enough of the training. One of the great joys of life surely is to be in possession of a fit body? And I was getting fitter by the phase, alternating my weight work with weaponry and static stretching.

Each month now, at the new moon's sighting, I would travel out to the hills above Braemar to meet with McCloed for practice in hand to hand combat, martial arts and wrestling. I went ostensibly to catalogue new herbs for the Medical Dictionary I was collating. And, since my affection for McCloed grew deeper with each encounter, I would be a liar if I did not admit that these trips were the highpoint of my existence.

Morangy enjoyed them too, for Isla, she of the triple breasts and the broad smile, had taken to coming with McCloed – for company – and she and the Healer had become firm friends. She would bring a picnic – fresh grouse and loganberries or some such – and after we'd eaten and while McCloed was putting me through my paces, the two little people would disappear among the dolmans carrying the empty basket between them, like children off on a morning mushroom cull.

All in all, precious few herbs got gathered.

McCloed was a punishing taskmaster. He let me get away with nothing, throwing me over his shoulder then making me get up so he could throw me again. The first time I threw him was one of my life's greatest triumphs. He rewarded me with a bear hug and then, remembering himself, blushed to the roots of his whiskers. I never loved him more than at that moment. He taught me to fall correctly at least, or I wouldn't have had a whole bone in my body. Lucky for me it was Ymer who slept nightly with the Maxwell. I would have had trouble explaining away the bruises otherwise.

Though we had trouble that way anyway, coming as usual, in the shape of Fergael.

She detested me as a forktail detests salt and went out of her way to make life uncomfortable for me, to the extent of setting a couple of her Secret Police to watch me clock-round, though the pair were so ineffectual I would take delight in tormenting them by leaving false clues to non-existent plots so that, when they eventually did come up with something, they were so discredited no-one believed them. They were cousins of the Chisholm Clan and a dimmer duo it would be hard to imagine.

But the dopiness of her henchmen made Fergael's intentions no less sinister. She loathed my guts and given half a chance would have used them for garters. Bad enough that I should possess the Maxwell's body (for so she thought) but I also had the Lady's ear which was much more dangerous. And I confess I used my position to curb the hag's excesses whenever I could.

Not that I could curtail all her iniquities. She spoke for the Mother Goddess and held absolute power over the Priest class at least. But in secular affairs I managed to put a spoke in more than one of her wheels. No longer could she with impunity point the finger at some innocent who, falsely accused of treachery by some spy looking to curry favour, would be delivered up to the diabolical torments of the Dark Tower for her perverse pleasure.

And the High Priest had become more perverse, if such a thing were possible, since my marriage to the Queen.

She had aye used powerful stimulants to induce her visions. Now the drugs began to use her. She became an addict who could no longer control her cravings. She shunned reality and dwelt increasingly in some twilight world of her own. Her body, never over-fleshed, wasted until she resembled a walking corpse, her face a deaths-head where black eyes stared from sunken sockets.

Her addictions brought with them strange and revolting preoccupations. She became convinced, having discovered some vampirical treatise, that human blood would restore her youth and took to creeping down to the cages in dead of night and bleeding the breed-beasts from a hole which she punctured in the jugular vein and then plugged with a pellet of dung.

She gave up eating solids altogether, existing solely on this blood which, mixed with certain root-based powders, hit her bloodstream like a thunderclap. She overdid it on several occasions and had to be brought to the infirmary, gibbering and foaming at the mouth, in the grip of some private Hell that had wiped the malevolence from her eyes and left only screaming terror. We had to swaddle her like an infant to prevent her from damaging herself and lock her in a padded room until the warp-spasms were over.

Ymer, who was by now well fitted for it, assumed the duties of High Priest in her absence.

It was my suggestion and I got the Maxwell to agree although some of the clergy were scandalised. Ymer had not yet been dedicated so it was not considered ethical.

The truth was that Fergael kept delaying the ceremony and Ymer was happy to let her do so. The Ceremony had built up in Ymer's mind to nightmare proportions rather as the marriage had previously in mine. And for the same reasons. She feared she would be found out.

Only the pure in spirit and body could be dedicated – with impunity – to The Source, and although Ymer pretended to be an agnostic yet her early training had left her with a sneaking

146

suspicion that there might be some rumour in the legend that anyone unworthy would, at the point of penetration, be consumed by all the tortures of the Damned. The Source, went the tale, would become a living entity, the huge penis sear through flesh and bone to immolate from within any person who was not totally inviolate.

Utter rubbish of course.

But Ymer, who had been penetrated by me and who cavorted nightly in the Queen's bed, had cause to fear that there might be some truth in the story. She was mistress of many unproveable mysteries and so could not rule out any paranormal possibility.

She still had visions but she had learned to control them now and could deliver at will any answer to an oracular demand. She also had the second sight and the ability to move objects, by power of thought alone. What she did not have was the Evil Eye. That was Fergael's province.

Ymer could be wicked, thoughtless, infuriatingly selfish betimes – but never evil. She and I had always been remarkably close in mind. They do say this is often the case with twins or lovers and we, of course, were both. But I was always the giver and she the receiver in these transactions. She could pick up my thought patterns at random from the far side of the Castle and would often come running to answer some question that I had not yet asked.

I, on the other hand, could never read her thoughts – except for that one occasion of which I will tell you shortly – and I learned afterwards that this was because she had conditioned herself to close her mind against intrusion. It was a survival technique which she had developed the first time she had felt Fergael trying to probe inside her head.

Fergael was a sadistic pervert who believed in the mortification of the flesh as a means of Holy ecstasy. Under her aegis, what had been a Life-cult had become a Death-cult and she took diabolical delight in inflicting such mortification on the bodies of her initiates under the hypocritical pretext that it was good for their souls.

If the Handmaidens of The Great Mother suffered, Ymer, as the next Fergael, suffered a hundred times more. The higher the office, the greater the responsibility. A High Priest needed to be able to withstand all things in defence of 'the Mysteries'. So

147

went Fergael's reasoning, not that it had much reason in it as I often said to poor Ymer.

Many's the time she's staggered into our cell, her wrists and ankles rubbed raw from straining against her bonds, her lips almost bitten through from trying to restrain her cries.

Comforting her at these times was a hard enough task. Making her presentable for the Maxwell's bed was even more of a problem.

Bruises, worse than any I ever endured at McCloed's hand, had to be hidden under make-up, grazed limbs camouflaged with heavy bracelets, before Ymer would don her blonde wig and take her place in the Queen's bed as Childe Rolande.

The whole thing came to a head one Summer's evening when she returned with her back a criss-cross of scarlet welts. Fergael had taken the scourge to her and for the first time had drawn blood. There was no question that we should camouflage such a mess, so I sent Morangy to say that I was indisposed and would be unable to join the Maxwell that night.

I set to bathing Ymer's wounds and salving them with antiseptic ointment to make sure they would not become infected. Then I gave her a posset of milk and honey laced with a sleeping draught.

When the Maxwell came to enquire after me, dogged as usual by the faithful Cameron, Ymer was already asleep and I abed in Morangy's dispensary, shivering with mock ague, fur rugs piled high against my chin though the night was as warm as goat's milk. My forehead, when the Lady put her cool hand against it, was hot and damp. But what she assumed to be fever was, in reality, a mix of sweat and sheer fury.

'The Childe is burning up,' she said, anxiously. 'Do something for her Morangy.'

'I am doing all I can, Ma'am,' the midget assured her. 'But she has a malfever and I don't see her up and about for a moon-phase at the least.

'A moon-phase. Mother Almighty. What has she got?'

'A virus of some description,' said Morangy. 'It maun run its course. I can relieve the symptoms – no more.'

The Maxwell bent to kiss me on the lips but Morangy restrained her.

'I wouldnae do that Ma'am,' he said. 'She'll be gae infectious.'

I smiled wanly and the Queen looked disappointed.

148

'You know best, I suppose,' she said, grudgingly.

'I do that,' Morangy confirmed. 'And just for good measure I think I'd better put her in quarantine.'

No sooner had the Maxwell taken her leave of me than I was up and out of bed like a catweazel.

I stormed through the corridors and slammed into the Inner Sanctum where I was just in time to interrupt Fergael in the act of undressing.

'What have you done to Ymer?' I howled.

'You dare enter my private chambers?' Fergael's face mottled at the insult.

'I dare, you Vulture. And I dare do even more.'

I yanked her forward by her cockscomb and with my free hand circled her scrawny neck and began to squeeze.

I was so incensed I think I could quite cheerfully have throttled her there and then no matter what the consequences.

Evidently she thought so too, for her eyes clouded with fear at the fury in mine. Then I saw her expression shift. Her eyes darkened and I felt an almost physical pain as she hooked her mind into mine and began to pull my intelligence into her own, smothering it.

I tried to wrench my head away but her gaze held me firm.

I have always been a sceptic, believing that humanity controls its own destiny. It was not until that moment that I realized that the power commanded by Fergael had something diabolical in it, something all-pervasive in its evil, stronger than anything merely human. She turned that black magick onto me, paralysing my will, draining me of my life-energy.

Her eyes grew rounder, darker, expanding until they filled the entire room. Then there was only a stygian vortex through which I felt myself falling into an even blacker infinity.

And out of that sulpherous hole a voice came to me.

It was Fergael's voice.

Not her vocal voice but the voice that hid behind it, her inner voice, putrid with menace, heaving with glee at having entrapped me in her sticky web.

'So Rolande,' The voice oozed like treacle. 'I have you at last. Soon now I shall scrape out the inside of your memory and vomit the contents of your futile little existence past the farthest reaches of the furthest stars. So far that it will never claw its way back home to the empty husk that it leaves behind. And I will parade your idiot body before the Maxwell so that she may see

149

what you have become. And I shall beg you for my experiment tomb and she will grant permission because what she sees will disgust her. And I shall take the greatest pleasure – for you will still have the ability to feel pain – in allowing you to live for the longest time. And when – finally – you hurtle screaming down to the grave, I shall consign your remains to the Holy Flame and do what I choose with your precious Ymer.'

I felt myself sinking further and further into the murk.

Reality receded but I was powerless to resist the mind-lock that Fergael had on me.

And then, suddenly, in the pinpoint that was the eye of the vortex, a small dot of light appeared. And it expanded until it became a face. My sister's face . . . wet with tears.

Ymer never wept. Even when she had returned from her ordeal that evening, her back laced with carmine ribbons and the nails torn from both her littlest fingers, she had not wept. But she was weeping now. For me.

Then I heard her soft voice overlaying the other, harsh one, as she sent her thoughts to me across the void of space to the edge of the pit where I hung by a thread.

'You can survive this, Rolande,' she said. 'Fight it. You have the power.'

'No.' My mind shook its head in defeat.

'You *can* do it,' she insisted, communicating with me soul to soul. 'Try. Try it for me. For Euan-Noag.'

His name and the sacrifice he had made for me pulled me back from the brink and I tried, with her urging me on, struggling up from the depths only to be sucked back down in a see-saw of mind bending forces.

'I can't,' I heard myself say.

'No, you can't,' It was Fergael, knowing she had me beat.

But in that moment of self-congratulation she let her concentration slip for the merest instant.

It was all the time Ymer needed.

'We are two, Rolande,' I heard her say. 'Two in one. Join with me. Together we can overcome the beast.'

And my mind leapt into hers and together the sum of our two parts overcame the single cell that was Fergael. I came out into the light with a rush and hurled her from me like a plague ridden excrescence.

She landed in a huddle atop the naked body of Scawthatch

who, I noted, had not made one move in her lover's defence and would no doubt suffer for it later.

The High Priest's eyes had blanked out as though some current had drained her internal batteries. She seemed to have shrunk and, as she pulled her knees into a foetal crouch, I thought she resembled one of those ancient mummies that are dredged up now and then from reclaimed bogland.

'When she recovers,' I told Scawthatch, whose already pale skin had taken on a distinctly greenish tinge, 'tell her I said to keep her carrion claws away from Ymer.'

The girl nodded mutely and I left – shaken and not a little stirred.

Fergael respected me more after that – but I would not say she detested me any the less.

She bided her time, that is all.

And her time was coming.

THE TRUE CHRONICLES OF THE REDEEMER

Now it happened that one day a Wildeman, a servant of The Redeemer known as McCloed, was taken captive in the High Hills and brought to Castle Ballater in triumph.

Chapter
17

AND THEN McCLOED GOT HIMSELF CAPTURED.

The whole of Castle Ballater – the whole of the countryside – was abuzz with the news.

A man – a real man, not a castrati – had been taken near Invernyess and they were bringing him to Ballater for trial.

Idiot. He had been playing the hero again – had stayed behind, to hold off the militia when his Clutch had been ambushed in a river valley. The result was inevitable and before he could kill himself – which had apparently been his intention – they had him in chains.

I nearly had a kiniption fit when I heard the news.

Morangy and I were dividing head-ease powders into paper twists when Ymer burst in to tell us.

'They say he's as tall as a horse,' she said, swinging her arms about. 'With balls like a bull, hair down to his waist . . . and a beard, would you believe it?'

I looked at Morangy.

The description could have fitted any of my Wildemen.

'I'll believe it when I see it,' I said, trying to appear disinterested. 'Does he have a name, this paragon?'

'They call him McCloed,' said Ymer. 'I can't wait to see him. They say they'll have him here before nightfall.'

After Morangy had cleared up the mess I made spilling half the powders, he 'suddenly' discovered he was short of elder bark which he needed, most urgently, to fill a prescription for liver fluke.

Would I like to come outwith the Castle and help him gather some?

Needless to say, I said I would.

So he and I proceeded to the gate and told Cameron, who was awaiting the prisoner, that we'd not be long.

'Which way are you headed?' she wanted to know.

'Oh . . . out in the direction of Braemar,' Morangy waved vaguely. 'I saw some well-grown trees up there the last time I was by.'

'Aye, well keep your eyes open,' said Cameron. 'You might see them bringing the Wildeman in.'

'Nae doubt I'll see him soon enough,' said Morangy.

'Nae doubt,' agreed Cameron. 'But if you wish to see him alive and kicking, I should get a look while the going's good. He'll no last long once Fergael hooks her claws into him.'

Naturally we never went next nor near the Braemar turn.

We headed instead towards Hillockhead and a small steading that served as a message drop.

As expected, a young loon was waiting there with news from Colluden. It was brief and to the point and he repeated it verbatim.

'The Redeemer must come to the High Hills,' he said. 'The time is now.'

We sat awhile, Morangy and I, trying to still our racing pulses, trying to work out a cohesive plan that might cover all aspects of this sudden emergency. Whether I should just cut and run or whether there was some way we could work it that allowed me to return to Castle Ballater after the deed, whatever it was, was done.

'It's handy to have you privy to all the Maxwell's secrets and policies,' Morangy ruminated. 'I think we maun hedge our bets 'til we see whether Colluden intends a rescue operation or a full-scale uprising.'

So it was decided that we should bring Ymer into the thing – persuade her to cover my tracks while I headed, post haste, for Colluden's lair.

It would be harder for her to impersonate me in broad daylight and we would have to find sufficient excuse for her to take the risk. Something plausible, for Ymer was no fool.

She knew nothing thus far of my alter ego as The Redeemer and I felt it prudent not to let her into the secret at this point. She was a woman, after all, and devoted to the Maxwell. Neither of us could judge what her reaction might be should we advise her of the anarchy of our actual intentions. What she didn't know – she couldn't tell.

155

So we decided to appeal to the romantic in her.

Morangy informed her that on our trip in search of elder bark we had encountered a young girl who had a bone-chill and needed some warm-nursing.

'Would you give cover if Rolande went absent for a wee whiley?' he asked.

'Why can't you do it?' was Ymer's immediate response – as indeed we had expected it to be.

'Because Rolande wants to see the kwine,' said Morangy, and he winked, as lewd and suggestive a wink as it has ever been my misfortune to witness.

Ymer was delighted with the intrigue.

'Rolande,' she hooted, flinging her arms around my neck. 'I do believe you're in love.'

And I hung my head and tried to look abashed while muttering some half-hearted denial under my breath.

'But won't it be dangerous?' Ymer was suddenly concerned. 'What will she say when she discovers you are . . . not what you seem?'

'Tsk,' said Morangy. 'She is a country kwine . . . and not overly bright. If Rolande keeps the light off she'll never work out what's going on.'

'In that case, of course I'll cover for you,' giggled Ymer. 'But only if you promise to tell me all about it when you get back. All of it mind. Every intimate detail,' and she stroked my cheek in anticipation of where these revelations might lead us.

And so it was arranged.

Morangy put it about that Ymer had contracted my fever and would be out of circulation for a while.

I, meanwhile, awaited my moment to escape, watching from my cell window until I spied the dust that heralded the platoon bringing in McCloed, rising up Ballater Brae. Then I hied my way down to the gateway – ostensibly to get a good look at the prisoner – and slipped out under cover of the melée that accompanied his entrance.

My heart rose in my mouth as they paraded him through, dragging him behind the Captain's horse, dirty but defiant. People jeered and threw filth at him, verbal and actual.

He had a great rent in his arm that needed attention and the healer as well as the lover in me impelled me to approach him. Instead, I shrank back into the crowd so that he should not see me as he passed.

It was Ymer that he saw then, seated by the Maxwell's side, when they hauled him before the Warlord and the Fergael for judgement.

He made a magnificent entrance to all accounts, snarling and struggling like the great wild creature that he is. His very size made him formidable, even before the Maxwell, who is tall for a woman. It took six Clanswomen to hold him down.

But on seeing Ymer, he became suddenly subdued.

He thought she was me, of course, and didn't want to show himself up in my presence. Also I daresay he was ashamed that I should see him come to such a pass.

Faced with the spectacle of McCloed, buck naked, his long hair matted with sweat, his muscles etched clear under the grime of the journey, Ymer's impersonation of me fell by the wayside.

I have always been reticent in my reactions, Ymer more transparent. And her reaction to McCloed was there for all to see. This was no simpering castrati, no half drugged breed-beast up from the cellars for a mock battle. This was something different entirely.

Morangy says she looked as though she'd been struck by a thunderbolt. Her mouth dropped open and her eyes . . . well.

As for McCloed, his eyes betrayed him too.

'If you'd seen the look that passed between them,' Morangy confided, shaking his head. 'It was so thick you could have cut it with a knife.'

The Maxwell was not amused.

She dismissed 'Rolande' from the council chamber and sent her to wait, in disgrace, in the royal bedroom until the judgement had been made.

Then she subjected her paramour to the most rigourous night of love-making that she had so far endured at the hands of the Warlord of Alba.

According to Ymer it was very exciting.

But a little late.

The damage had already been done.

My sister had fallen in love. And with a man, of all things.

Not that it looked like a love with much future. As the Maxwell took great delight in telling her that night, McCloed was as good as a dead thing.

Charred flesh.

Just as soon as Fergael had succeeded in extracting some

names and locations out of him he was to be consigned to the Holy Flame.

Alive.

THE TRUE CHRONICLES OF THE REDEEMER

And Rolande assumed his Man-guise and donned the battle armour of The Redeemer and took Enfidion and the Gae Bolga and rode forth to rescue his servant McCloed. And the feat having been accomplished, being oppressed by a thousand Clanswomen, Childe Rolande took the shape of a great golden eagle and flew away into the High Hills.

Chapter
18

IF FERGAEL THOUGHT MCCLOED WOULD CRACK EASILY, SHE WAS sorely mistaken. She was still heaping torments on him and he had still not broken his silence by the time I reached the Highlands.

I had been forced to steal a horse from the Militia outpost at Braemar in order to get there at all and I had been pursued half-way to Glenavon before shaking off most of the battalion.

I could have done with a bath and a sleep and a good, hot meal, but of course there was time for none of these things.

'You must rescue my General,' Colluden wheezed, controlling the fit of coughing that had heralded my arrival. 'Take six men of your choice and get McCloed out of there – dead or alive – if you're too late to save him at least we can bury him with dignity. I'll no have that hag consigning him to the radar dishes and the corbies.'

So with the assistance of Blossom and Isla's nimble fingers I donned my war-armour and girded on my weapons. There was no time to stand on ceremony so I called out those who were to accompany me at the same time.

Competition was fierce for the honour, but I knew already whom I wanted. McCann and One-Eye for old times' sake; Cormac, a youth of my own years, a formidable fighter who was regularly pitted against me in training; Finlay and Finool, two brothers from Botchersgate in the Lowlands and young Euan, Blossom's other boy, who was old enough to sit a horse but still small enough to slide through a back window and slip a door-latch. With one son in chains already, Blossom was loathe to see him go but I promised her I would guard him with my life and so, in the end, she consented.

It was one of those golden days that we get up here in the Maytime and the sun warmed our bones as we mounted up and headed down the mountain. Above us, Griffens spread their tawny wings in the warm currents, their shrill cries mingling with the encouraging shouts of the remaining Wildemen who, with Colluden, crowded the cave entrance to cheer us off.

We must have been a fierce-looking bunch, me all in metal and leather, my face concealed by Susuki, my troop bearded and hedgehog-bristled with weaponry, faces flushed with the expectation of battle, eager for their chance to get a crack at the Maxwell at last.

A smell of heather and pine rose to our nostrils, mingled with hot horse sweat and as we forded the rushing torrent at the dip of the hills, a salmon leapt to salute us and wish us well in our enterprise.

I took off my helmet and slung it to the saddle pommel. The warm wind caught my hair, and pulled it out behind me in a singing stream. We were off to rescue McCloed.

I never doubted we would do it. Around me my Wildemen shrieked and whooped and thus we galloped all the way to Braemar, the grouse rising in clouds under our pounding hooves and the jackrats darting in panic from our approach.

Thereafter we were forced to exercise more caution, drawing heavy woollen cowls athwart our heads to conceal us from the prying eyes of the occasional farm labourer who stopped to stare as we rode by.

Nearer to Ballater it was worse. The countryside was fairly bristling with Militia out for game after the recent capture and we had to take to the hedgerows. Several times we were forced to dismount and lead our steeds through the tangled undergrowth skirting the main thoroughfare. It was time-consuming but better than being caught in a skirmish – or worse – captured before we got next or near our destination.

We came, about nightfall, to the bottom of the Castle Brae, dismounted, and bided our time until it was as truly dark as the early summer eve was likely to get.

It was on just such an evening that I had had my innocence so rudely shattered by Corbie, the Tax Collector. The same silence, the same smells, the same sense of magic in the dusk – as though something extraordinary was about to happen.

We tethered our horses in a clearing and made our way up

the hill to where the great grey pile of Castle Ballater stood outlined against the sky.

The climb was steep.

I led the way and the others scrambled behind, McCann bringing up the rear with Euan perched on his shoulders, clinging to his grizzled hair like fungus to a tree-bark. We had to proceed with the utmost caution. The night air was heavy and so deathly still that the voices of the sentries fell down around us in a waterfall of words. A dislodged stone would have echoed like a thunder-crack and so we picked our steps with all the daintiness of heelers at a Highland wedding. I was convinced that, should the sentries cease their banter, the harsh sound of our breathing would rise to their ears like the call of the Marsh-wraithe and all would be lost. Luckily for us, the female of the species has aye had the talent for saying a lot about gae little, so the occasion, like the breath-sound, never arose.

We kept on climbing until we reached the foot of the granite walls. Once there, we edged around the perimeter until we came to the heavily bolted door which led to the kitchens. Here, as far away from the main gatehouse as you could go, provisions were regularly taken in and slops thrown out.

On either side of the door were set two small, slit windows. The one on the left, which was almost obscured by a steaming midden, had been left agape.

Cockroaches crunched under our feet and a fat jackrat scuttled away as we skirted the pile of refuse to flatten ourselves on each side of the door. On my signal, McCann hoisted Euan up and in through the aperture.

It was but a few steps to the door and the great iron bolt that secured it from within and I trusted that Euan would have strength enough in his child's fingers to move the metal back before the watch-sentry, whom I suspected would be ale-swilled and snoring, came to her senses and alerted the guard.

There was a heart-stopping clatter as Euan dropped to the ground. Evidently he had displaced some keg of provisions during his descent. We held our collective breaths but there was no responding challenge, only the grating of the lock followed by a moment of silence. Then the heavy metal door swung open and there stood the wain, well pleased with himself and grinning like a Ben-Shi from ear to ear.

The grin soon turned to a scowl when I packed him off down the hill with instructions to hold the horses and 'get himself out of it' if we failed to return with or without McCloed by the first cock-crow.

The watch-sentry lay sprawled in a corner, wrapped around her jar as though it were a lover.

Finool had slit her throat and heaved her on to the dung-heap before I could move to stop him.

'One less to bother our backs,' he grunted, in response to my protests. 'This is no game, ken? It's them or us.'

'Stay here,' I said, grimly. 'Don't move a muscle until I get back. There are at least a hundred armed Clanswomen on the premises. I don't want them roused if I can avoid it.'

'Where are you off to?' grumbled McCann. 'And how long should we stand here like lilties? I canna put up with too much of this thumb-twiddling.'

'I have to find out where they're holding McCloed,' I told him. 'If he's in the dungeons we stand a chance. If they've got him in the Dark Tower then we're in trouble. Wait here for me. I'll be quick as I can.'

There was some mumbling – but they waited.

And I – stealthy as a blood-bat – flitted through the corridors until I came to Morangy's cell, and let myself in.

Placing one hand over his mouth, I wakened him by pressing my fingers into the pulse spot behind his left ear. His eyes opened with a snap, incomprehension and fear mingling in them as he strove to adjust his brain from the sleeping to the waking state.

I raised the visor on my helmet.

'It's me,' I hissed. 'Rolande. I'm going to take my hand away. No noise. Nod if you understand.'

He gave a weak inclination of his head and I took my hand from his mouth. He drew a deep, shuddering breath.

'You scared the living daylights out of me,' he complained. 'Where's McCloed?'

'They have him in the Dark Tower – what's left of him.'

'Damnation,' I said. 'Then we're beaten before we start.'

'Why?'

'I have no card to break the door-seal.'

'Wait here.'

Morangy was back almost before he had gone, pressing into my palm the green card that would be our passport to Fergael's domain.

'Aurora's new love is a Handmaiden,' he explained. 'She keeps the card in her slipper.'

'How do you know that?'

'Because I watch them betimes,' grinned the Healer. 'It passes the time if I canna sleep. I've bored a hole in the wall so I can see them but they can't see me. It can be very enervating . . . if you like that sort of thing.'

The notion of Morangy as 'voyeur' was one that had never occurred to me before but I had no time to discuss it further at this juncture.

There were more important things afoot.

I hurried back towards the kitchen.

But this time I was not so lucky.

Neither was the Clanswoman with whom I collided rounding the final corner. She had been on a nocturnal visit to the privy and was still fumbling with the buttons on her trews when I appeared from nowhere and knocked her off her stride. Her eyes opened wide, then her mouth, and to silence the coming yell I was obliged to strike off her head with my drawn sword. It left her shoulders and spun off down the hall like a football in search of a goal. Blood spurted in a huge fountain from her severed neck and she collapsed to her knees before rolling over onto her side.

She was the first human being I had dispatched since Euan-Noag but I hadn't the time to dwell on it. Instead I took to my heels and made the distance to the kitchens in double quick time.

Gathering my forces about me, I led the way out of the Castle proper and up the uneven pathway that led to the Dark Tower.

Silently, I slipped the entry card into the slot. Slowly, and just as silently, the door in the metal casing swung inwards. In single file we climbed the stair. It was black as pitch in there but we did not dare light a taper. We went, the one behind holding on to the one in front, ever onward, ever upward, 'til we emerged, through the trap-door, into the temple itself.

It was deserted.

Such was their faith in the security of the locks that they hadn't even left a guard to oversee the prisoner.

Only the keeper of the eternal flame was there – and she had nodded off.

She would never wake.

McCann snapped her neck as he might have snapped a bantam's. She never knew what hit her.

McCloed lay on the altar before the statue of the Great Mother. He was in a dreadful condition, his body a mass of burns where Fergael had taken the branding-irons to him. The tear in his arm had been deliberately kept open and probes inserted to worry the raw flesh. A couple still protruded from the wound. Blood had congealed around their barbs welding them into the gash. One of his eyes was puffed shut, the other held open by a sliver of bone. But at least they hadn't been gouged free of their sockets, one of Fergael's favourite tricks. However he had lost a canine. Blood dribbled from the hole in his gum where it had been torn out by metal pincers.

He was conscious – but only just.

I sent Finlay and Finool to search the premises for Fergael while I unlocked the chains that restricted McCloed's movements and chafed the blood back into his numbed limbs. Three more handmaidens were discovered and dispatched before they found the High Priest, drugged to the eyeballs and dead to the world, on a pallet behind a screen.

She was fit for nothing, so we gagged her and wrapped her in McCloed's chains and left her where she was.

My Wildemen wanted to kill her out of hand but I said no.

She was so befuddled that she wouldn't even have noticed. And I wanted Fergael to be conscious when she met her end, to suffer the agonies she had inflicted on McCloed and countless others before she was allowed to tasted the blessed relief of death.

I am powerful but slight of build, so it was Cormac, as the strongest among us, who hoisted McCloed across his shoulders so that we could make off down the stairs with maximum speed.

I took a light this time, to avoid accidents on the way down – and that's how the trouble started. In the hurry to get out, I neglected to douse it fast enough as we exited the Dark Tower. One of the sentries on the main building was alert enough to spy the flickering flame and the figures that it illuminated.

At her cry of 'Who's there?', I hurled the brand to the ground and trampled it out. But the damage had already been done and the cry of the slughorn calling the Clanswomen to arms reverberated round the entire valley.

Hampered as we were by the near comatose McCloed, we

165

had barely reached the head of the brae before the Clanswomen came pouring out of the main gate to challenge our retreat.

The Wildemen had their thirst for action satiated with a vengeance in the affray that followed.

'Take McCloed down,' I howled to Cormac. 'We'll hold them 'til you get away down the hill.'

And while he slithered down the incline, unheeding now of what din he made, McCann. One-Eye, Finlay, Finool and myself laid into the guard.

It was hard going, but although they had the advantage of superior numbers we had the element of surprise in our favour. Apart from that, my Wildemen were well used to night forays so their dark-sight was far superior to that of our adversaries.

We laid at least a score of them low before Cameron emerged from the Guard-House carrying a lighted brazier.

She couldn't have done us a better turn.

The light fell across my armour, sparking off the sword and the Gae Bolga, and the shiny black depths of my face-concealing headgear.

One look at my bared breasts and the padded codpiece and the Clanswomen dropped back in disarray.

'Good Godfathers,' Cameron swore. 'What is it?'

'Go now,' I hissed to McCann. 'Get back to the Highlands with McCloed. I can handle this rabble alone.'

'There are too many . . .'

'Do as I say. They fear me. It is all the edge that I need.'

And while my Wildemen melted away in the darkness, I illustrated my point by drawing myself up to the full height and raising my sword above my head in a gesture of power and defiance.

'I am The Redeemer,' I roared, and my voice, distorted by the Susuki, bounched off the Castle walls in sepulchral echoes. 'I have come to claim what is mine.'

The Clanswomen crowded together. One actually fainted. Encouraged, I moved towards them and they retreated in fear of the unknown.

But Cameron was made of sterner stuff.

'Attack, you bitches,' she yelled. 'If it's human we can kill it – if it's an apparition it cannae harm us.'

'Locheil.'

It was the Maxwell.

Her voice cut through the hysteria like a cold douche. She

had come from her bed naked to see what all the fuss was about and as she stood, silhouetted in the arch of the great gateway, her red-gold hair loose and falling across her magnificent breasts, she drew the gaze like a magnet.

All heads turned in her direction.

But she had eyes only for me and in her gaze was a mix of uncertainty, disbelief and dread.

'What is it, Majesty?'

Ymer emerged from out of the dark, rubbing the sleep from her eyes with the backs of her hands. She, at least, had taken time to fling a linen wrap about her. As she stood there, in her long blonde wig, I felt suddenly displaced, as though I had stepped from my body and was now observing myself some distance away.

'Go back to bed, Rolande,' said the Maxwell . . . and I almost found myself obeying.

But Ymer had already caught sight of me and her reaction was as extreme as it was instantaneous. She was to tell me later that I was her vision made flesh from the afternoon where the snow-bear had run amok in the courtyard. The sudden sighting threw her into a fit. She fell on the cobbles and began to foam at the mouth.

The Maxwell dropped to her knees beside her stricken lover.

'Capture that . . . creature . . . whatever it is . . .' she shouted to Cameron, then she bent to pull the tongue from Ymer's mouth so that she might not choke in her frenzy.

It was time for me to disappear. I had done what I had come to do, and by this time McCloed would be well away.

I raced round to the back of the Castle, Cameron close on my heels and a trail of shrieking harpies hallooing behind her. Through the scullery door I went, along corridors that I luckily knew like the back of my hand, remembering only at the last minute to sidestep the corpse of the headless trooper.

Cameron, of course, was expecting no such obstacle. She stumbled over the body and slid to her knees in the still sticky blood and the careering crowd behind collided with her as she fell so that they all keeled over like so many skittles. While they were disentangling themselves one from the other I had time to reach the dispensary. Morangy was not there so I rushed instead to his quarters.

There I dived under the bed.

167

When Cameron and her crew crashed-in in pursuit, the Midget was waiting, craning through the open window, a look of utter disbelief on his face.

'Where is it?' screamed Cameron. 'Where did it go?'

'It flew out the window,' croaked Morangy.

Cameron stopped dead in her tracks.

'Flew out?' she echoed, uncertainly.

'Changed into an eagle and soared away over the valley,' confirmed Morangy.

There was a stampede for the window and herb-pots that had been months in the growing were scattered hither and yon as the Clanswomen craned for a gleek at the sky.

A moment before my entrance, Morangy had been observing a golden eagle swooping over the lowlands in search of stray lambs. Frustrated in its attempt to find an easy supper, it was soaring now, back towards its eyrie in the mountains.

As the women jostled for space, the clouds drifted back and, for a moment, the great golden bird hung silhouetted against the paler circle of the moon.

'There it is,' shouted Cameron – and the Guards began to twitter, like birds themselves, in superstitious awe.

Morangy sat down heavily on the bed causing me to duck my head sharply and affording me a wonderful view of his bare feet among the jackboots.

'I would never have believed it,' I heard Cameron say, shakily, 'if I hadn't seen it with my own two eyes.'

THE TRUE CHRONICLES OF THE REDEEMER

So the Warlord of the Clans went forth to do battle. And the Priest, Fergael, called the Great Dragon-beast from its watery lair in Loch Nyiss that the Maxwell might ride him into the fray. And Aife sent a cold wind to raise the Battle-Standard Hraefn. And Morrigan, Goddess of War and Death, laid her hand on them all.

Chapter
19

THE MAXWELL, DETERMINED TO QUELL ANY PUTATIVE INSURREC-
tion before it took hold, decided on a show of force.

She mustered her Clanswomen and, flanked by Fergael and
myself, set off at daybreak for Loch Nyiss, there to call up the
Waterhorse which the Warlord traditionally rode into battle.

With us we brought the jewel-crusted Kelpie Mask that
normally hung above the antlered throne in the Council
Chamber. Also the magic Battle-Standard Hraefn, furled tight
in its rune-worked casing. The standard, depicting a giant raven,
was reputed to flutter in victory, droop in defeat. Cameron was
honoured with its guarding and carried it like a new-laid egg
which she feared might crack.

The weather stayed fair for us and the sun was up and
shining as we filed out of Castle Ballater to the skirl of the
pipes and the well-wishing shouts of those remaining. Women,
children and castrati, all lined the battlements. Even the breed-
beasts were there. Normally a feature when the Maxwell took
the field, it was thought impolitic (considering the nature of the
enemy) to include them in this particular campaign. So they were
to be left behind. They stood, huddled in a clump by the main
gate, uncertain of what was expected of them but cheering all
the same, to be on the safe side.

We made a brave show. Gold braid, tassels and buttons
flashed in the morning sun. Dress uniform rather than battle
fatigues was the order of the day and blue vied with red, red
with green in the interwoven colours of the Maxwell tartan.
Boots and weapons gleamed with last minute burnishing. Spirits
were high.

The cavalry rode in the van, each mount a great antlered

stag (gelded for managibility), harnessed in tooled leather, horns newly gilded. The riders wore trews and jackboots and great ballooning capes and bonnets with griffen feathers to keep their hair in check. Behind them the footsoldiers strode out in heavy kilts that swung jauntily with the sway of their hips.

And before all rode the Maxwell, tall and imposing on the King Stag, her helmet crowned with the antlers of the Warlord of the Clans.

In the shadow of the Dark Tower Ymer stood, surrounded by kneeling Priests praying for our safe return. As we passed under the main gate she let loose a flock of finches. They whirred away in the still air like so many coloured lights.

We had spent the night together, Ymer and I, the Maxwell being embroiled in her battle plans, and Ymer confessed her interest in McCloed and begged me spare him should our paths cross in the coming conflict.

She chose a point in our activities when I could refuse her nothing but I would have reassured her anyway. I confessed in my turn that I felt much the same way about the man as she did herself.

Then Ymer told me a curious thing.

I pass it on to you, for what it's worth.

All my life I had been taught to believe that the Fall had been brought about by the cursed War-Machines built by men for the destruction of Humankind. Fire rained down from heaven, so the story went, laying the land waste and setting up a poisoned cloud whose rainfall killed most of those whom the fire had not already claimed.

Now, from my sister's lips, I was to learn that this was not the whole truth.

A great plague had also swept the world, she told me, and this is what drove men to madness and self-immolation. It was carried in the blood and sperm of the males but could be passed on to women – even to children in the womb – and those afflicted died of many diseases at once which riddled the body like the Backshi and ate the victims alive from within.

There was no cure.

Which was why, when the women took power, the men were castrated. Not merely to subdue them but to halt the spread of the plague. It was also discovered that the pure love of woman for woman was the only sexual relationship which did not carry fear of the disease. Their coupling was approved by the Goddess

171

in that She made it possible, from that time forward, for women to bear children without the aid of man, taking over the task herself in her manifestation as The Source of all life.

It was one of the Mysteries, Ymer said, and she should not be telling me since I was not an Initiate, but she did so that I would know that any intercourse with a man held the danger of contracting the affliction. She had not known of it, she said, when she had contemplated coupling with Buchan, nor indeed when she had first seduced me. But she knew it now. Clearly I had not been touched by the poison, but she could not promise that McCloed did not carry the germ in his blood.

I pictured McCloed as I turned to wave Ymer a final farewell and found it hard to imagine that such a perfect specimen of manhood would hold within him the seeds of destruction. Still, it gave one pause for thought.

'You must dedicate the Lady Ymer to the Source.'

The Maxwell's voice brought me back to myself, even though she was addressing Fergael.

'I will do it when we return,' the High Priest assured her, albeit reluctantly.

'See that you do. If she is not ready to learn the truth now, she never will be. Besides, I am heartily sick of the squabbling and jealousy that govern the Inner Sanctum. The Priesthood should show a more responsible face to the populace. As should others that I might mention.'

She glanced sideways at me from under her helmet.

She was still offended at my supposed behaviour towards McCloed the previous day. As a mark of her disapproval she forbade me to join the expedition and had only been persuaded otherwise by Fergael who told her that I would make a good impression since the people loved me well. The hag spoke true but she had, as usual, an ulterior motive. She was hoping I would not survive the battle and, from the glances that she continually darted at me, I realized that I would have to look as much to my back as my front in the coming affray.

I muttered something suitably contrite and the Maxwell thawed a little, patting my hand and giving me the makings of a smile.

I smiled back, wondering what excuse I might dredge up should she decide to exercise her droit de seigneura during the excursion.

But all thoughts of self soon faded as we began to pass

through the settlements en route to the black stretch of water known as Nyiss.

It seemed the whole countryside had turned out to greet us and I was once again struck by the line between affluence and abjectedness that ran, straight as a sword-thrust, through the centre of the society. On the one side stood the women. Well-fed, well-garbed, bursting with well-being, they came out to cheer us as we passed, rosy cheeks wreathed in smiles as they threw flowers in our path and ran forward to press sweet-meats and good luck charms into our palms. On the other hand the men, emaciated and work-weary, hung back like thin shadows on the periphery of the crowds. Sullen, malnourished, their eyes dulled with fatigue.

Yet in some eyes I saw, for the first time, a hint of something new.

Hope . . . or, if hope was too much to hope for, at least the beginnings of resentment . . . even hate.

It was a start.

The weather began to worsen as we passed through Cults and turned up towards Queenswells. Clouds covered the sun and sudden sharp spats of hail flung themselves upon us only to finish almost before they had begun. By the time evening came and we stopped to make camp in the lee of the Cairngorms, clouds were rolling in from the west, threatening more pro-longed rain.

The secret of my sexuality was saved that evening by the first skirmishes of the Wildemen.

The four of us, the Maxwell, Fergael, Cameron and myself, were dining in some style and I was desperately trying to invent excuses why I might not lie with the Queen later, when my dilemma was resolved by the sounds of fighting outwith the Royal tent.

The camp was in an uproar.

Several clutches of Wildemen had caught the Clanswomen at their supper and had dispatched a number of them while they ate, stealing their arms, and, to add insult to injury, their food, before melting back into the rain. Panicked and disoriented, female fought female in the dark and it took some time to separate and subdue them.

The remainder of the night was spent hunting the raiders without success. Not a single Wildeman did we catch, though they picked off stragglers at their leisure so that we lost many more of our troops before the dawn brought lightening skies.

Thereafter sentries were posted at each stop – a case of shutting the barn door after the horse has long gone.

Two evenings later, towards dusk, we came at last to Loch Nyiss.

There cannot be a more desolate stretch of water in the whole of Alba. A haunted place, hung about with stories of the great Sea-Worm said to inhabit its depths.

I had never seen the Dragon myself – nor met anyone who had seen it – but young boys were regularly sacrificed at the water's edge to keep the monster content and away from the crofts and cattle-stations of the bordering farmlands.

It was Fergael's task to coax the Kelpie from its lair that it might be harnessed and mounted by the Monarch who would then ride it into battle and presumably scare her enemies to death before they had even drawn sword.

All this was the stuff of legend. Except for the occasional infiltration of maurauding bands from the Poisonlands to the South, peace had reigned in Alba for as long as anyone could remember. No Maxwell had had to take to the battlefield since the punitive wars after the Fall. No Fergael had called up the Worm since that time either and I was interested to see how this Fergael would rise to the challenge. She had become more nervous the closer we had got to the Loch and this evidenced itself in her increasing bad temper. By the time we reached Nyiss she had worked herself up into a kind of apopleptic frenzy which I am sure (together with the powder she kept sniffing) was the only thing that got her through the ordeal.

Although it was more of an ordeal for others.

The young boy, for instance, brought from a neighbouring townland to be sacrified to the Waterhorse.

His death, screaming and begging for mercy, sickened me.

Human sacrifice is forbidden in Alba now. It is a barbaric practice, unacceptable in a civilized society. Though I admit it has not been easy to stamp out and one still sometimes comes across a pathetic huddle of bones, that can only be human, on some wayside altar to the Mother.

People had gathered from far and near to witness the sacrifice and the calling-up. The weather could not have been more appropriate if Fergael had ordered it herself which, from what I witnessed later, she may well have done.

As she cut the child's throat, a great jagged shaft of lightning rent the sky, illuminating the sacrificial knife as she proffered its blood-dripping point towards the Loch.

A warm wind had sprung up, exciting the dull waters into ripples and, as she exhorted the beast to rise from the fathoms, a rumbling was heard across the Loch. Distant thunder I thought then, but still it sounded as though the Kraken was stirring in the bowels of the tarn.

Eviscerating the boy with a practised hand, Fergael gathered his guts in both arms and, striding to the very point of the rocky outcrop, allowed the stinking mess to slide down into the waters.

'Arise, Great Snake,' she howled. 'Kelpie of the Loch. Come forth and carry the Maxwell to War and to Victory.'

Silence followed the High Priest's pronouncement. It hung over the dark surface like Summer mist.

The waiting populace held their breath.

Time passed. Nothing occurred. People began to shuffle their feet and mutter amongst themselves. The rhomboid muscles in Fergael's upper back started to harden with the strain of holding her bloodied arms aloft.

I turned to look at the Maxwell. Her face was tense under her tan. A small tic worked under her right eye.

And then there was a sudden churning in the water, a bubbling, a swirling. Preceded by a waterspout of gigantic proportions, a monstrous apparition surged up from the depths. Bloody entrails dangled in fronds from between the jaws of its lizard head. The King Stag reared in alarm, the Maxwell pulling him back into line with a well-aimed clout of her spurred heels. Someone in the crowd screamed and the crush moved back, those in front, who had a view too close to be comfortable, treading on the toes of those behind who strained forward to see.

Up until that moment I had doubted the truth of the Kelpie's existence. I have aye been sceptical of such tales. Now the living legend hung, house-high before me. And its reality was infinitely more awesome than any drink-embellished story I have ever heard. Here was a creature of nightmare made flesh.

Give Fergael her due, she did not flinch.

Probably she was relieved that the monster had put in an appearance at all – and too drugged to realise the danger.

Still, she did not flinch, even when the monster, water cascading from its back, gave a deafening roar, blasting us with the stench of rotting fish and twisting its snake-neck from side to side in search of the rest of its supper.

As the head darted out to snatch the body of the child, Fergael slung a double harness athwart its neck and pulled it tight.

The creature flicked its head, flinging her away like a troublesome fly. She flopped on the grass some distance away, screaming to the Clanswomen to catch the bridle and hold it hard.

It took fifty souls, me amongst them, to subdue the beast, which we did by cutting off its air supply so that its tiny eyes glazed over and it fell senseless, half-way between land and water.

Then stakes were driven into the ground and the carcass dragged free of the shallows and secured with ropes lapped and overlapped across the monstrous grey hulk.

I got a better look at the creature then.

On its side it was as high as the highest stockade, with a humped torso, stubby legs and a head which, though disproportionately small for its body, was still the size of a full-grown warrior. The hide was like that of a hairless seal and it had a long, flat tail, half-fin, half-rudder, stretching out at the back. Triple rows of razor teeth filled the lizard-jaw and a cockscomb of skin ran, like a frill, from the base of its curved spine to a point halfway between its wicked red eyes.

The locals crowded in for a better look but Cameron drove them back with curses and blows and, while the beast was still recovering its wind, the Maxwell hauled the Dragon-Mask over its head, pushing the bit between its jaws (a task I would not like to have tackled), and fastening the whole contraption under its chin.

I had thought the Mask merely decorative.

Now I saw that it had a purpose. It was a muzzle and bridle combined, allowing a rider to exercise a modicum of control over the Water-beast.

We left it there for the night with a handful of nervous guards overwatching it.

Rumour had it that a family of the monsters dwelt under the Loch — as indeed they must, unless this particular beast was immortal — and we didn't want (as Cameron put it) a whole gaggle of them descending on us during the night.

We slept were we lay and were awakened just before dawn by a tremendous commotion. The Kelpie had managed to work its head free of the noose and the long, sinuous neck was thrashing around, keeping the sentries at bay, while the creature heaved and strained against the ropes.

The Maxwell was immediately in charge.

I had not seen her in this guise but clearly it was the role for which she was born.

First she sent several troopers to kill and cut up a stag. Then she instructed Fergael to marinate the great gobbits of meat in a mixture that was known to quieten unruly horses.

While this was going on she approached the crazed Kelpie and, flinging herself across its snapping head, wrestled it to the ground. Lying across it, a hand-span from the slavering mouth, she began to croon, half-singing, half-talking to the beast. And when she wasn't crooning, she would blow up into the dilated nostrils. By the time Cameron arrived with the prepared meat, the Maxwell had the creature all but subdued.

She poked the pieces of flesh through the lattice-work in the Mask and sat, fondling and stroking the neck until the giant Worm lay semi-sedated and ready for her to mount. Then she straddled the neck, which was as thick as a horse's back at the point where it joined the trunk, and ordered Cameron to cut the restraining ropes.

Grasping the reins that ran from the Mask and gripping tight with her powerful thighs, the Queen held on as the Guard Captain sliced through the binding and the great beast lumbered upright.

Its first instinct was to make for the waters which had spawned it. But the Queen had made preparation for that.

A human wall bristling with drawn spears separated the Kelpie from its home. A few well-placed jabs sufficed to persuade it to change direction and the Beast turned, to loud cheers from the relieved crowds, and plodded off inland.

The Clanswomen fell in behind and Cameron rode up brandishing the Battle-Standard which the Maxwell unfurled and held high for all to see.

And here something occurred which I cannot explain.

The wind had dropped in the night so that the morning was calm and clear as a bowl of freshly drawn water. The flag drooped sullenly in the breezeless air, the Raven fashioned on it hanging forlornly, its wings folded, its head bowed.

A bad omen.

Then Fergael galloped forward, Death on a black horse, and she raised her arms to the Heavens and she uttered a piercing cry.

'Blow winds of Alba,' she shrieked. 'Come Aife, Spirit of the East. Breathe life into the Morrigan – the Great Goddess of War.'

And a sudden sighing sound filled the sky that chilled the blood and raised goosepimples on the flesh of all who heard it. And a biting cold wind came out of nowhere to lash the surface of Loch Nyiss to a frenzy. And the scarlet standard unfurled so that the raven appeared to open its wings and raise its black head. And it fluttered bravely on its bloody field, high above the heads of the cheering Clanswomen as the army strode for the High Hills in search of The Redeemer.

178

THE TRUE CHRONICLES OF THE REDEEMER

Now at the Lady Ymer's initiation it was discovered that she was impure. And great was the wrath of the Mother Goddess. So the black witch Fergael put Ymer to the torture and buried her in a black box in the Dark Tower.

Chapter 20

WE HAD NOT GONE FAR BEFORE FERGAEL COLLAPSED. EVIDENTLY the effort of calling up the Kelpie and raising the heavenly wind had been too much for her. The Maxwell sent her home with instructions that she should dedicate Ymer to the Source forthwith.

'Two Sorceresses are better than one,' was the way she put it. 'And with such as Dragons and Chimeras abroad, we need all the Magic we can muster.'

So Fergael returned to the Dark Tower.

And I went on with the Maxwell and so was not there when Ymer needed me most, to comfort and encourage her, as she had done for me so many times, in the extreme hour of her need.

In the Inner Sanctum, before Fergael, before the Priestesses and Initiates, before the very Source itself, she was to be exposed as a fraudulent creature – a violate virgin who had betrayed her most sacred vows. And as such her life would be forfeit – her body subjected to the most exquisite tortures before – as the dread speech proclaimed at her naming had promised, she was brought . . .

> '. . . in hideous agony,
> to the dishonour of an unmarked grave.'

Morangy did his best in my absence.

He inserted a small bag of chicken blood into the vagina so that, at the appropriate moment, the skin would burst and blood flow to simulate the breaking of the hymen.

This covered the mundanities well enough.

But that was not what Ymer feared. She had seen too much

180

in her time as an Initiate not to believe in the Source as a living Entity. Three in One. The Maid, the Mother and the Crone (a part played to perfection by Fergael). Ymer feared the All-Seeing eye and her own inadequacies.

For when all was said and done she had broken her vows, even though she had crossed her fingers when she had made them. She was not virgin, knew herself violate both in body and soul and, in her heart of hearts, she could not believe that the Great Spirit could condone her behaviour.

As they winched Ymer up on the harness that would lower her onto the idol's phallus, she looked up into the golden eyes and she swears that they had become living eyes that held in them the knowledge of all her blasphemies. Her whole body contracted as the eyes bored into her and the bag slithered from between her legs and burst with a soft plop at the Source's feet.

'I was petrified,' she told me later, 'I had never felt so exposed, so helpless, swinging above the heads of the Inner Circle, naked as the day I was born, impaled on that malevolent gaze like a worm on a hook.

'I tore my eyes away and looked down at the scarlet splotch. When the bag had hit the floor there had been an immediate, awful hush. Even the barron fell silent and the air grew chill as a Winter funeral.

'Scawthatch and Ailill, who had been guiding the harness, let go of it as though it had become red hot. I hung there, the straps biting into my groin and underarms and in spite of the chill, I began to sweat.

'Fergael turned white as the blood drained from her face, then livid purple as it rushed up through the corded veins in her neck to explode into her head in a flood of righteous wrath.

'She was holding the ritual scourge in her hand and she fell upon me, lashing my cringing flesh and howling that I was forever damned, that my body might rot but that my spirit would languish eternally in the fiery pits of the Underworld, begging for a forgiveness that would never come. She cursed me for a whore, a bitch, an unbeliever. She crossed my name from the Book of Life.

'I looked away into the eyes of the Godhead, scarcely feeling the blows from the whip, searching behind them for some sign of understanding. But the golden orbs held no hope. The life that had burned remorselessly from them had died, leaving once again the blind stare of a statue, hard and unflinching as the stone from which it had been carved.

'I bowed my head in despair and once again my gaze fell on the blood and as I gazed another drop fell to join it (from the wounds in my back, I suppose) and suddenly it seemed to me that it was raining blood, that it fell and was met half-way by a fountain of blood that bubbled up from the floor and oozed out to cover the matting in a viscous flood. And the red of the blood became the redness of flame that spread through the Dark Tower, licking upwards to coil around my bare legs and engulf my body.

'And I began to scream, not with the pain of it, but in the knowledge that these were the flames of my future, rising from the Underworld. A vision of Eternity sent by the Source to show that I was forever damned. That I would never be forgiven and that those self-same flames would sear my scorching soul until the end of Time.'

They cut her down, writhing and foaming at the mouth, blood running red from the whip-wounds in her back.

Then they strapped her to the altar and Fergael administered hot irons to the tenderest parts of her flesh.

Even though she was delirious, still the torture went on. Even though she was mad with a fear greater than anything the irons could engender. Even though she was not responsible for anything that she said or did. Even so they tormented her.

And in the end she betrayed us both.

Morangy and myself.

I, for that I had violated her in the first place, and Morangy for that he had known and condoned it all.

She told of the chicken blood, of the marriage ceremony, of the first day at the Summer Palace when she had discovered that I was a hermaphrodite. She told them everything.

Except that I was The Redeemer.

And she would have told them that too, had she but known.

Then they took her, still raving, and enclosed her in the small black coffin where she had been imprisoned after the Buchan affair.

Morangy, spying on Aurora when her paramour burst in with the news, learned of his danger a beat before Fergael crashed in to arrest him.

He escaped by the skin of his teeth, fleeing the Castle in fear of his life, since neither the Maxwell nor myself were there to save him from Fergael's fury.

As for Ymer, she came round in pitch blackness, aching in body yet thankfully unaware that she had revealed all and signed, not only her own death warrant, but ours as well.

THE TRUE CHRONICLES OF THE REDEEMER

Then the Redeemer went out to do battle against the Maxwell with his Wildemen and his Wardogs and the great Sno-bear, Invincible, by his side. And he slew the great Kelpie beneath the Warlord of the Clans and took from her the Battle Standard Hraefn and claimed it as his own.

Chapter
21

I AWOKE TO DEATHLY SILENCE, THE CAMP STILL AS A GRAVEYARD — not even a bird heralding a morning pure as the scent of pine needles.

We had camped in a hollow in the High Hills, posted sentries at the passes and fallen asleep, exhausted, after the long march from Loch Nyiss.

I sat up in my sleeping-plaid, the vestiges of the night's dreams dissolving like dew in the morning sun. I had dreamt we were surrounded, no hope of escape, doomed, defeated, disgraced.

Looking up into the face of the dawn, shading my eyes against the purple and gold-flecked sky, I saw that the dream had become reality.

The Wildemen had broken all the established rules of combat — had not waited to be 'called out' as honourable adversaries would have done. They had descended, stealthily in the night, dispatched the sentries and retreated to the hilltops where they stood now, silhouetted like bristles on a porcupine against the lightening sky.

At their epicentre, on the topmost point of the rising ground, sat Colluden, supported on a hide litter by two strong youths. To his right stood a tall figure and my heart lurched as I recognized McCloed. To his left Euan, alias Cuchullain, struggled to rein in a pack of ferocious, twin-headed War-Dogs.

Folk began to stir around me, unnerved by the silence, aware that something was wrong. I could hear gasps of comprehension as the enormity of the situation hit them and the clash of weapons, hastily grasped and buckled on.

We had left ourselves in a woefully vulnerable position and

it gave me no joy to murmur 'I told you so', even though I had cautioned the Maxwell the previous nightfall that to camp in a dip in the hills was to leave ourselves open to ambush. She, not realising the extent of the opposition (as I clearly did), shrugged my objections aside. Even the normally canny Cameron had felt I was being cautious to the point of cowardice.

'Let them come,' she had scoffed. 'We'll be ready for them.'

So come they had – and caught us with our kilts down.

The truth was that the Maxwell's proud army, resplendent in their tartans and braid, were no more than a bunch of toy soldiers, weakened by soft living, picturesque on the parade ground perhaps but with neither the guts nor the skill to deal with a real confrontation and no match for the bloodthirsty bunch who faced us, fired by the desperation of the underdog.

Cameron was cursing now, calling the Maxwell's troops to arms, harrying and chivvying.

'They didna play fair,' she complained, belting on her broadsword in haste.

'They're not interested in fair,' I told her. 'All they want is to win.'

'Then why didn't they slit all our throats in the dark, like they did the sentries?'

'I expect they want to rub our noses in it,' I said.

'Battle stations,' roared the Maxwell, desperately attempting to rally her panicked troops.

'Form a square, you stupid eejits,' shouted Cameron. 'Protect your backsides.'

These were all the directives they had time to issue, for as the Maxwell struggled to mount the Kelpie and haul it upright (still semi-comatose from its drug-induced sleep), Colluden gave the order to attack and with a collective blood-curdling roar, the Wildemen surged down from the mountain-top engulfing the camp in a human avalanche.

After that I was conscious merely of defending myself, trying to stop being hurt without hurting – a well-nigh impossible task – my eyes assailed by the carnage, my ears sickened by the screams of the wounded, the howling of the dogs and the War-whoops of the men.

Above the din I suddenly heard the voice of the Maxwell crying out my name and then I saw her bearing down on me, riding the Kelpie, a couple of hounds hanging from its flanks like fleas off a dog.

'Climb aboard,' shouted the Queen, laying about her with her battle-axe – and I would have done so gratefully had not a blow to the back of my head felled me and dissolved the world to black.

I came to on the side of the mountain, bedded in purple heather and hidden from the affray below by a high stand of fern. Blossom was sponging my head. Colluden sat by her, rheumy eyes regarding me with concern. A little way away Cilla, the bearded lady, kept watch for stragglers who might inadvertently crash into our hiding place. Hunkered next to me, near but not too near, sat McCloed.

'He's coming to,' said Blossom.

'And about time too,' the old man was unsympathetic. 'Away back down, McCloed. He'll live.'

McCloed rose reluctantly.

'I didn't mean to hit you so hard,' he said, gruffly . . . and then he was away, sliding through the heather on his belly, like a snake.

'Get up, Rolande,' sad Colluden. 'The battle goes badly. It's time the Redeemer put in an appearance.'

'It didn't look like it was going badly to me,' I winced, feeling the lump on my head which I firmly believed to be the size of a boulder and was astounded to discover was no bigger than a bantam's egg.

'You underestimate the Maxwell, damn her hide,' said the old man. 'She's managed to rally her troops to the standard.'

'The Raven flutters high,' announced Cilla from her vantage point.

'A bad omen for us,' grumbled Colluden. 'You must take the Raven, Rolande, otherwise the cause is lost. With their superior numbers it's only a matter of time before they overwhelm us. We had the element of surprise but only the nucleus of our band is strong. The rest are ill-fed, ill-trained rabble, fled to us over the last two moon-phases. They'll tire easily and no be much good in the hand to hand combat.'

'Let me help you on with this.'

It was Blossom again, staggering under the weight of my armour and weapons. The helmet, Susuki, rolled off the top of the pile and I caught it just before it hit an adjacent rock.

'How did you come by these?' I asked, allowing her to assist me into my breastplate. 'The last I saw of them they were stashed under Morangy's bed.'

'Aye – the wee mannie managed to smuggle them out to us while you and the Maxwell were poncing about round Loch Nyiss.'

'Well done, Morangy,' said I, adjusting the helmet straps and picking up my weapons. 'Well, how do I look?'

'Awe-inspiring,' said Blossom, giving me a hug.

'I wish I felt so,' I said, turning to Colluden for instructions. 'What now, Prophet?'

'What now?' Colluden looked as though he might suddenly be taken with an apoplexy. 'Get out there and do what you were born to do of course. Beat the Maxwell. Hammer those murdering bitches into the ground.'

'There seems to be a good deal of murdering going on on both sides,' I said, feelingly. 'I'm not sure that this is the right way to go about affecting change.'

'For pity's sake,' roared Colluden. 'This is a fine time to be getting second thoughts.'

Standing there on the mountain in my burnished armour, I could hardly tell the old man that I had always had second thoughts, could not see the virtue in replacing one tyranny with another. What I wanted was the best of both worlds. But to Colluden everything was so clear cut. Black or white, no greys. I envied him his certainties.

'If you fight for nothing else,' he said in disgust, 'fight for your balls – and theirs – the ones that still have them.'

I had a sudden vision of a small boy who had died bleeding from a botched castration during one of my mercy tours. And I knew then that something had to be done. It was the method that I questioned. Not the validity of the cause.

But the guiding force that governs our lives moves in mysterious ways. I might have dithered there forever had not my mind been made up for me in a curious and unnerving fashion.

A huge bellow shook the hillside and a great Sno-bear suddenly lumbered from a concealed cave among the heather, two small cubs gambolling in her wake. A She-Bear. The female of the species twice as deadly as the male, she made a bee-line for my bright armour, singling me out as the intruder who was threatening the sanctity of her lair.

I sprang from the covert with a yell that echoed round the

189

hills and brought the fighting down in the valley to a momentary halt, as all eyes turned towards the source of the sound.

So there I was, high above the killing-grounds, sword upraised, armour and weapons afire in the fully risen sun. What an effect I had on those below. The legendary Redeemer, half-man, half-woman, who, it was now known, could change at will into the form of an eagle and escape into the High Hills.

Of course I was holding the sword aloft to defend myself against the rampaging Sno-bear but with the sun at my back and the dark Susuki giving me a semi-human air, it must have seemed to those looking up that the very Source itself had risen to rally the Wildemen against the Maxwell.

'The Redeemer,' someone shouted, and the cry was picked up from throat to throat as though I had not come alone but had a thousand re-inforcements at my back.

Then the Sno-bear crested the rise for all the world as though she had come to fight at my side.

As for me, I set off down the incline with her at my heels and the pair of us hurtled into the heart of the battle to shatter the morale of the Clanswomen and drive the remaining Wildemen into a veritable fury of battle fever.

I had come into the field precisely as Ymer's dream had foretold – with a great Sno-bear as my companion – and as I headed for the Maxwell and the Battle Standard Hraefn, an avenue opened up before me just as if a swathe had been cut through the combatants by a magic sword.

I dodged behind the Kelpie, putting its bulk between me and the maddened bear. And the beast found something else on which to unleash it's spleen and dived on the Water-Horse, raking its flanks with razor claws and sinking rabid teeth into the amphibian's tough flesh.

The Dragon let out a howl somewhere between the sound of a slughorn and the bray of a jackass.

Parrying the blows being aimed furiously at me by the Maxwell, I rushed round to the head of the Beast and fired the Gae Bolga through one of the apertures in the Dragon Mask and in through the trumpeting jaws. The barbs sprang to life in the open throat, piercing the gullet, cutting off the air supply.

The great creature flung its head wildly from side to side, trying to shake the obstruction loose, but the spikes only bit more deeply until they protruded through the scaly neck like a metal collar.

The Kelpie bleated like a frightened goat and collapsed on its forelegs before rolling over with a crash that rocked the whole valley and trapped the Maxwell by one leg under the long, grey body.

She screamed with pain but I had the lust of battle on me now. Tearing the standard from her hand, I raced up the side of the fallen beast to stand on the hillock of its bloodied flank and hold the fluttering flag aloft.

'I have the Raven,' I roared. 'I am the Redeemer. Together we are Invincible. The day is ours.'

THE TRUE CHRONICLES OF THE REDEEMER

Then Morangy came to the victory camp with the news that the Redeemer's sister was to be put to death by slow fire. So McCloed was sent to Ballater to trade the Maxwell, who was alive but sorely wounded, for the person of the Lady Ymer.

Chapter
22

Morangy arrived in the middle of the celebratory feast.

Much whisky had been drunk and not a few of the proud King Stags had ended up on the roasting-spit, leaving their unfortunate riders to escape how they might.

On foot, harried and hounded over terrain with which they were unfamiliar and which the Wildemen knew like the backs of their hands, a great number of the Clanswomen fled the battle proper only to perish in the fastness of the High Hills, slaughtered out of hand, despite my orders to the contrary, by men eager for revenge.

Some of the things I had seen that day had turned my stomach. I confess I had drunk more than was good for me in an attempt to blot out their memory. So when Morangy staggered into the tent which had been commandeered from the Maxwell, I was, to put it mildly, feeling very little pain.

The sight of the Healer soon sobered me up.

He was a hairsbreadth from collapse, covered in filth and sweat from his long, perilous journey. He flung himself to the ground at my feet, pouring out the grim story that had driven him to seek us here in the back of beyond.

It was a gory enough tale. For he described in graphic detail the punishments that Ymer would endure (was at that very moment enduring) before death released her from the clutches of Fergael.

And such a death.

She would be rolled in soft clay and roasted like a hedgehog over a slow fire until the baked earth cracked and dropped from her bones, carrying the cooked flesh with it.

I was reaching for my weapons and calling for a horse before he had finished.

But Colluden restrained me.

'You cannot go, Rolande,' he said, raising himself on one elbow from his couch in the corner.

'Don't tell me I can't, old man. I am going. Nothing you have to say could stop me.' – I was already at the tent flap.

'The men need you.'

'Bollocks. Ymer needs me more.'

'Rolande.' Colluden's voice was very sharp. 'You are a Leader now. And a Leader cannot afford the luxury of private griefs.'

'Then I resign. Let them fend for themselves. I never wanted to be the Redeemer anyway.'

I flung the tent-flap aside, jamming Susuki on my head as I did so.

Outside, a group of Wildemen were engaged in drunken horseplay around the campfire while more of their number amused themselves by taunting and baiting the thirty or more female prisoners lodged in the makeshift stockade. Most of the women I had known since childhood and it sickened my heart to see them brought to such a pass for my sake. As I looked on with mounting disgust, a stocky individual, legs bowed from a bout of infantile rickets, broke away from a staggering victory dance, to vomit up the contents of his stomach not a strides-length away from me.

'Look at them,' I said. 'Savages. The whole bunch. Fifty of them together are not worth my Ymer's life.'

McCloed came up behind me. He had been drinking dram for dram with me since the fighting stopped. Now he, too, had sobered up.

'Let me go, Rolande,' he said and he placed his hand on my arm. His touch ran through my veins like molten gold and I felt the woman in me surface so that I ached to turn and bury my face in his shoulder. Instead I permitted him to lead me back into the body of the tent.

'You canna be spared,' he said. 'The men need someone to hold them together. Otherwise the whole uprising will disintegrate and today will have all been for nothing.'

'You hold them together,' I said, shaking his arm free. 'You are their General.'

'And you are their God,' said Colluden. 'You canna desert them now.'

'And would you have me desert Ymer?' I asked him.

'What is Ymer?' he countered, 'Just a hussey who's shared your bed and softened your brains.'

'She is my love,' I shouted.

'She is his sister,' announced Morangy.

I felt as though the mountain mist had descended to swirl around my senses and fade the sounds of celebration outwith the tent into the periphery of my hearing. In the unnatural calm that followed it, I turned towards the Healer, waiting for him to qualify his statement.

As he did, describing to us my birthing, much as I have described it to you, it seemed that I had always known in my heart of hearts that what I felt for Ymer was stronger than mere ties of affection. Many times in the course of our coupling I had felt so close to her that it seemed to me our flesh was the same flesh, our blood the same blood.

And so it proved.

When he finished, I looked from Colluden to McCloed.

'Blood is thicker than water,' I said. 'I must go.'

And neither of them had the heart to contradict me.

But once again fate intervened with the sound of screaming from outside. I rushed into the warm, torch-lit darkness, Morangy and McCloed at my heels.

A soft wind was soughing through the heather bringing with it that overpowering scent of the earth's fecundity that is the smell of Summer. That, laced with the exhilaration of victory and the surfeit of strong liquor, had proved too much for certain of my warriors. Half a dozen of them had dragged a young Clanswoman from the stockade and were preparing to rape her.

This was the supposed crime for which Euan-Noag had died and now I saw it, in all its ugliness, for the abomination that it was.

They had thrown the girl to the ground. She lay spread-eagled in the mud, held fast by ankles and wrists. One of the gang had clamped a hand over her mouth to still her screams but the terror in her eyes, as she struggled to free herself, could not be hidden.

Another leant forward and, grasping the waistband of her trews, tore them from her body in a mighty heave that left her exposed from waist to thigh. Then he hoisted his skin tunic to bare his naked genitals. His penis stood erect, huge and menacing. Gorged with blood, the tip had thrust through the foreskin, mushroom-head purple against the pink of the shaft. He sank to his knees between the Clanswoman's splayed legs and in doing so, half-turned towards me.

It was One-Eye.

Beside me, McCloed's breathing had quickened, a heavy, unnatural sound. Then the circle closed around the girl and all I could see were swaying backs.

At the very edge of the crowd, young Cuchullain attempted to push his way through the forest of legs for a better view of the spectacle.

It was this more than anything that galvanised me into action. This childe had been named for Euan-Noag at his birthing. I could not let him grow up feeling that such behaviour was excusable.

I still held Enfidion in my hand. With the other I grasped the lighted torch from the tent-pole and swung into the sea of bodies, flailing the brand in front of me as I went. I hacked a few ears and singed a few heads on the way through. No matter, I got there.

Not before time.

One-Eye was at the very point of penetration.

I pressed the sword-point into his throat and his erection withered at the root.

'One move,' I hissed. 'And it will be your last.'

So he stayed where he was, a ridiculous figure, his tunic hoisted above his hairy rump, flaccid pudenda dangling pathetically between quivering thighs.

I helped the girl to her feet. She stumbled against me and I handed the brand to McCloed, using my freed arm to support her.

'Listen to me and listen well,' I said, icily . . . and I had not even to raise my voice, so total was the silence that had fallen over the abashed gathering. 'I am the Redeemer, am I not? And I have come to free you from the yoke of servitude, have I not?' and I looked around as though expecting some reply. When none was forthcoming I continued. 'Never forget that you . . . men . . . are but a part of my people. Never forget that I have come, not to replace one dictatorship with another but to bring justice to all. When I rule it will be over an Alba where everyone is equal. No sex more dominant than the other. It will be, as far as I can make it, a fair society and no-one, male or female, shall have the power or the right to violate another.'

I lowered my voice to lash them with all the scorn I felt. 'Today I am ashamed to be a man. Today I can almost understand why women have castrated men all these years. If those of you with balls behave like animals no wonder you have been gelded to protect the female of the species.

'I am the female of the species . . . If you ravish a woman, you defile me, for I am her as much as I am you.

'Get up,' I prodded One-Eye.

He scrabbled awkwardly to his feet, defiant in his humiliation, appealing to McCloed.

'You said men and women were meant to couple,' he complained.

'By mutual consent,' said McCloed, turning red with embarrassment. 'And with affection . . . not like beasts in rut.'

'We have our urges,' grumbled One-Eye, and I could feel a stirring of sympathy for him amongst the spectators. 'It's only natural.'

'Do not play upon our former friendship,' I warned him. 'Urges are natural. Rape is not. Next time you feel the urge find a willing woman. Otherwise have a wank. Self-violation is your privilege. Now go to bed – the lot of you – and pray that the morrow does not bring you the hangovers you deserve.'

The Wildemen dispersed, drifting away into the dark to sleep it off and I led the distraught Clanswoman back to her companions in the stockade, assuring them that, while I was there to protect them, they need not fear any repeat performances. The words were no sooner out of my mouth than I realised that I had committed myself, that I could not go to Ymer's aid after all.

But someone would have to go.

'You'll not find it difficult to penetrate the Castle,' I told McCloed as we walked away. 'Provided you take Cuchullain along. Put him through the window like we did when I came for you. There's no more than a skeleton guard overlooking Ballater. The pick of the fighting force came out with the Maxwell.'

'But she'll no be in the main Castle,' said Morangy, as we came into the tent. 'Fergael will have her in the Dark Tower.'

'Then McCloed will have to get a green card from someone in the hospice. That will let you into the Inner Sanctum,' I explained. 'Use whatever force you deem necessary. Just get her out of there.'

'No need to use force at all.' Colluden spoke up from his place in the corner where he had all but been forgotten.

'How so, Prophet?'

'We have the Maxwell.'

'So?'

'So. Use your brains. She is a burden is she not, wounded, with a leg that may fast succumb to gangrene?'

Morangy looked expectantly at me and I nodded to indicate that what the old man said was true.

'Furthermore, she is the cause of much discontent. The men want her blood. Sooner or later they will expect to get it.'

'She is my prisoner,' I said. 'I will not let them take her.'

'No need. Offer a swap. The Lady Ymer for the Warlord of the Clans. Fergael dare not refuse such a trade.'

'We canna give her back,' protested McCloed. 'Without her the women have no leader. Give her back and they have someone to rally to.'

'Would you rather they rallied to that bitch Fergael?' countered Colluden. 'Besides, she's very weak. She may not outlive the journey. And if she does, with that leg she'll be in no fit state to lead her troops, what's left of them, anywhere in the near future.'

'If she's that weak can she go at all?' I asked.

'That's up to the wee mannie,' said Colluden.

'I'll need to see her,' was all that Morangy would say, 'before I can pass an opinion.'

So I sent McCloed to commandeer a farm-cart, just in case – and Morangy and I went to the lean-to behind the stockade where the Warlord of the Clans lay under close guard.

The Queen was stretched out on a makeshift pallet of straw and furs, her face pale and sweat-beaded, her bad leg, which I had tended myself while she was unconscious, oozing blood from the multiple fractures that I had bound together as best I could with splints cut from a nearby sapling.

Morangy pursed his lips when he saw her.

'Tis much worse than I anticipated,' he said.

'We have no medical supplies,' I explained, defensively. 'I tried to persuade the Lady to bring along a medicine wagon – but she would have none of it.'

'Aye, the poor deluded kwine didna believe that blood

would be spilt. She figured a show of force would be enough. Weel, weel, she knows better now.'

He placed his hand on the Warlord's forhead. She opened her eyes and stared at him glassily.

'Morangy?' she said.

'Ma'am?'

'My leg hurts, Morangy,' she whimpered, then checked the sound, as though recollecting what was expected of her. 'Can you ease it any?'

'Rest quiet, Ma'am,' said the Healer, gently. 'I'll do my best.'

The Queen sighed and closed her eyes again. She had not noticed me standing in the shadows and Morangy led me outside so that she would not hear our conversation.

'It's hard to know what to do in the circumstances,' he said. 'I havenae my bag with me . . . and you with no supplies . . . Have you nothing? No drugs at all?'

'Only the stuff that was used to dose the Kelpie. But that could fell a horse.'

Bring it,' Morangy ordered – Healer to apprentice. 'We'll dilute it with some whisky. It'll put her out of her pain until I get her back to Ballater.'

'You canna go back to Ballater,' I protested. 'Fergael will have your blood.'

'That's a chance I'll have to take. If I don't get the Maxwell back she'll be dead by the next dark of the moon.'

He turned to look into the interior of the tent and the ravaged features of the Lady.

'She was aye good to me,' he said, wistfully. 'But for her I'd no be here this day. A life for a life. I owe her that.'

'I owe her much too,' I said, biting my lip. And then I thought of Euan-Noag and my heart hardened. 'But many more owe her their death . . . and not a man in this camp but would have her guts if I let them. So she has her life of me . . . that's the best I can do.'

'It's the best any of us can do in times like these,' said Morangy. 'Tell McCloed to be ready at sunrise. I'll sit with her til then.'

'You'll do no such thing,' I said. 'What you need is some sleep. Take it in my tent. I'll sit with her.'

So we dosed her and Morangy slept and I sat by her as I had promised, holding her cold hand in mine.

She only came to once, but when she did it was to smile at me with a relief that curdled my heart.

'Rolande,' she said. 'You are safe.'

Then she dropped off to sleep once more, leaving me to weep alone, for that which was past and would never come again.

THE TRUE CHRONICLES OF THE REDEEMER

When General McCloed came to the gates of Ballater Castle, he spoke with the black hag, Fergael, offering up the Maxwell in exchange for the Lady Ymer. This the witch refused. Then Cameron, the Warlord's commander, had the Princess brought forth and the deal was done. But the Maxwell's wound became rotten and festered so the Healer Morangy cut off her leg. And seeing the Queen's weakness, Fergael plotted to take her place as Ruler of Alba.

Chapter
23

IT IS A WINDY, EAST COAST DAY, THE SUN SPARKING OCCASION-
ally through bleak cloudbanks that carry scatterings of sleet. I
pause in this narrative because lately I have begun to tire easily
and find it difficult to concentrate on anything but the coming
birth.

Besides, it is time for me to hand over the telling of this tale
to Ymer and McCloed and Morangy who were witness to it
whereas I was not. I have asked my Secretary, Dumfrees, to
document this part and hope that what they recount is true and
not embellished with too much hindsight and, in Ymer's case,
romanticism.

Yesterday I slept clockround, exhausted by my literary
labours, and Ymer stole my manuscript and read it and woke
me with tear-stained face to tell me that it had revealed to her
many things about me that she had not known before.

Strange.

I had thought she knew everything about me.

And I her.

But I am reminded by her reaction that such an assumption
is pure arrogance and that no one person can ever know another
– only guess – from hints gleaned by observation. Inaccurate
hints, laced with self-delusion, for one's impression of the other
(especially if that other is a love-object) are inevitably coloured
by what one wishes them to be, not necessarily what they are.

At best the human ability to deceive leads to misinterpret-
ation, at worst to infidelity, jealousy, rage, hate, murder, war.

Without it, however, there would be precious little joy. Or
peace.

Life would be exceedingly predictable.

And excessively dull.

But I digress.

Let me loose the reins of my story now and for a moment pass them over to my dear husband McCloed, my strong – if unimaginative – right arm and the father (funny how that word still sits awkwardly on the tongue, like a curse) of the future heir of Alba.

McCloed's Narrative

It was a dreath sunrise. Everything dripped. Rolande would have said the world was weeping. The Redeemer was aye poetic.

Me?

I believe in calling a corbie a corbie and all I could gleek was that it was a foul morning to be travelling – especially wi a woman who wasnae well.

I had a clutch of twelve loons wi me – not counting the drover, who sat atop the mule-cart, and the Healer, who rode inside to tend the Maxwell.

The Lady was in sair condition and I had my doubts whether she'd complete the journey. Sometimes, when the cart hit a particular deep rut, she'd give out a soughing sound, half-way between a whimper and a sigh, and I could tell that the wound-agony had got through the sleep-potion to grip her in it's teeth. Apart from that, there wasnae a peep out of her.

When we stopped that night, she was so pale and still, I thought she was a goner. Not that I was fashed either way. But I'd promised Rolande I would get her to Ballater, dead or alive, and bring his sister out (in similar condition) and I was damned sure I'd stick to my word.

If she corpsed on the journey it would make my job that bittie harder. That's why I spent most nights working out contingency plans in case our bargaining power should peg out. But the wee mannie managed to keep her going right enough. He's a powerful fine Healer that Morangy. I'm fine pleased he'll be around to deliver my son.

It was a bothersome journey, slow and at times downright dangerous. At one point we were set upon by a bunch of robber women and, at Fryersfort, the Captain sent out twenty of her best Militia to face us so that we had to waste good time dispatching them before we could go on.

All doors were bolted agin us so we were forced to forage for food which kept us back even more. What wi the weather and the welcome, we were all bloody glad when we got to Ballater.

I had thought to talk to Fergael. If I could have got hold of her I'd have wrung her scrawny neck – but it was Cameron who appeared on the battlements.

I hadnae seen her since the battle and supposed her dead and buried. But here she was, still breathing, though she'd lost her swordarm below the elbow and had the stump supported across her chest in a mesh sling.

'What do you want?' she roared – the loss of the arm had done nothing to improve her temper – or dampen her spirit.

'I hae the Maxwell wi me,' I roared back. 'I'll exchange her for the Lady Ymer.'

'Wait.'

Cameron disappeared and came back not long after with Fergael in tow.

'Speak your piece,' she said. 'And make it brief.'

'The Redeemer has sent me to make a trade,' I told her. 'The life of the Maxwell for the Lady Ymer.'

The witch's eyes narrowed.

'What does the Redeemer want with the Lady Ymer?'

I am not a diplomat. Nor a good liar. I am a plain man – as anyone will tell you. I decided the best I could do was tell the truth as much as possible and avoid the bits I didnae think Fergael should know.

'Dinna ask me,' I said. 'If I had my way the both of them could go rot. Two bitches less to pollute the air with their stink.'

Fergael grinned.

What a face that woman had. A deathshead with pointed teeth. Like nothing human.

'Show me the Queen,' she said.

So I had two of the loons lift the pallet out of the mule-cart.

By this time the battlement was ringed wi faces. Few Clanswomen, I noted. All that were left in Castle Ballater, besides the odd sentry – were the very old, the very young, the Medics and the Priests.

They stared down at the still figure of the Lady and no-one spake a word.

'Is she alive?' said Fergael, finally.

'Only just.'

'Send her in and I'll send the girl out.'

But I was having none of that.

'The Lady Ymer first,' I said. 'Then you shall hae the Queen.'

Fergael spat.

'Do you take me for a fool, Wildeman?' she said, managing to get enough bile into the pronouncement to curdle cream. 'Is it likely I should send the Lady Ymer out so that you can then slaughter the Maxwell in front of my eyes?'

'Don't judge others by yourself, hag,' I shouted. 'I gave my word that no harm would come to the Queen while she was in my custody.'

'The word of a Semi-human is not acceptable currency.'

To tell you the truth of it, at that point I was ready to storm the place and beat the shit out of the lot of them – Rolande or no Rolande. I'm a hard man to rile but once my dander's up I'm difficult to stop.

This story might have had a different ending if Morangy hadnae stepped in.

'In the name of the Mother, Fergael,' he pleaded. 'Make the trade and hae done with it. Otherwise the Maxwell is as good as dead. If I don't do a procedure right now she'll no outlast the forenoon.'

That was enough for Cameron.

Her red head disappeared frae view, the witch greeting at her to come back, to wait for orders, threatening her wi all manner of deaths if she didnae return.

The next thing we knew the main gates were opening and half a dozen veterans emerged carrying a black coffin shoulder high. Cameron was right behind.

I suspected a trick, thought that the box might be full of weapons, so I stood the loons to alert, just to be on the safe side.

But my fears were ill-founded.

As they came abreast of us, one o the women stumbled. The box tippit and the lid opened spilling the contents to the ground.

It fell, like a sack of neeps and lay there, eyes screwed tight shut.

It was a kwine. Stark naked. Bruised. Scarred. In a dour state.

'Take that to your Redeemer,' said Cameron, and she

didnae seem too proud o the package. 'Much good may it do him.'

I told the men to cover me and I went forward to pick her up. She had long black hair and when it fell away from her face I was looking at the living spit of Rolande. The Redeemer's dark shadow.

This was the one who had eaten me wi her eyes, the day that I'd been taken. But what a change. That arrogance had gone. I recognised Fergael's hand in her condition. I've not seen such terror in a human being's gaze afore or since.

My heart went out to her, pathetic scrap that she was. I could see why Rolande was so taken wi her. She needed protecting. And I kenned it was up to me to protect her now. For she wasnae fit to protect hersel.

Ymer's Narrative

I don't remember much of it.

I recall voices, coming and going, and thinking I was dreaming, and waking up and finding I was not, and screaming a lot.

I might have saved my breath.

Nobody took a blind bit of notice.

Though it was me who was blind.

Stuck in that black hole.

Buried alive.

I've had trouble with my eyes ever since.

Something happened to them in the box. My pupils dilated so much (opening to cover the entire iris, trying to find a chink of light in the dark) that they lost their ability to shrink again. Now my eyes can't abide bright light. Or light at all. Even the glare from the clouds on a dull day is too much for me to tolerate, gives me headaches and double-vision. That's why I wear the veil and the big hats. It's also why I stay up nights and sleep in the daytime. People have spread all kinds of tales about me. That I'm hideously scarred. That I'm totally unhinged. But it's just that my eyes are very sensitive to light.

I used to love the sun . . . the feel of it on my body.

Now, when it comes out, I have to burrow in under the blankets and hide. The curtains are always drawn in my room. Sometimes I even lock myself in a cupboard with a cloak over my head.

I'm explaining this to dispel the rumours going round that the Redeemer's Sister/Wife is mad.

Though I suppose I did go a little crazy while I was in the box.

I seemed to be in there forever.

I thought I was going to be left to rot . . . I'd resigned myself to it really, by the time McCloed arrived.

I'd also screamed myself hoarse and wet myself so many times that I couldn't stand the smell of myself any more. I'd sunk into a kind of trance. I remember I chewed my fingernails down to the quick. I was hungry and there was nothing else to eat. Self-cannibalism. I used to have beautiful nails. Like little shells. But they never grew back properly. They're ridged now and uneven. Except for the little fingernails. The ones Fergael pulled out. They never grew back again at all.

I had resigned myself because I was riddled with guilt. I genuinely felt that this was the beginning of the punishment that I would have to endure for all eternity. I felt I was getting my come-uppance. The Source, who sees all, had seen through me, had been scrutinising me all these years, recording my sins of omission and commission and emission, and now I was being made to pay for all that enjoyment.

Now, of course, I realise that it wasn't the Source taking revenge at all.

Only Fergael.

But I got my own back in the end up.

Yet even now, I still can't rid myself of her memory. Even now, when my mind tells me that it was all superstitious non-sense, I still wake up at times, terrified out of my wits at what lies in store for me after my death. Will I return to the earth as Rolande says, or is the fiery pit laying in wait for me?

If it is dark when I wake, I sometimes fear I am back in the box and then Rolande and McCloed have to be brought to comfort me – which leads to some interesting situations. Compounding the felony. I can't win really. I think women were born to be guilty.

Anyway, when the baby comes I don't suppose they'll have the time to indulge me so much. More's the pity.

Don't ask me how long Fergael kept me in the box. In the end I believed that the part of my life that had occurred since Buchan's death was something I had made up in my head to amuse myself. Time ceased to exist. I ceased to exist. There had always been the box and I had always been in it.

And then, when I was past caring, I became conscious of movement. Someone was lifting me up and carrying me somewhere.

Shaken out of my vacuum, I felt the fear come rushing back.

What if they had decided to bury me, really bury me under layers of dark, damp soil? Or worse, throw me on the sacrificial flame and burn me to death? I fought for breath, suffocating. I could almost hear the worms burrowing through the wood, smell the fire singeing my flesh. I began to scream again. A silent scream, for no sound came from my dry throat, only a kind of premature death-rattle. But I was not dead yet. Did not want to die. I started to beat against the box lid with my nail-less fists, hammering with all my strength which, by that time, wasn't much.

And then the world was filled with light . . . and I was in the courtyard of the Castle and Fergael was there with all the Handmaidens and Initiates and there was a great fire burning and a pot hanging over it and the smell of sulphurous clay.

That much I saw before I covered my eyes against the brightness.

'Get her out,' I heard Fergael say.

Then rough hands lifted me and half-dragged, half-carried me (for my legs were useless) to the altar stone and laid me flat on the cold granite.

The light hurt. The stone hurt.

I began to shiver.

I was naked, as I had been when they hoisted me up on the harness . . . how many lifespans ago?

Fergael was wearing full ceremonial regalia. Black and gold. The death-robes. She carried the Holy Staff, the one cut from the first thorn tree to flower after the Fall, and she beat it three times on the flagstones before she pronounced sentence on me.

'Nameless and defiled,' she said, 'who have sullied the Inner Sanctum with your adulterated presence, now must you pay the ultimate penalty for your sins. Your foul form will be clad in clay and roasted over a slow fire. Only when your putrid flesh has fallen from your undeserving corpse will your bones be fit to be offered to the Great Mother.'

She made a sign and Ailill and Scawthatch took poles and

unhooked the cauldron from the tripod athwart the fire. The molten clay, laced with coagulants, would be poured over my body and left to set hard before I was skewered, like a porker, and hung over the fire.

I could only hope that the hot mud would be the death of me. But I doubted it. Fergael did not have it in her to be so merciful.

I recall forcing myself up on my elbows. I suppose I was trying, instinctively, to get away. But even the effort of raising myself that far was too much for me and I fell back, banging my head against the granite and stunning myself.

So again I thought I was dreaming when I saw Cameron dash into the courtyard. Cameron with only one arm.

'The Savage is here,' she shouted. 'With the Maxwell. He's offering to trade the Queen for her.' She pointed to me and even with my impaired vision I could see the look of distaste on her face for my condition.

The courtyard emptied as Fergael followed Cameron back to the battlements.

Unbelievably, I was left alone.

Once again I tried to get up.

I had a vague plan that I might crawl away and hide before they came back.

But I had just managed to struggle into a sitting position when Cameron returned with half a dozen veterans in tow.

Somewhere in the background I could hear Fergael screaming and shouting. The light was searing my eyeballs. I was almost relieved when the Clanswomen bundled me back into the box and closed the lid.

I felt it being raised again and then I was being jolted every which way, banging off the sides of my prison as they carried me . . . where?

I reached my hands out to try to steady myself and then the box tilted alarmingly and the next thing I knew I was pitched out onto the grass.

And I heard Cameron say . . . 'Take that to your Redeemer, much good may it do him.'

Then someone was lifting me into the light.

I looked up and saw McCloed.

Now I knew I was dreaming.

McCloed, my beautiful savage, who had spoken to me with

his eyes in the Council Chamber. McCloed, my phantom lover, had come to rescue me from the wicked witch.

He held me, tenderly, like a mother does a new-born girl-childe, and for the first time in my life I felt totally secure, totally safe.

I fell asleep.

Morangy's Narrative

It's a miracle I got the Maxwell hame at all.

And then all that kerfuffle at the gates afore they would bring the Lady Ymer out and admit us. If it wasnae for Cameron, the Maxwell would've died out of hand.

I wasnae inwith the confines of Ballater long enough to draw breath afore Fergael was calling on the Captain of the Guard to clap me in irons.

'Have a titter of wit,' Cameron tellt her. 'You can have his hide after he's mended the Maxwell – not afore.'

So wi' that heartening prospect hanging over me, I had the procedure room made ready and Aurora hersel' came to assist me in the operation.

By the time we got her on the table the leg was in an advanced state of putrefaction. When I unwound the bandages the stench was enough to knock you down. There was nowt for it but that I should take off the limb.

I reported this to Cameron who reported it to Fergael who came flapping into the sterile area like a dose of the black plague. She would have it that the Queen be asked permission before I severed the leg. Silly bitch. I tellt her the Lady had been prepared and was only semi-conscious, but she insisted that I slap the poor kwine awake so she could get her spoke in.

'Majesty,' says she, shaking the woman to stop her from dozing off again. 'The Healer has a mind to amputate your leg.'

The Queen looked at her but you could tell she wasnae taking much in.

'She doesnae hear you.' I said. 'Or if she does, she doesnae understand.'

'Your leg, Maxwell,' Fergael ignored me. 'The Midget says it must come off.'

The Maxwell made a supreme effort to speak. Her words

were so low we all had to crane forward to catch their meaning. But it wasnae the leg she was interested in. It was something else entirely.

'Rolande,' she whispered. 'Is there word of Rolande?'

'What nonsense is this?' Fergael was brusque. 'Your leg, Majesty – has Morangy permission to proceed?'

She might as well have been talking to the wall. The Queen took no note of her. She turned instead to Cameron.

'I dreamt I saw her . . . and she was well. Have you heard anything, Locheil?'

But Cameron shook her head.

'There was some talk of her being struck down by the savage, Maxwell . . . the one who brought you hame.'

The Queen grasped my hand, held it tight.

'Morangy,' she pleaded. 'Has she been brought in from the field perhaps? Wounded?' She dared not say 'Dead.'

Her eyes held a hint of desperation and I was sorely tempted to tell her that her beloved Rolande was alive and well but I couldnae. She still had no notion that Rolande was the Redeemer and this was no time to tell her. The shock would have killed her if the leg didn't.

It struck me then that Fergael must know the truth by now. Ymer wouldnae have tellt her about Rolande and the Redeemer being one and the same because she didnae ken it hersel', but she had let on about his male and female organs and, since the Redeemer was known to be twin-sexed, the witch must have put two and two together and come up wi' five. I peeked at her out of the side of my eye, expecting her to say her piece and land us all in it, but her mouth was set tight as a fish's arse. So I shifted back to the Queen and tellt her 'No', Rolande hadnae been brought in wounded. It was no more than the truth and I left her to draw her own conclusions.

'You can do what you like with me, then,' she said, closing her eyes in resignation. 'It makes no difference. If you could amputate my heart while you were at it, you'd be doing me a real service.'

Fergael stormed out at this juncture but went no further than the ante-room. From there I could hear her voice, shrill and ugly as she tore into Cameron about ayething or other. I ignored it for as long as I could, dosing the Queen with a sleeping-drug and scrubbing up her leg in preparation for the procedure. Aurora fussed about sterilising knives and sharpening the hacksaw that I maun use to cut through the bone. But in the end even she couldn't stand the din and began dropping things . . . like some nervy apprentice.

The leg would have to be removed just below the hip to make sure none of the poison remained to seep into the trunk. There were arteries in the groin and I kenned well I would need the whole of my skill to cut just right or the Queen might bleed to death.

Just before I made the first incision I was forced to go out-with the procedure room and tell the two women to shut up.

'I hae a gae delicate operation to perform,' I told them. 'If you maun act like fishwivies then go and do it somewhere where you won't put me off my stroke.'

Cameron took it well enough but Fergael looked at me as much as to say 'You wait'.

At the time I couldnae care less. If I didnae get the leg off soon, the Maxwell would be so weakened she'd die under the saw anyway. And me for the chop before she was half cold. Her mental state was gae poor and, if her physical condition was allowed to deteriorate alongside, then there was scant hope of saving her.

It was only when the procedure was well over and the Queen safely removed to the comfort of her great antlered bed that I had time to sweat over my own future.

The Lady needed constant minding and I figured the safest place for me was at her side. Apart from that I couldnae very well put her in charge of an auxiliary. So, even though I felt like a wet week in Auchtermaughty, I had them set up a cot for me by her bed and I collapsed into that and was out like a light before my head hit the pillow.

Sometime during the night Fergael shook me awake.

'Get up,' she ordered, throwing her weight around as usual. 'Rouse the Maxwell.'

'I cannae do that,' I protested. 'She needs her sleep. She'll need be let bide if her mind and body are to mend.'

'Get up, you undersized excrescence,' says Fergael. 'There's a war on. The army's waiting orders.'

'What army's this then?' says I. 'Did Cameron no tell you? The army's scattered. The war's over.'

'Not while I have breath in my body,' she said, her eyes goggling out of her head like a frog. 'No damn upstart is going to tell me how to run Alba. (She was talking like she was the

Maxwell all of a sudden.) I sent word to every outpost in Alba, to send half of every military detachment in the land to Ballater. They're arriving in droves. And they need orders before they go out. Wake the Queen like I tell you. I have to speak to her. Now.'

'Speak on, Fergael. Just try not to do it so loudly.'

The Maxwell had woken, disturbed nae doubt by Fergael's ranting. The hag turned on her without hardly drawing breath.

'Your battle-orders, Majesty. Your new army is assembling. They'll need briefing.'

'Indeed? And since when has the High Priest been in charge of the army, Fergael? The Kirk is your department. The Clanswomen answer to the Maxwell.'

'But my Lady is not fit . . .'

'I will decide whether I am fit or not. And should such be the case then control of the forces passes to the Captain of my Guard.'

'Cameron?' Fergael was furious. 'You would place Cameron over me?'

'In this instance, yes. She is my Second-in-Command,' said the Queen, adding, pointedly. 'She is also my most loyal subject. I trust her implicitly.'

'My loyalty is suspect I take it?'

'Have a care Fergael,' said the Queen, softly. 'I am weak. But I am still Warlord of the Clans. And I will recover.'

'I live for the day, Your Majesty,' said Fergael, her mouth speaking one thing and her eyes saying the very opposite.

'You may go.' The Queen dismissed her. 'And send Locheil in.'

I would like to have been a fly in the wall during that confab but I had to be content to wait outside cooling my heels while the Maxwell and Cameron held their council of war.

I was out there, listening at the keyhold, I confess, when Aurora came slithering round the corner, looking over her shoulder as though she feart she was being followed by the Arch Fiend.

'I need to talk to you, Morangy,' says she in a cracked like voice.

'Talk away,' says I. 'I'm all ears.'

'It's Fergael,' she said. 'She's taken leave of her senses.'

'Have you only just noticed?' I said.

'She wants me to poison the Maxwell,' said Aurora.

Now that really did rock me back on my heels. Fergael must

have gone really mad at last to blurt out such obvious treasons to the Queen's Chief Medic. Either that or she thought herself so invulnerable as to be beyond touching.

'She says it's for the good of the state,' said Aurora. 'She says the Maxwell's not fit to rule Alba. She says I maun slip her a mickey finn.

'You? What makes her think you'd do a thing like that?'

'We've been . . . lovers,' At least she had the good grace to blush when she said it. 'And anyway, she says if I don't she'll have me . . . removed . . . She says she'll tell the Maxwell that you and I were in league with the Redeemer and that she discovered a plot for us to poison the Queen. She would do it too . . .' and she started to bawl.

I put my arms around her. It wasn't an entirely unpleasant experience. She's a big kwine, Aurora.

'Dinna fash yesel,' I told her. 'She'll nae get the chance. What poison did she suggest?'

'One of her own damn make-ups. She says it has no taste, nor smell. She says if I put it in the Queen's sleeping-potion she'll drift off and nobody will be any the wiser.'

'The crafty devil,' I said. 'And she would rule Alba, I suppose?'

'There's more,' Aurora said. 'She says she can rally the women like no-one else. She says that she can give them potions that will make them fight like Ben-Shi. She says then she'd show this Redeemer what stuff we females are made of.'

'And what about you?'

'I'd be Chief Midwife . . . and you'd be killed.'

'You wouldnae last the day out, kwine,' I told her. 'Once the Queen was dead, Fergael couldnae afford to have you around . . . in case you had an attack of the consciences and let on in a fit of remorse.'

'I know that,' said Aurora. 'What's to be done?'

'You'll hae to pretend to go through with the thing,' says I 'There's naething else you can do, for the time being . . . if you want to stay healthy that is.'

At this point Cameron re-emerged and Aurora scootered off, sniffling.

It was a measure of Fergael's megalomania that it never struck her Aurora might go to someone with her story. Or that someone would pass the story on.

Needless to say I spilled the beans to Cameron double-quick. The upshot was that a clock-round guard was put on the Maxwell's apartments and no-one was allowed to prepare drugs or administer them except me.

They locked me in with the Queen and allocated us a food-taster.

I felt a bittie safer that way.

Poor Aurora died mysteriously in the night. I couldnae be sure, nothing was ever confirmed, and of course I couldnae get out of the Queen's chambers to perform an autospy, but I hae a sneaking suspicion it might have been poison did her in.

THE TRUE CHRONICLES OF THE REDEEMER

Then McCloed brought the Lady Ymer back to the camp of the Wildemen and put her in the care of the Clanswomen who were prisoners there. And the Redeemer assumed the aspect of woman and brought McCloed to bed. And a Childe was conceived of the union. And in that self-same time, the Prophet Colluden passed away.

Chapter
24

I HAD NOT BARGAINED FOR SUCH TROUBLE FROM THE WILDEMEN. I had thought myself well aquainted with their natures. Now I found myself sorely mistaken. For I had judged them by my own criteria and by the temperament of Euan-Noag, whose character was, I now discovered, the exception rather than the rule. The men's behaviour, after the battle, all but obliterated what was left of my sympathies for the cause of male supremacy and left me torn with agonies of doubt about the beast I had unleashed.

My female half was frankly appalled at the boorishness displayed. The drunkenness and lewd brutality offended me somehow more than all the barbarism I had witnessed during my time at Ballater. There was a crudeness, a sheer brutish nastiness that I had not anticipated.

Although what I had anticipated, I can't be sure. That the Wildemen would be magnanimous in victory, perhaps? That they might embrace their enemies and forgive them? Vain hope. Generations of cruel oppression had ingrained too deep a hatred in them for that. And the women prisoners did not help eradicate this attitude by hiding their fear behind an aggression that invited confrontation.

The escalating unrest was partly my own fault. My mind was elsewhere, with my sister and McCloed and my fears for their safety. But the problem lay also in my character. I had been trained in diplomacy, in the rule of reasoned argument. Hostility and mistrust were not easily stayed by such methods, and though I strode around the camp trying to keep some kind of order, I found it increasingly difficult to contain the seething mass of ill-suppressed resentment that greeted my continued support of the female captives. At any moment, I felt, things might degenerate into an orgy of blood-letting.

I went to Colluden to ask his advice and found him dying. The journey and the battle and the sheer effort of willing himself to stay alive had taken their toll. He was an old, old man and, suddenly, he looked it.

I was chastened that I had not noticed the change in him before – and that I had sent Morangy away without even asking him to oversee the Prophet.

I said as much. But Colluden patted my hand and reassured me.

'He couldnae have done athing, Rolande,' he said. 'It's the mechanism. It's worn out. There's nothing left now but to die.'

'You'll not die yet,' I protested. I think that until then I had thought the Prophet immortal.

'I've seen what I wanted to see,' he said. 'The first great victory. Athing else would just be an anticlimax.'

'There may not be athing else,' I told him. 'I doubt I can control the Wildemen. If they run amok we're banjaxed. We're a small enough force as it is. Divided we'd be for the high jump.'

The old man propped himself up on one withered elbow. His white brows hung like snow-heavy sedge over eyes that had sunk far back in his head.

'Which ones won't see reason?' he said, a little of the old irascibility re-entering his voice.

'One-Eye for a start. And I fear McCann. People I'd not have expected it from.'

'Always rebels,' chortled the Prophet. 'They need a firm hand is all. Round them up and bring them to me. I'll show them.'

So, in McCloed's absence, I went out into the camp selecting from each knot of dissent the troublemakers who were fast becoming a thorn in the side of the revolution. I told them their Prophet wished to speak to them and they came, albeit reluctantly, like unwilling children hanging back from an anticipated tongue-lashing.

'I hear you're behaving like spoiled wains,' he laid into them when they were all assembled. 'I didnae swipe you from the Maxwell's midwives and spend my valuable time teaching you the difference between right and wrong so that you could show me up at this juncture.'

He looked around for rumblings of revolt. There were none.

'Do you not see what you're doing?' he asked. 'You're lowering yourselves to their level. If you behave as badly as they've been doing you're no more worthy of power than the basest of them. If you act like beasties then that's what you are. Unless you can respect yourselves you cannae expect the world to respect you. And the world's eyes are on you now, make no mistake.

'Soon you'll have to journey to Ballater and confront the wounded she-lion in her den. The arch-bitch Fergael will be with her. By your behaviour at this hour will the world – and history – judge you.

'So which is it to be? Will future generations look back on you as reasonable men, who took a rotten society and turned it into something better? Or will they say you were just a bunch of barbarians, replacing one tyranny with another?'

His speech faltered and he began to cough, the spasms wracking his stick-thin body and twisting his face against the pain.

McCann knelt by him, holding the whisky-jar to his lips so that he might drink, but the Prophet pushed him away.

'Leave me be,' he said. 'You disappoint me – the lot of you – I would have hoped for a bit of head-ease in my dying time at least.'

One-Eye sank to his knees by the old man's pallet. Tears stood in his good eye and he made no attempt to blink them away.

'You willnae die, Master,' he said.

'We'll all die,' Colluden told him, testily. 'Only some of us will get less peace at it than others . . . Where's Rolande?'

I stepped forward to take my place at his side.

'Stay by me,' he ordered. Then he stared at the Wildemen, reducing them to the size of ants with the scorn in his eyes. 'This is the Redeemer,' he said at last. 'Into his hands I commend your welfare.'

There was some muttering, not much, and what there was he quelled instantly.

'Dinna think, he roared, 'that any man among you is fitter than this Childe to be the Redeemer. The Redeemer has been chosen by a higher power than you or me. And for good reason. There is a strength in Rolande but there is also something more.

Something that not one of you skivers possess. Compassion. A far more important commodity than brute force and ignorance if this revolution is to succeed. This Childe has the vision to carry Alba out of the Dark Ages. And if you could only raise your expectations out of the mire you would see that.

'Rolande is the Chosen of God.

'And he who raises his hand against the Chosen One is damned to Hell and back again and don't any of you forget it.'

He began to cough again and lay back, exhausted by his efforts.

'I canna bully you any more,' he said. 'I'm dying. But before I die peaceful, I shall hae your oaths that you will follow the Redeemer faithfully. It shames me to have to ask it. I thought I had brought you up better. But you leave me no option.'

So they swore the oaths of fealty, through him, to me, pledging allegiance and undying loyalty to the Redeemer and the Cause, filing past, one at a time, to mumble their promises and accept the Prophet's last blessing.

He placed a gnarled hand on each bowed head and one could almost see the power passing from him to them. Each rose renewed and revitalised and I knew that, thanks to Colluden, I need not doubt their support in the future.

'You maun each deal with your clutches howsomever you may,' he said, finally. 'Rolande will have the overall picture to attend to. You canna expect him to sort the petty details as well. Deal with others as you would be dealt with yoursells mind. Punish if need be, but do so fairly and not in anger. And never strip a man of his dignity. It is a form of murder and debases the punisher as much as the punished.'

He lay back with a sigh, closed his eyes and died.

It was so sudden and so peaceful that, at first, we none of us realised that it had happened.

I felt for the pulse and found none.

'He is gone,' I said, and crossed his hands over his chest.

One-Eye began to sob, loudly, like a disconsolate bairn. And then a general wailing broke out, not unlike the greeting of women. The Wildemen gave vent to their grief unashamedly and it was good to see them cry, weeping for a great prophet and a greater man. Colluden. Father of the Revolution, who had started the whole thing when he saved that first boy-childe from the knife.

I gave them their time with him and then I dispatched them

223

to their various clutches to break the news and prepare for the wake.

Much drinking would take place before dawn, with the health of the corpse toasted and many stories, apochryphal and otherwise, told and re-told during the long night of mourning.

Colluden's pallet was removed to the centre of the campsite, raised on a boulder and a fire built beside it so that all might have a chance to view the remains.

One by one the Wildemen shuffled past, each reaching out to touch the dead Prophet's head as though, in the gesture, they were taking into themselves a little of his memory.

I stood beside the bier and the routine never varied. A touch for Colluden and a salute for me. In his dying the old man united us and his passing had had a cathartic effect, purging the desire for revenge that had threatened the very heart of the uprising. Even the women were permitted to view the corpse and none offered them insult as they payed their last respects.

I made a speech — one of my better efforts — eulogising the old man and what he stood for, assuring them that at the end (though here I paraphrased a little for he had been predominantly pro-male in his outlook) his greatest wish had been that the sexes be united in friendship for the common good of Alba.

Then I left the sexes to become better acquainted and went back to the War-tent to air my grief in private.

It was there that McCloed found me when he returned with Ymer.

She was still delirious and exceptionally weak so we took her to the tent where the Maxwell had lain and left her in the care of a couple of older Clanswomen.

Then I accompanied McCloed to the dead Prophet's side and stayed by him while he said his farewells.

McCloed had been closer to Colluden than anyone but he bore his grief with dignity. In fact he wanted to stand vigil through the night but I persuaded him that the old man would have wanted him to rest and be in good shape for the coming assault on Ballater.

Colluden's 'General' held himself aloof until we were alone together in the War-tent. Then he broke down and cried like a baby and it was my pleasure to comfort him, stroking his neck and murmuring words of endearment into his long hair. It seemed the most natural thing in the world for me to kiss away his tears and he did not dissuade me when my mouth moved down to his. To be frank he responded with a passion made more powerful for having been denied so long.

Afterwards we lay in each other's arms like a pair of virgins. Neither of us spoke. There was nothing to say. But I kissed McCloed's eyelids and he smiled. And the smell of him was in my nostrils and the feel of his skin against me was like swansdown and I knew deep in the centre of myself that I loved this man more than life. And somehow I felt that Euan-Noag would have been pleased.

It is true that Birth and Death are closely related.

A life for a life.

The self-same night that Colluden passed away I conceived the Childe which, as I write, moves within me.

THE TRUE CHRONICLES OF THE REDEEMER

And when the Lady Ymer discovered the lovers together, her jealousy turned her against her twin, for she also loved the General McCloed. In her rage she loosed the female prisoners and fled with them to Castle Ballater.

Chapter
25

So we made love, McCloed and I, and for me, as well as him, it was something extraordinary and new. The smell of his body, sweat-sweet and warm as baby's breath, filled me with a kind of madness that made we want to swallow him whole.

I was down on my hands and knees in front of him trying to translate the desire into reality, when Ymer made her entrance. I did not hear her come in. I was too preoccupied. But McCloed suddenly pulled away and I turned my head to see what had caused such a dramatic change of mind.

My sister stood in the arch of the tent-entrance, holding the flap high with one emaciated arm. She looked terrible. Her eyes were bruised black in her pale face and there was a growing fury in them that I could not fathom.

Ymer, the sensual, who had taught me that there was no shame to be found in the human body. Nothing distasteful. Nothing taboo. Why was she looking at me like that and beyond me, at the discomfitted McCloed?

It never occurred to me that she might disapprove. On the contrary, I was sure she would be delighted, would want to share in my happiness, for had she not told me that she, too, desired the Wildeman? Ignoring the storm-warnings, I rose, walked naked towards her and attempted to put my arms round her shaking shoulders. She pushed me away from her as though I was covered in plague-sores and her lips drew back from her small white teeth.

'Traitor,' she croaked, and then, her voice becoming louder with each epithet, 'Freak. Degenerate. Whoremonger.'

She began to hammer at my breasts with her clenched fists and I was forced to grasp her wrists. The breasts are a tender enough area and do not take kindly to such pumelling. But if I found her battering of this part of me uncomfortable, I was nowhere prepared for what came next. She raised her knee with a sudden jerk, carrying the point of the knee-cap into my groin.

The searing fire that filled my body is impossible to describe. Think lucky if you never experience it. They tell me childbirth is a painful process but I approach it with the equanimity of knowing that it can be nowhere near as incapacitating as that knee-jerk. The pain shot through my stomach and chest, past my throat and up to the top of my head where it collided with the interior of my cranium. From there it ricocheted into every corner of my being, evading not a single cell. I could neither breathe nor speak. I fell to the ground with a rabbit-shriek singing in my ears. It was my own voice but I had no realisation of having cried out. I was too busy holding on to my testicles, convinced that they had been sheared from my body and would, should I release them, drop off.

The agony echoed and re-echoed within me and such was its intensity that if Fergael herself had entered at that moment with a stake in her hand and the intention of driving it through my heart, I would have been powerless to prevent her.

Gradually the waves diminished to the point where they were almost bearable. The mists began to clear and I saw McCloed holding Ymer's thin shoulders and trying to shake some sense into her. I wanted to tell him to go careful, that she was not the strongest after her ordeal, but no sound emerged.

Anyway, he was having little success and the look in her eyes, half-hate, half-longing, at last gave me the clue to her extraordinary behaviour. It was a look that had stared back at me from the looking-glass on the day that Ymer had told me of her love for the Maxwell, disregarding my feelings, not realising that I would be in the least put out. Now I had inadvertently payed her back in kind.

Ymer was jealous.

'You're overwrought, kwine,' McCloed was saying, his face flushed with embarrassment and the remnants of our passion.

Ymer spat in his face.

'Poofter,' she screamed.

McCloed blanched. Then his eyes hardened and his lips set in a grim line. Tucking Ymer under one arm, he marched with her to the bed, swung her across his knee and began to wallop her behind.

She kicked and howled, calling down the curses of the Mother on his unworthy head, dredging words and threats up from the dunghill of her rage that no human being should ever hurl at another.

Still he thrashed her.

And I lay, in a slowly reviving heap, trying to pull the vestiges of my pride together.

Not the most auspicious beginning to a great love affair and, in that moment, there was very little sign of the triumphant triumverate that we have become. But, hate being akin to love, as the old wives will have it, it all came right in the end.

Now that she is included in the circle of our love, as if it had ever been my intention to exclude her, Ymer has quite forgotten her jealousies of that first night. But no amount of soothing words or loving reassurances could penetrate her fury at the time.

When McCloed loosed her at last, to raise me from the floor, she stood four-square in the centre of the tent and screeched her defiance at us.

'A fine pair,' she shouted. 'A freak and a pander. You think you can play false with me? I am Ymer, Childe of the Blood Royal. I will see that you roast for this betrayal.'

And she turned on her heel, almost bumping into McCann on the way out.

The big man had come to see what all the ruckuss was about and, finding us both buck naked and a woman fleeing the tent, jumped immediately to the wrong conclusion.

'Beg pardon,' he said, a lewd grin spreading across his features. 'I didna mean to break anything up.'

I flung a cloak about me and made to follow Ymer but McCloed put out a restraining hand.

'Convey the Lady Ymer to the stockade,' he ordered, stiffly. 'She is to have the same privileges as the other prisoners. No more. No less . . . And wipe that silly smirk off your face.'

'Yes, Sir,' chortled McCann, ducking out through the tent-flat just in time to miss the drinking-horn that McCloed flung at his head.

'I must go to her,' I said, turning to McCloed. 'She has a fearful temper and is prone to fits. She may harm herself if she's left alone.'

'Not that lady,' said McCloed, grimly. 'That lady has much

230

too high an opinion of herself to do damage to her person. Whit she needs is a bit of healthy ignoring. She'll soon come around.'

I should have argued with him, maybe even pulled rank and saved us all a load of bother after, but at the moment McCann came back into report Ymer secure and tell us that it was Sun-up and time to bury Colluden.

McCloed was the first person who had ever suggested that Ymer's 'fits' might be self-induced rather than involuntary. He's nobody's fool, McCloed.

We did not bury Colluden. I for one have a particular aversion to putting anything in the cold ground. Nor did I wish to see the old man burn. Cremation was the woman's way and I felt the Prophet deserved something more particular than that. The Eagle of the High Hills should not be brought low by death.

So I had the men construct a cairn, a platform of stones atop an adjacent hill. There was a wonderful view from the place down over the valley where our great victory had been won. It seemed appropriate.

The hillock was built high enough to dissuade any wilde-creatures from attempting the climb and an awning of hides was slung over it to discourage the corbies and fend off the worst of the weather.

The old man's litter was laid out on the summit and we left him, sleeping his last sleep, half-way between earth and sky, overlooking the heathered hills and bottomless tarns of Alba.

McCloed gave the funeral address, and he spoke reverenti-ally of Colluden's wisdom and grit and his uncomplicated belief that the Human Race was essentially good. And the Wildemen stood, attending to their young General, hair blowing, heads bowed, while the warm wind carried his words to where the egrets swooped over the old man's beloved Highlands.

It was as we trudged downhill again that the first hint came that something was amiss.

An unhealthy silence seemed to have blanketed the whole area and, as we rounded the last rocky outcrop and came into full view of the camp, our worst fears were confirmed.

The place was deserted.

The flickering fire that centred the encampment was the only live thing in it. Around it the sentries lay sprawled like a necklace round a central stone. Each had a spear protruding from between his shoulder-blades.

To one side of the clearing, the stripped carcass of the great Kelpie lay bleach-boned in the morning sun, heightening the graveyard feel of the place. The beast had been carved up the day after the battle, its flesh laid out in carpet strips to dry. The dehydrated meat would be sliced and used as sustenance on long marches. The liver and lights had fed the War-Dogs for days, while the entrails had been polished off by carrion birds.

The gate to the stockade lay open. The paddock had been emptied of the last remaining King Stags.

Of Ymer and the women, there was no sign.

The rumbling came like a single threat from the collective throats of the men. They surged downhill, palming weapons as they went, ready to commit wholesale slaughter in revenge of their fallen comrades.

There was no sense in trying to stop them. I left them to their foraging knowing that they would eventually trickle back, sullen and unsatisfied, to see what plans McCloed and myself had made for them.

Ymer's life, I knew, would not be worth a cow-pat if any of these men reached her prior to me. And if she got to Ballater, whence I was sure she was headed with her troops, then her life would be worth even less. Fergael would see to that.

It was up to me to save her from herself . . . and everybody else . . though I must admit that I was beginning to come round to McCloed's view that she was a 'silly, spoiled kwine who needed thrashing at least twice a day to knock some sense into her'. This, I promised him and myself, was the last time I would get her out of any scrape into which she had got herself through thoughtlessness, carelessness or sheer bloody-mindedness.

I had clad myself in the armour of the Redeemer for the funeral ceremony and, to make sure that everybody could see me, I clambered up atop the Kelpie and struck a straddle-legged pose to deliver my address.

'Wildemen of Alba,' I roared, in what I hoped was suitably heroic style. 'This is no time for petty revenge. The world lies before us. Ours for the taking. But only if we keep together and show the Clanswomen a unified front.

'You mean you're going to let the bitches go?' someone shouted.

'Never,' I said. 'They will face justice at the right and proper time. For now, we must march on Ballater.'

232

There were some mutterings in the front about me having a female bias and a foot in both camps. I pounced on these. They were all the cue I needed.

'Someone here says I am half-woman and this is our weakness.' I pointed in the general direction of the dissenting voices. 'But he is wrong. I am half-woman. This is true. But it is our strength. I will go ahead, disguised as a woman, and enter Castle Ballater. Can any of you do this?' They were listening now, intrigued. I had them. 'At the appropriate time I will open the gates to you and you shall enter Ballater as victors.'

A cheer went up. I quelled it with a raised hand.

'McCloed has procured me a horse,' I told them. 'I will ride ahead. You must gather your weapons and all the men you can muster on the march and follow on to Ballater with all speed.'

'What if they capture you, Redeemer?' shouted McCann, aye ready with the awkward questions.

'Capture the Redeemer?' I smiled. 'You forget. I am the eagle. If they get too close I shall simply do as I did before and fly away.'

THE CHRONICLES OF THE REDEEMER

So The Redeemer left the army under the command of McCloed. And entering Castle Ballater in woman's guise, found Ymer captive and Fergael, with all the clan of Alba gathered about her, preparing to usurp the antlered throne.

Chapter
26

I REACHED BALLATER UNMOLESTED, REMAINING HOODED AND answering on the odd occasions that I was asked that I was on my way to join the Maxwell's army, like any other loyal Clanswoman.

The entire country was up in arms and I passed scores of small troops, anything from a douzaine to a demi-century, all headed in the same general direction as myself. It was when I reached the Castle proper that my problems began. I found the gates barred against me and a vast army of women encamped outwith the walls. There was nothing I could do immediately, so I decided to sit it out, waiting for the darkness to add cover to my attempts to gain entry.

The females around me were from all arts and parts and this stood me in good stead since there was little danger of my being recognised as might have happened inside the gates where everybody knew me. I found no difficulty in attaching myself to one of the many campfires that smoked in the dusty air. There was a spirit of cameraderie abroad with bread and ale being shared freely – just as well considering I had not eaten in a clockround – and from my vantage point in the middle of the crush I was able to pick up the latest gossip.

There was much talk about The Redeemer. Wild exaggerated stories that gave me anything from three legs to a bird's beak and invested me with magical powers that, had I the half of them, would have negated the necessity of fighting at all. I could just have waved my magic wand and the walls would have parted and we could have walked into Castle Ballater, no trouble.

But this speculation, while entertaining, was useless to me.

I wanted facts, not fairytales. In the end I had to elicit these by asking the relevant questions myself. I assumed the soft accents of the north, posing as a country bumpkin who lived too far away from the hub of things to know anything about court intrigue.

'When will the Maxwell show hersel'?' I wanted to know.

'Never, at this rate,' said the woman on my left, a weather-beaten farmer from Carnoustie. 'She's been put under a sleep-cure by the Great Healer, Morangy. He's an eveling, did you know?'

'You don't tell me,' I sounded suitably amazed.

'As sure as I'm sitting here. A wee mannikin no higher than my sporran. But a great one at the doctoring, for all that.'

'He'll need all his skill this time,' snorted another. 'She's lost a leg.'

'The Maxwell?'

'Aye, and Cameron, her top woman, has lost an arm. What a nation. A pair of cripples in charge.'

She was shushed into silence by the huddle of women who looked around nervously in case this blasphemy might have been heard and associated with the rest of them.

'What if The Redeemer attacks before the Maxwell recovers?' I asked.

'We'll be ready for them,' said the woman from Carnoustie, scornfully. 'A bunch of castrati led by a freak. No contest.'

'But wi' no leader . . . ' I said, doubtfully.

'Dinna fash yersel', we hae a leader. Fergael.' And the rest of the circle rallied round to reassure me.

'A strong leader.'

'No nonsense about her.'

'Aye. You should hae seen her when the Lady Ymer came back. She got short shrift. Clapped her in irons straight away.'

'Serves her right, traitorous vermin.'

'She's mad they say.'

'Who? Fergael?'

'No, Ymer. Blind as a bat and given to fits. Has the evil eye.' The woman made the gesture with two fingers said to warn away evil spirits.

'What'll happen to her?' I asked.

'Oh, Fergael will think of something fitting,' said the farmer and she spat as if what was fitting brought a nasty taste to the mouth.

Hardly had this self-appointed oracle finished speaking than the witch herself came out onto the battlements to address the troops.

She had forsaken her normal black robes for a bright scarlet surcoat which contrasted sharply with the sallow skin and picked up the carmine that smeared her lips and dotted her sharp cheekbones. If the colour was intended to soften her stark image, it did the opposite, making her look more predatory than ever. She held in her hand the Battle-Standard Hraefn, which some enterprising Clansman had snatched from our camp during the great exodus, and she held it high so that the women could see the great Raven fluttering proudly in a promise of victory.

Her appearance was greeted with subdued clapping. Fergael inspired fear rather than affection. It was the way she wanted it. She surveyed the thronged masses with eyes that bored to the bone and the clapping died away to leave an expectant hush.

Fergael let the silence hang in the early evening air, savouring the moment, until she knew that she had the attention of every last woman in the crowd.

Then she spoke.

'Clanswomen of Alba.' She pitched her voice high, throwing it across the heads of those nearest so that it reached also those at the very back. I recognised it as an old theatrical trick. But it was very effective. 'The Lady Maxwell, Warlord of all the Clans, has placed on me a singular honour.'

'Where is the Queen?' piped up some brave soul at my elbow.

'She is still abed,' said Fergael, seeking out and pinpointing the voice with her eyes so that I, standing too close to the speaker for comfort, pulled the hood closer around my head as though shielding myself from the north wind's chill. 'But she is still able enough to issue orders. In the absence of Cameron, who is herself suffering from a wound received in battle, the Maxwell has appointed *me* Leader of the Armies of Alba and laid on me the responsibility of quelling the forces of this upstart, The Redeemer.'

Sporadic cheering greeted this announcement.

'We are in a position of extreme strength,' Fergael told them. 'We can see the enemy coming from any direction from our vantage point on the Brae, for we hold, not only Ballater, but the heights that surround it.

238

'Added to that, I have information that the Leader of this scum, this slave rabble that dares outface the might of Alba, this self-styled Redeemer . . . is a fraud . . . ' She paused for effect and to allow the information to sink in. The women looked at one another, wondering what was coming next. Then she let them have it. 'He is a common freak,' she roared. 'An eveling who has lived out his life in subterfuge under the patronage of our beloved Maxwell. This man/woman . . . this "thing" . . . is no other than Childe Rolande . . . the Queen's consort.'

Good timing, Fergael, I thought. Give the devil her due she had a sense of the dramatic.

A gasp greeted her revelation, followed by a hum of disbelief. Fergael raised her voice to hammer home her point.

'And this ingrate,' she said, 'who has for years passed himself off as a woman, is now biting the very hand that fed him so lavishly. This traitor is infecting our country with heresy and rousing semi-humans to challenge the rule of law and decency. Are we going to tolerate this?'

'No!' The roar of the women filled the valley.

She had them now.

'You may be wondering how this monster achieved his aims?' yelled Fergael – and indeed they were. 'I will tell you. He had an ally. Here. In Castle Ballater itself.'

Fergael dealt her trump card.

'One of our own,' she screamed. 'A traitor to her sex . . . the Lady Ymer.'

In the stunned silence that followed this pronouncement, Ymer was led forth in chains. She was alive at least. But only just. Her head had been shaved and her body stripped of all but the briefest loincloth. She had been scourged and her body still carried a livid criss-cross of welts across breasts and shoulders.

Hissing and booing greeted her appearance and some people at the back began to hurl missiles, clods of earth and stones torn hastily from the ground.

'This deviant,' shrieked Fergael, 'who was to follow me as the next Fergael, who had everything that life could offer, sold her birthright in exchange for sordid sex with a man . . . or half a man . . . for she is the paramour of the freak, Rolande.'

'Kill her,' shouted someone.

'Killing's too good for her,' said another.

'Roast her alive.'

'Tear out her eyeballs.'

239

'Carve her up and feed her to the pigs.'

'Kill! Kill! Kill!'

The cry was taken up by the entire army. Bloodlust filled every eye. And my small, frail sister shrank back from the sound of her approaching doom.

This was precisely what Fergael needed. A sacrifice. Something to unite the army, even if it was only hate. She allowed the Clanswomen sufficient time to work themselves up into a frenzy. Then, at the zenith of their fury, she raised the Battle-Standard high to silence them.

'I hear,' she announced, solemnly. 'And I obey. At first light tomorrow . . . the Lady Ymer dies.' Then she swept from the battlements with her cohorts dragging Ymer behind.

She left the women plenty to talk about – none of it very complimentary to Ymer – and when the traitoress was brought from the gates to be transferred to the confines of the Dark Tower, the rush to get close to her created a momentary confusion which allowed me to slip through the archway unnoticed and secrete myself in one of the storerooms.

I could do nothing for Ymer in the face of such a mob and my plan was now to find the Maxwell and either to persuade her to intercede on her daughter's behalf, or to hold her hostage and trade her as I had done before. I still did not realise that the balance of power had shifted so radically. But I was soon to learn.

I made my way, by fits and starts, to the Maxwell's bedchamber, where I was amazed to see Cameron herself, standing guard over her sovereign's quarters. The big woman was semi-comatose from lack of sleep, her head drooping on her breast. Had Fergael, or indeed myself, wished to dispatch the Warlord of the Clans, this would have been the time to have done it.

But Fergael was still playing out her little charade with Ymer and I could hear the noise associated with that, the screams and shouts of the Clanswomen's righteous indignation, even through the thick granite walls of the Castle.

My original plan had been to hide out somewhere until I heard that the army was approaching, then to open the gates to McCloed and the Wildemen as I had promised. And indeed I still intended to do that – after I had dealt with the problem of Ymer – but what I had not bargained for, and neither would my General, I was sure, was the number of the gathered army and the strength of their position. McCloed would be forced to fight

240

uphill and dispatch a vastly superior force before he even reached the gates of the Castle proper.

And this time he would not have the element of surprise. The Maxwell's band-box army had been smug and sure of victory. This had made them easy to topple. The women I had sat among were more aware of what they had to lose and that, together with the hate so carefully churned up in them by Fergael, made them a different kettle of fish altogether. By her oratory she had succeeded in rousing their battle rage and debunking my reputation in one fell swoop.

Very clever.

All this I thought as I watched Cameron's head fall slowly onto her chest. A couple of times she pulled herself out of it, her head snapping up and back and her eyes regaining focus as she struggled up from the depths of sleep. Once she raised her maimed arm as though to wipe her eyes with the non-existent hand. She muttered something and let the stump fall in disgust – and her head began to droop once more. She had been standing, knees locked, back pressed firmly against the door for support. Now her legs gave under her and she slid slowly into a sitting position before toppling sideways across the entrance to the Queen's bedchamber.

I tiptoed stealthily to her side and undid the keyring from her belt, selecting from it the horn-handled gold key that I knew so well. Hadn't I passed it on to Ymer night after night for longer than I cared to remember? I used it to unlock the door.

The Guard Captain barely stirred as I replaced the ring, stepped over her body and slipped inside to be greeted by a knife in the lower back.

'Don't stir.' It was Morangy's voice. 'Or I'll fillet your kidneys where you stand.'

'It's me,' I hissed. 'Rolande'.

Across the room, in the great antlered bed, the Queen lay sleeping peacefully. There was colour in her cheeks and she looked a good deal healthier than the last time I had seen her, but the narrowness of the ridge below her trunk denoted that the gossiping Clanswomen had spoken true. She had, indeed, lost the leg.

'Bless us and save us,' said Morangy, scuttling round to get a look at my face. 'Is it really you? How did you get in?'

'It's an ill wind,' I said, grimly. 'Fergael and the whole band

241

of harpies are busy vilifying my unfortunate sister – and your sentry is fast asleep.'

'Then we'd better lock ourselves in,' said Morangy, opening the door and peering out. 'Here, give me a hand with her.'

So I took her head and Morangy took her feet and together we manoeuvred Cameron inside the room, securing the door not only with the key but a double bolt on our side.

'Poor kwine,' said Morangy, looking at the sleeping soldier. 'She's had nae rest in a moon's phase. One by one they've all deserted us and gone over to the side of that black bitch. Even Cameron wavered when Ymer came back with the news of The Redeemer's true identity . . . but in the end, duty overcame inclination, and she stayed loyal.'

'And the Maxwell . . .?'

'Knows nothing yet. I have her on the sleep-cure. What did you do to that sister of yours anyway? She came back here like a raving lunatic and just played into Fergael's hands.'

'It's a long story,' I said. 'Anyway I'm here to let her out and the Wildemen in.'

'You'll be lucky,' snorted Morangy. 'Fergael's to sacrifice her tomorrow.'

'I heard.'

'Aye, but you havnae heard the worst of it. The bitch intends to bathe in Ymer's blood. She has some powerful spell concocted and she believes it'll make her immortal.'

'Do you believe it?'

'I believe what I've always believed, that she's stark, staring bonkers,' Morangy paused . . . 'And yet . . .' he looked thoughtful and when he spoke again it was almost as if he were talking to himself. 'I am a Healer,' he went on. 'And I know healing to be a practical trade, rooted in knowledge and truth. But I also know that some of the feats I perform must seem like magic to the untutored. So who am I to say that there are not others privy to secrets that I may not know . . . that seem like magic to me?'

'I don't understand you.'

'I really don't understand myself . . . that's the problem . . . but I cannae afford to dismiss the notion out of hand.'

'You can't be serious,' I snorted. But Morangy continued to look grave so that I realised to my discomfort that he was all too serious.

'I am older than you, Rolande,' he went on, at last. . . '
'More than twice times your age. That is a fact. How old would
you say the Queen was?'

I looked over at the Maxwell, at her smooth, unlined
features, the glossy abundance of her red-gold hair. I ventured
a guess.

'Thirty Summers?'

'My estimate exactly. That would make her some fifteen
Summers younger than me . . . and yet . . . ' he paused. 'And
yet when I was a childe, maybe three Summers old, no more . . .
and cured her of her Falling Sickness . . . and in return had my
eveling life spared . . . she looked precisely as she does now . . .
no older . . . no younger . . . the same . . . By my reckoning that
makes her seventy-five at least.'

'But that's not possible.'

'Maybe not . . . But it's a fact. And let me tell you something else. Once every which while, say each ten Summers or so,
since I have been Chief Midwife anyway, the Queen has
retreated to the Inner Sanctum for a period of some thirteen
cycles. No one was ever permitted to visit her there except Fergael, and, each clockround, one of the thirteen Priests of the
Source. It was given out that she was in retreat, praying and
fasting and renewing her spiritual entity with the Godhead.'

'I remember,' I said, excitedly. 'It happened just after I
arrived at Ballater.'

Morangy nodded. 'Quite so. And is due to happen shortly
again. At the end of the retirement she emerged . . . not wasted
and wan as is normal after a long fast, but renewed . . . restored
somehow.'

'What are you trying to say?'

'I'm not sure, except that her re-emergence has always co-
incided with the appointment of thirteen new Priests. The old
ones never come out of the Dark Tower.'

'That's monstrous . . .' I was horrified. I looked across at
the Maxwell and shook the idea away.

'Monstrous,' agreed Morangy. 'But if it works . . .'

'If it works then it's doubly important that I get Ymer out
of there.'

Morangy shuddered.

'Too right,' he agreed. 'That kind of power in the hands of
Fergael doesn't bear thinking about. The bitch might live forever. Then where would we be?'

THE TRUE CHRONICLES OF THE REDEEMER

And the Redeemer walked through walls and found, in the magic land between, a powerful weapon, a stick which breathed fire and sent metal sparks into the hearts of all Alba's enemies. And in the Dark Tower the Childe joined battle with the Black Hag Fergael. And the witch was vanquished.

CHAPTER
27

Morangy moved to the antlered bed and took the Maxwell's limp wrist in one hand, testing her pulse.

'She's due to surface about now,' he said. 'I'll need to see how well she's fared before I decide whether or no tae put her under again.'

As if on cue, the Maxwell's eyelids fluttered, then lifted over eyes glazed and disorientated by her drug-long sleep. She dropped her head gently from side to side, gazing this way and that as if familiarising herself with some unknown scene.

And then her look lighted on me.

It was as though the sun had come out. Her face lit up with a smile that was all loving relief and she raised herself on one elbow and spoke my name as though the saying of it brought me back from the deadlands.

'Rolande, you are safe.'

Her eyes clouded and she fell back, weakened by even so small an effort.

Morangy was suddenly all business. He hoisted the Queen's head off the pillows, supporting her with his small sturdy chest while he held a cup of honeyed herbtea to her lips. She drank thirstily.

'Subjects get gae de-hydrated on the cure,' he said, using even such a moment to broaden my healing-knowledge. 'They hardly ken if they're here or the other place when they come to. It's a drastic business and not to be used lightly. Still, in dire cases it gives the poor souls time to mend.'

He laid the Lady back and she sighed, as if remembering something she would rather forget and reached down and felt for the place where her leg had once been. The covers gave way beneath her questing hand and she sighed again, more heavily.

'No dream then?' she said, closing her eyes against a large tear which squeezed itself from under her lids and ran down her cheek to bury itself in the coruscations of her red-gold hair. She wiped it away with the back of her hand then held the self-same hand out towards me without opening her eyes.

I sat beside her, this strong proud woman, now crippled and wasted by her long fast and she clasped my hand with a fierceness belying her frailty so that my knuckles stood white under her grip. And although it was hardly the time I told her of Fergael's treachery and Ymer's danger and how the witch believed that if she bathed in the Childe's blood she would become immortal.

I waited for a denial – but none came. Instead the Maxwell opened her eyes and gazed steadily into mine.

'And you must believe it too,' she said. 'She has the power to work such magick.'

I snatched my hand away.

'So you have used it,' I said, my gorge rising at the thought. 'That is why you are ever young. That is why the Initiates are replaced every decade. That is why Morangy remembers you – just as you are now – when he was a stripling of three Summers.'

The Maxwell's voice hardened and she turned her accusing gaze on the discomfited Healer. 'You know little and presume much,' she said.

'Do you deny it?' I demanded.

'I have no need to justify myself to you,' said the Queen, coldly. 'But I do deny it.' She elbowed herself up again, her face greying with the effort. 'Help me dress. I must squash this internal insurrection before the Freak arrives at my gates.'

'You're too late,' said Morangy, 'the whole Castle's gone over to Fergael. She commands the army. And right now she's in the Dark Tower guarded by her cronies, preparing to sacrifice your daughter and bathe in her blood.'

'No way in,' I added. 'Without running the gauntlet of the entire Guard.'

'Where is Locheil?' demanded the Queen and, in reply, Morangy nodded over his shoulder to where the Guard Captain lay, sleeping peacefully in the lee of the locked door.

The Maxwell snorted and, taking her full body-weight on her fists, sat up properly.

'Raise me,' she commanded and then, when we hesitated. 'Come on, come on. We don't have time to act like gormless loons. Raise me up when I tell you.'

So between us we raised her, though not without a struggle. Even in her depleted state, she weighed more than both Morangy and I put together. As we stood, panting in an effort to hold her upright, the Queen stretched forth one of her long, pale arms and grasping the extreme right point of the great royal spread of antlers which hung over the regal bed, bore down on it with all her strength.

There was a rolling, grating sound and the room trembled as if shaken by a quake. Then a portion of the wall behind the night-table swung inwards to reveal a gaping hole and a set of steps disappearing down into the dark.

'It leads to the Tower,' said the Queen, as we lowered her thankfully back onto the bed. 'Go rescue my daughter and bring me that troublesome Priest. If she comes willingly – all well and good. If she resists, you have my permission to dispose of her.'

Morangy grabbed a lighted taper and preceded me into the tunnel, but the Queen held me back.

'You are unarmed,' she said, gruffly. 'Take my sword – if I know Fergael, you'll need it.'

I unhooked the great war-weapon from its stand beside the bed and turned it once in my hand to get the balance of it before I strapped it on. It was not Enfideon, but it would do very well. With a final salute to the Maxwell, I plunged after Morangy and the door swung shut behind us with a clang.

It was pitch black inside, the faint light from the taper barely making a dent in the graveyard air. Morangy's language was nothing ordinary. He employed expletives I have never heard before or since, calling Fergael every imaginable kind of a monstrosity, hiding his own fear in bluster. I was afraid too but strove to contain it in different fashion, keeping silent, hugging myself to myself lest the terror of the dark and what I should find in the Tower bubbled out to overwhelm me. Small, many-legged bodies slithered away under our questing heels as we began our descent, holding on to each other and the slime-slicked walls in the absence of anything remotely resembling a bannister.

After what seemed a veritable life-cycle the steps levelled out into a narrow corridor piled high with packing-cases bearing strange hieroglyphics and some printed words. 'Ammunition', said one. 'MI5 rifles' another.

I searched my memory for where I had seen those words before, then remembered. It was in one of the Euan-Noag's books – where else? These were old style weapons from before 'the fall'. I recalled the drawings I had seen often enough in the flickering half-light of my night-time candle flame. The long, sleek, dark green objects were called 'guns' and were said to be able to project metal pellets with such velocity that they could tear through stone walls. Far-fetched nonsense, I was sure. Still, I made a mental note to investigate the claim when I had the time and, since one of the boxes lay open, I took out one of the weapons plus a boxful of the metal objects called bullets, and carried them with me as far as the head of the stair.

Morangy, who had gone on ahead of me, called back for me to 'get a move on'. Easy for him to say. Being the size he was he had little difficulty slipping through the narrow apertures between the packing cases. As for me, I was out of breath, had grazed my body in several places and had a large rent in the bodice of my gown by the time we reached the end of level ground and came at last to the opposing rise of the steps leading upwards. These terminated at the top in a metal door on which had been written the legend 'Fire EXIT. Keep closed'.

Ignoring the warning, Morangy undid the rusted bolts and pushed inwards. Nothing happened – except for the fact that Morangy began to dance up and down in rage and kick the heavy door with small, frustrated feet. I thrust the rifle at him.

'Take this and go back,' I said, sternly. 'You're more of a hindrance than a help to me in this state.'

'What is it?' he asked suspiciously.

'Never mind what it is.' I pressed the box of bullets into his hand. 'Take these too and hide them under the bed. I don't want the Maxwell to see them.'

That was when I had my brainwave. Snatching the weapon and the box back I unbuckled the Queen's sword and handed him that instead.

'What are you doing?' he demanded. 'You're surely not intending to face that madwoman wi' nothing but an old green stick?'

I sat down on the top step and began to prise open the box, removing the ammunition and turning the gun over until I found the aperture where, if my memory served me well, the clip should be inserted.

'Hold the light up, can't you,' I said, my own temper fraying as my fingers fumbled with the unfamiliar mechanism.

Morangy did as he was bid and the clip slipped into place with a click. I stood to tuck the long folds of my frock up into the Queen's sword-belt.

'Get going,' I told Morangy – and he grumbled – but he went.

'I don't know which is worse,' I could hear him grumbling, as the light from the taper faded with his retracing steps, 'To face Fergael or the Maxwell when I tell her I've left her lady-love to tackle the witch unarmed and unaided.'

But I could tell from the tone of his voice that he was secretly relieved. And I knew I had done the right thing, because, if my hunch was correct then the weapon I now held in my sweating palm was all I would need to frighten Fergael out of what was left of her wits, and give me the edge to alter the balance of power once and for all.

I leant my shoulder to the door. It didn't budge. Obviously it worked on some powerful hinge mechanism. I remembered my strength training and put my back into it, bracing my trunk against the door and adding extra force by exerting all the power of the great quadriceps muscles down the front of my thighs. The door began to move. Slowly it gave, a mere fingerswidth at a time, till I had it wide enough for me to slip through sideways.

It slammed behind me with a hollow thud that reverberated up through the building. I stood rooted, waiting for the inevitable hue and cry that must follow such a din, but when nothing happened I realised that clearly I was still deep enough underground for it not to have penetrated up into the apex of the Tower. The break had given me a chance to regain my wind and I started up, in the all enveloping blackness. As much as I could judge, the stairs were similar to those which rose from the front entrance to the tower proper. Certainly they felt as though they were constructed of the same, paint-flaking metal. The bannisters, for this time, thankfully, there were some, felt rough against my hand and they spiralled as they rose so that, by the time I was half-way up and stopped to take a short rest, I felt quite disorientated. When my breath had quietened somewhat, I continued on. My knees were feeling the strain and those same muscles in my thighs which I used to open the door began to feel soft and rubbery. I judged the tunnel to be as deep again under the ground as the Tower itself was high, and I had just got to the point where I felt I would have to sit down again, when I became conscious of a pinpoint of light somewhere above me. The knowledge that I had almost reached my destination spurred me on, and I continued to climb, despite my wobbly legs, until I suddenly emerged into the dim light of the Tower proper.

I was on a narrow ledge, high above the temple area. It jutted into the room, three times human-height and about as wide as a windowsill. It was without protective railings and to one side lay a coiled rope ladder, presumably for descending into the tower itself.

The pungent smell of votive flames assailed my nostrils and I felt my stomach heave in protest as I hunkered down to get the lie of the land and weigh up the opposition. Below me, Initiates and Priests scurried back and forth like so many ants intent on their chores. No-one noticed me, hung as I was between floor and ceiling. All eyes were directed at the sacrificial victim, my sister, who until recently had been one of their exalted circle and had now fallen so spectacularly from grace.

She was chained to a pillar, hard by the great altar where McCloed had been bound, and she was naked, her pale body lying slack against her bindings, her eyes closed, her head lolling sideways over scourged breasts. To one side of her, a bath of noxious liquid steamed and bubbled and it was to this that the women of the Inner Circle scurried and retreated, depositing in it phials of salts and sulphurs which raised clouds of hissing steam from it's surface.

Ymer looked dead. Her creamy skin had taken on a hypo-thermic pallor and if she breathed at all it was an infinitely shallow process. For one horrible moment I thought I was too late and, in reflex action, I flung my mind out to her in an attempt to gauge whether or not there was anything left of her life-force. Was it my imagination or did I perceive the slightest movement, the merest rising of the chin?

I hurled my thoughts at her, willing her to stay alive, realis-ing in my desperation that if she died now then the War, what-ever the cause, would not have been worth the winning.

Whether or not she heard me I will never be sure. The feeling that I had of something reaching out to me was cut short as the deep red curtains immediately below me parted, drawing

251

my mind away, severing my tenuous, telepathic link with my unfortunate twin.

I flattened myself out, more in instinct than in fear, as all eyes turned towards the witch. I had a wonderful view of the top of her cockscombed head as she emerged from the robing-room, flanked my Scawthatch and Aillil, the former bearing the sickle-shaped killing-knife on a brocaded cushion, the latter carrying the carved bowl fashioned from a human skull which would catch the victim's life-blood.

Never had Fergael more resembled a carrion bird. Evil emanated from her like a living thing as she stalked towards Ymer, fustian robes aflap. Even the Inner Circle, used to her mad rages and erratic behaviour, drew back as she padded by, silent as a panther, deadly as a scorpion.

Ymer's head snapped up suddenly to face her executioner. Eyes locked eyes and, for a single disorientating moment, I was one with my sister so that her vision was my vision and I found myself facing the image of Fergael, saw her triumphant leer, felt the black eyes boring into mine. A brief impression of the knife and the bowl proffered and then I was back within myself, whirled across the void by a great push from my sister.

I saw Ymer shudder and draw herself upwards and away from the knife that Fergael now held in her hands. The witch raised her hand to strike and I scrambled up, grabbing the rope ladder and flinging it over the ledge's edge.

In that instant, I found myself immobilised and the knife in Fergael's hand hesitated as though some force, stronger than the witch's physical power, had stayed her hand.

My sister was not dead. She was fighting back. Bound and helpless as she was she was not going to go gently into the dark night that awaited her. It was only later that I realised that it was her fear of eternal damnation and not a love of a life which by that time she would have been glad to relinquish, which spurred her on, enabling her to dredge up a power from the depths of her battered spirit that even she, until that moment, did not know she possessed. Her mind's strength, fuelled like those of the martyrs of old, by physical deprivation, torture, hunger and thirst, had risen to another level, where human frailty made no impression. Lack of food, sleep, love, humiliation, and the sure knowledge that she was one, alone, against the world, had unfettered Ymer from the prison of her flesh and allowed her to soar with the strength of the universal spirit behind and within her.

So she threw her challenge at the High Priest's head, forbade her to use the knife, stayed the power that was in the killing gesture so that the hand holding the murder weapon fell uselessly to the black hag's side.

Fergael ground her pointed teeth and drew back, spreading her arms wide until they became corbie wings. She screeched like a banshee and, from her hooked claws, flung two lightning bolts of clearest blue energy flashing towards my sister's eyes. I know it was hallucination, a mirage brought on my some hypnotic hold which the witch had taken on my mind, on the minds of all of us held in thrall in that Dark Tower, but I swear, as those bolts seared across the room, I not only saw them, I felt the heat of them and the wind of their passing.

Ymer dropped her head, squeezing her eyes shut, concentrating, and the inhuman flame, instead of slicing through her, dissipated against her tortured flesh to flow around her body in an azure glow that trickled away into the air leaving behind a small trail of firefly sparks.

My sister's green eyes opened, wild, starting from her emaciated face. They seemed to widen and then to multiply, growing and glinting in the gloom like so many sparkling emeralds. An ever-changing pattern viewed through the end of a kaleidoscope, they formed and reformed, now spiralling, now advancing until they appeared the size of trenchers, now sinking to mere pinpricks as they retreated into the distant dark.

From my vantage point on the ledge it was disorientating enough. Closer to, on the temple floor, Priests and Initiates were collapsing one upon another, screaming and shielding their eyes against the unbearable brightness of the vision.

Fergael threw her hands across her face to ward off the pain and she screamed, a hollow piercing shriek pitched so as to puncture the illusion. The sound tore the eardrums and severed the thread of Ymer's concentration.

The emerald lights vanished, the eyes shrank back into their sockets and in that one single, heart-stopping moment my sister dropped her guard and became again a small childe at the mercy of a merciless monster.

Fergael needed no more than that single moment. Ripping the bowl from the mesmerised Scawthatch's hand, she raised her arm for the mighty slash that would rip through the jugular vein.

I leapt from the balcony, landing in a cat-crouch, and as I landed I screamed the witch's name and Fergael whirled towards me, killing knife still raised, and rushed at me with all the fury of a wolf let loose in a sheep-pen. In her mad eyes were the years of resentment that had been mounting steadily against me since I had first come to the Castle bringing with me the memory of my detested mother.

'My wish has been granted,' she howled. 'The Source has delivered the Redeemer into my hands.'

Then she was on me, teeth and nails clawing like a wild-cat, knife flailing in search of the opening that would allow her to rip out my gizzard. Even though she had the power to blast me where I stood, clearly she wanted to see my guts spilled, wanted physically to tear and hack. She needed my blood to satisfy her hatred of me, a hatred so strong that it stopped me dead in my tracks.

The ferocity of her attack forced me back and I defended myself as best I might, raising my unaccustomed weapon like a stave to ward off the torrent of blows.

Suddenly my foot caught against a votive bowl, dropped in haste by a retreating Initiate. I stumbled over it and fell awkwardly and the gun clattered from my hand, leaving me defenceless.

Fergael raised the great sickle-dagger above her head with both hands to ensure that the full force of her body would come into play when she drove the point through the folds of my gown and into my heart.

The Maxwell's cry was the only thing that saved me.

It came from the ledge where, until but a minute before, I had been standing myself. Now the Queen had taken my place, supported by a newly awakened Cameron. She had drawn herself up to her considerable height and, even in her mutilated state, the strength of her forceful personality dominated the whole room.

'Drop the knife,' she commanded.

And Fergael, back arched like a bending bow, looked for one moment as though she might obey. Then the years of suppressed hate and rejected ambition sprang to the surface overcoming any remaining feelings of duty and she screeched her defiance at the Warlord of the Clans.

'Who are you,' she shrieked. 'To tell me yea or nay? You half-creature. You love-sick ninny. You . . .'

The words stuck in her throat, cut off by the knife haft that had appeared, as if by magick, in the hollow beneath her scrawny neck.

Cameron, outraged at the Priest's blasphemies, had snatched the skean-dhu from her sock and sent it homing with all her force and deadly accuracy, into the witch's voice-box.

Fergael took a step back, dropping one knife and clutching at the other. With superhuman strength she tore it from her gullet and held its dripping blade up towards the huge statue that was The Source.

Her howl of supplication was drowned in the blood bubbling from her throat as she swayed for a moment in the long shadow of her God.

Everything else passed in a blur. One moment Fergael was lunging at Ymer, the next I had grabbed the rifle, pointed the hollow end at the witch and pulled back the curved bit of metal which I have since remembered is called the trigger. There was a deafening noise and a great burst of flame shot from the end of the machine and Fergael was lifted up and back as though by an unseen hand. She smashed against the great statue, blood spurting from a hundred holes in her body.

The Source shifted and shuddered on it's plinth, hesitated for a moment, then toppled forward. Fergael raised the skean-dhu upwards in a pathetic effort to protect herself, but the gesture was a futile one. The blade of the knife slashing through the billowing blue skirt afforded me one brief glance of a huge, erect phallus as the statue collapsed, crushing the black hag of Alba to the floor.

THE TRUE CHRONICLES OF THE REDEEMER

And the Maxwell discovered the true identity of The Redeemer and told of the Truth and the Way. And Rolande was offered the chance to become woman and to reign in the Maxwell's stead. But the Childe chose not to choose, preferring instead to take the central path.

Chapter
28

THE MAXWELL HAD YMER UNBOUND, WHAT WAS LEFT OF HER, and taken back to the Royal bedchamber. I would have taken her myself but the Queen forbade it.

'You and I maun talk,' she said and then, when Cameron objected. 'I have nothing to fear from Rolande. What must be said is for this Childe's ears alone. Your duty is to see Ymer safely to my rooms, Morangy's to make her well.'

She touched Ymer's dark head, the touch of a mother to a much-loved childe. It was the first affectionate gesture I had ever seen her use and my sister smiled a wan smile before sinking back into her stupor.

Two Initiates did the carrying, on a makeshift litter made from the Queen's own plaid, with Cameron striding in front and Morangy bringing up the rear, skean-dhu at the ready to ensure that no harm should be offered my sister on the way. Then the rest of the Priests were rounded up and sent after and I found myself alone in the Dark Tower facing the great Chieftain of Alba.

She sat awkwardly athwart the granite altar stone where Cameron and I had set her after manoeuvring her, not without difficulty, down from the ledge. I could have dispatched her there and then, with a single burst from the rifle which I still held, cradled in the crook of my left arm. But something stayed my hand. Curiosity. The look in her eyes. The feeling that what she had to say was of immense importance.

'I know all about you, Rolande,' she said, and my face flushed red, like a small childe caught with a hand in a biscuit barrel.

'Cameron?' I asked and she nodded, patting the altar beside her, indicating that I should sit.

I hesitated for a moment. I don't know what I expected in my long awaited confrontation with the Maxwell. Anger. Resentment. Horror. Disgust. Certainly not this meek acceptance of the status quo. Were there to be no recriminations, no challenges, nothing? Discomfited I made my way to where she sat, stepping around the great fallen statue, almost tripping over Fergael's bloodied hand which protruded from beneath the golden head like a mutilated spider.

The Maxwell took my hand in hers and began to speak, holding my attention, not only with the captivating quality of her personality, but with the content of the tale she had to tell.

'This is not how I had expected it would be,' she began. 'I had hoped to be able to rejoice in your arrival, to guard your growing, to prepare you for the Monarchy as I myself was prepared. But no matter. In the end it all comes to the same conclusion.'

I must have looked as astonished as I felt for the Queen actually laughed. A dry laugh to be sure. But a laugh for all that.

'Fergael was right after all,' she said, indicating the broken hand. 'She was certain that it was The Chosen who was expected that hard winter so many moons ago. All the portents spoke of it. The darkness over the Sun. The new star above Ballater. And the bones. The Castle stank with the smell of sacrificial blood that season. So many lives lost in vain it seemed at the time. The childe was a girl after all. Ymer. Fergael was furious. I was desolate. The most important life lost had been that of your beloved mother. And for what? Alba still had no heir. Or so we believed.' She looked at me slyly. 'Morangy has a lot to answer for,' she said.

'He saved my life.' I could not let this go by unchallenged. 'I am an eveling. A hermaphrodite.'

'And I,' said the Queen. 'As all the Maxwells have been since "the fall".'

This was too much for me. The Maxwell was a woman. I knew. I had seen her often enough at her bath. I made to protest, but she held her fingers up to my lips and continued.

'Mark me, Rolande, and listen well, the tale is long and there is little time for the telling. The enemy is at the gates and you must make the choice. When you know the truth I am confident you will choose wisely . . .

'Once upon a time, the world was ruled by men. It was a place of wonders then. The species had progressed to the point where it could fly like the eagle and negotiate the depths of the ocean like the legendary leviathan. The populace lived in huge cities whose buildings were so tall they would make even the Dark Tower pale into insignificance. There were machines which enabled people to speak to each other over great distances and magic boxes which brought storytellers and circuses to every hearth. And yet this world was not a happy place but filled end to end with disharmony and strife. For instead of using these great and wonderful inventions for the good of all, men chose instead to make war, building weapons of the kind you hold in your hand, to kill and maim each other. At the last they constructed a doomsday machine which killed whole nations at a blow and poisoned the skies South of Alba so that nothing normal could live there. And the Great Mother punished such wickedness by sending a plague which killed many more who had survived the poison-winds and those poor remnants remaining had no leader or purpose in life but to squabble amongst each other for the food and shelter that was left.

'Then rose the first Maxwell, a hermaphrodite from whose likeness the statue of the Source was carved. And that Maxwell pulled the threads of what was left of Alba into one coherent skein and weighing life in the balance, and seeing that all the world's sorrows were man-made and that poison lurked within, had the man part cut away and became woman and ruled as woman. This is the choice. And each Maxwell since that time has made the same decision. We have all become women in truth.

'So now the choice is yours, Rolande.'

She told me then of the Great Lie, how it had been devised and orchestrated by that first Maxwell to break the ancient bonds of servitude and give the women of Alba a strength and belief in their own superiority.

She told me too that all the Maxwells had been sterile and so, unable to reproduce their own kind, had had to wait until another freak was born naturally. Nature usually threw up a hermaphrodite once in every hundred years or so.

'You talk of the evil in men,' I said, bitterly. 'You, who to retain your longevity, bathe in the blood of slaughtered Priests (here I pointed to the great vat which still foamed and bubbled hard by the fallen idol). Yours is a dynasty more steeped in gore than any you have replaced.'

'Not so.'

'Then what of the thirteen who disappear every decade?' I demanded, hotly.

'Ritual suicide. It is in their vows. And each one knows before she binds herself to the Great Mother that if the Mother's representative is not re-born in their span they will be required to offer up the ultimate sacrifice – themselves – in supplication for the Source's re-incarnation.' She looked at me accusingly. 'So you see, Rolande, you might have spared the last batch. Had you not chosen to live a life of deception and lies, had they but known that the Chosen had risen again, they need not have died at all. Their blood is on your hands – not on mine.'

The blow struck home. Guilt for all the half-truths I had ever told, for all those who had suffered and died for me, from the repulsive Corbie to my own beloved Euan-Noag, surged through me, turning like a knife in my guts. Then I remembered who had been responsible for my mentor's death and anger replaced remorse. I leapt from the altar and stood, straddle-legged, facing the Maxwell in challenge.

'I don't believe you,' I yelled. 'You are lying to bring me to your way of thinking because your plans have gone sorely aglay. You thought to take me, a twinned being, and raise me in the woman's way, so that when the time came, I would think like a woman and this "choice", as you call it, would be a foregone conclusion. But I have not been raised so. Thanks to the man you murdered I have seen the other side of the coin. I know first hand the iniquities perpetrated by this regime. The Backshi death, the castrations, the death-dishes, the camps. And I reject them. For I am man as well as woman. Two halves of the whole. And I will stay so. I will not make the choice.'

'You must.' For the first time the Maxwell began to look flustered. 'There is no other way.'

'There is,' I said, waving the gun at her. 'I could blow your head off any time I choose. Rid the world of you and your kind once and for all.'

'Rolande.' The Maxwell struggled up, grabbing my arm for support. The gun barrel pressed against her stomach. The slightest movement from me and her insides would decorate the walls of the Dark Tower. She knew it. Yet no fear showed in her eyes. Only concern. 'Think of Alba,' she said. 'The land which bore you. I have served this country all my life. I have lived for it. Now it is my turn to die for it.'

'You should have died long ago,' I spat. 'You unnatural thing. You and your tall tales of a suicide pact. Without the blood of Priests to bathe in you would not be alive at all, let alone still so young and fair.'

The Queen looked down at her single limb and gave a harsh laugh.

'So fair? You jest. I am a thing now. Half a thing. That is why you must choose. Alba needs a Leader – a strong leader – to hold her together in this time of crisis. In the name of the Mother, Rolande. The country itself is a female. She has need of you.'

'I am a Healer. I will not bathe in the blood of others. If that is what Alba needs to survive then she can go hang. She is not worth protecting.'

The Maxwell sighed. 'The longevity thing has nothing to do with blood,' she said. 'It comes with the genes. You too will live to be old like me, Rolande. And like me you will grow tired of life, pray for the day when a successor comes to relieve you of the burden of responsibility – the thanklessness of rule. I have many lives on my conscience. Your dear mother was one of the few people who could relieve me of the black moods which accompany that knowledge. Many lives. Not least that of my predecessor.'

'So you think I will kill you to take power?' I snarled. 'Well you think wrong. I will take power anyway. And I will keep you in a cage, like a breed-beast (here she flinched as though I had struck her) for the world to jeer at and mock. There are worse things than death, Lady, as any freak in your kingdom could tell you.'

I flung her from me, hating myself as I did so, hating her more for what she was doing to me. She landed in a heap, striking her head on the Source's outstretched arm, and lay there stunned by the blow.

I went to her then and eased her up, ashamed at the ferocity of my reactions. How could I hope to keep the male element of the populace in check, appeal to their sense of justice and fair play, persuade them to be magnanimous in victory, if I could not control my own baser emotions?

For a moment I was tempted by the Maxwell's so-called choice. As a woman I could still control the world. As a woman, free of the aggressions induced by my male hormones, might I not right the wrongs perpetrated by the preceding Maxwells and restore balance to the community anyway?

I raised the Queen gently, wrapping my arms around her and placing her, lengthways, on the altar. The wound in her groin had begun to seep matter and so I untucked my skirts, tearing strips from the folds of my gown, wadging them against the raw stump to staunch the flow. It would have been better to let her die so, from loss of blood, but Morangy's lessons and the oath I had taken as a Healer would not allow me such an easy solution.

She looked up at me, eyes pain-clouded, and she must have seen the indecision in mine for she pressed home her advantage, threading her fingers into my hair and pulling my face down to hers.

'A Maxwell cannot die, Rolande,' she said. 'Barring accident and murder, we are immortal. Free me from this life of pain, I beg you.'

I shook my head. 'I cannot,' I said.

'You must. There is only one way to send me to the Great Mother, a way which reverses the longevity process.'

'What way?'

I was curious despite myself. As a hermaphrodite I had a vested interest in the knowledge. Besides, the closeness of her body, the sweetness of her breath, was producing a reaction in me which I regretted, but was unable to control.

'The antidote to everlasting life is found in the male sperm,' she said. 'The ceremony is simple. You must rape me, Rolande. Thus the ritual begins. The sperm reverses the process and, permeating the organism, brings about almost instant death. I abdicate. You assume the rank and titles of the Maxwell. The dynasty goes on.'

'And the castration?'

'A natural progression. Rape is the male prerogative. It will be your last act as a savage. Afterwards you will have the offending organs removed. The Fergael performs the ceremony.' She looked down at what was left of the High Priest. 'Ymer is the new Fergael. She is privy to the mysteries. Only the Maxwell and the Fergael in all of Alba know the truths that I have revealed to you today. Ymer will do her duty as is expected, when she recovers her strength. Only begin the ritual now. I am tired, Rolande. I am ready to die.'

263

Heaven help me, in that moment I wanted to take her. There was something titillating about her helplessness, her subjugation. The great Maxwell, at my mercy. I could easily have done the deed and afterwards kept my balls intact.

'You think you could, but in the end you will not,' said the Maxwell, reading my thoughts. 'The act in itself produces such feelings of self-loathing that you will be glad to submit to the knife. It will go some way to expiating the guilt. But it will not erase it all. For the rest of your life – and it may be a long one – you will find your feelings altered towards the male of the species, because you will know, first hand, the depravity of which they are capable.'

As she spoke these last words she began to stroke me, coaxing my incipient erection into throbbing life. I had forgotten everything. McCloed, Ymer, Colluden, The Revolution. My life was full of this woman, her red-gold halo of hair, her provocative mouth, her mesmeric eyes, her soft, insistent, stroking hands.

A moment later I would have taken her.

And then my head was full of shouting and clamour. Cameron had returned. She leapt from the ledge, sword clashing against shield as she shouted aloud the battle-cry of her clan.

'Get awa frae her, you murdering freak,' she howled, coming at me with all the fury of a Ben-Shi in heat.

I whirled and caught the Guard Captain a blow to the side of the head with the M15. It had all the power of my frustrated sex drive in it and, big though she was, it floored her. Her knees buckled and she fell forward, eyes rolling up in her head, and I scrabbled up the dangling rope ladder and flung myself into the secret passage with the Maxwell's supplications still ringing in my ears.

264

THE TRUE CHRONICLES OF THE REDEEMER

Then The Redeemer loosed the Breed-Beasts and took the magick fire-stick and opened the gates of Castle Ballater to the Wildemen and the Evelings. And when the final Battle was fought and won — Childe Rolande to the Dark Tower came.

Chapter *29*

I WENT DOWN THOSE SPIRALS FASTER THAN A FART AT A BEAN-feast and through the fire door in double quick time, scraping lumps off myself and what was left of my gown as I shoved my way past the packing-cases in the pitch black. My language was as bad as anything Morangy had come out with on the way through, particularly since I fell a couple of times on the stairs up to the Castle, grazing my knees and, at one point, dropping my rifle. It clattered all the way back down and I was forced to half jump, half slither to the very bottom and grope around in the dark, putting my hand on things I'd rather not remember, before I found it and could clamber up again.

If I hadnae been so fit and in such a state of high arousal I'd doubtless have destroyed myself. As it was, hammering on the reverse side of the secret door for somebody to let me out, I silently thanked the ancient inventor Nautilus, without whose machines I wouldnae have been in sufficiently good nick to put up with all this aggravation.

Morangy took forever to let me through and he got the sharp end of my tongue when I eventually burst into the Royal bedchamber, dustcovered and bloodied from my ordeal.

Needless to say, he wasn't the least bit fashed by my fury.

'Oh aye,' he said. 'As if I hadnae enough trouble reaching the damn mechanism, moving tables and hoisting chairs and taking my life in my hands balancing on the both, now I have to put up with abuse too.'

I snorted and told him to forget it but he wouldnae let it lie.

'Less of your language if you don't mind,' he said. 'There's a Lady present. Two – if you count yersel.'

266

'How is she?' I asked, giving thought for the first time to my sister, who lay tucked up snug in the antlered bed.

'Well enough considering,' said Morangy. 'Sleeping as you can see. Best thing for her.'

As my heart-beat stopped pounding in my ears and my breathing started to return to normal, I became conscious of the battle-sounds filtering through the granite walls; shouting and screaming and the clash of weapons, noises I had latterly come to know so well. In my mind's eye I could just picture the Wilde-men, trapped at the bottom of Ballater Brae, struggling against superior odds. McCloed would be to the fore no doubt, wearing the white wolf-skin that was his battle garb and swathing rings round him with the huge double-edged claymore that nobody but him could lift.

I grabbed Morangy by the crook of his elbow and he winced but didn't pull away.

'Have you your keys?' I demanded.

'Haven't I always?' he said, aye one to answer a question with a question and he fished in his sporran to produce the great round ring.

'Lock Ymer in,' I told him. 'She'll be safe enough for now. Then get off downstairs and loose the breed-beasts. I want you to take them to the armoury, give them whatever weapons you can grab and have them round at the Keep as fast as maybe. McCloed's expecting us to open the gates for him.'

I started tearing off the remnants of my robe – it was in tatters and would only hinder me.

'You're no going outwith the house like that?' Morangy stared at me in disbelief as I reached up to grab the slug-horn on the wall.

I had intended to wrap myself in the Maxwell's discarded plaid, the one they had used to transport Ymer from the Tower, but now I kicked off my underbreeks too. Morangy's reaction had given me an idea. I had none of my battle accoutrements to hand to give me presence. No armour, no Susuki to distinguish me as The Redeemer. What better way to identify myself than to flaunt my dual sexuality for all the world to see?

'Why not?' I said, grinning. 'With a bit of luck I might scare half of them to death.'

'Catch your own death, more like,' snorted Morangy. 'Going out bare-assed in this weather. You need your head examined. The wind out there is enough to cut you in half.'

McCloed's Account of the Battle

It wasnae going just great, ken? Small wonder. We were fighting uphill against a load of hard-cases from the bogs, instead of the Castle softies we were used tae tackling. These were country kwine battling for their steadings as much as their lives and, leaderless though they might be, making a canny stab at it.

We'd had the element o' surprise on the field in previous encounters not to speak of Colluden tae oversee us and give us a bittie inspiration. You might say we were as leaderless as them. Naebody to show off for. The Redeemer hadnae put in an appearance – might be dead (perish the thought) – for all any o' us kenned. The gates werenae opened that's for sure and rumours were going round that we'd been sold short. All in all morale wasnae all that high.

We'd started well mind you, in a great rush that had knocked the kwines back up the hill. Our front ranks were strong and well held taegether and the War-Dogs went through the opposition like a dose o' salts. Kwines are afeart of dogs as a rule. We'd kept the animals hungry on the march to make them more ferocious, but that was a mistake in the end. The beasties were wild enough to begin wi' but as soon as they'd ripped off the odd arm and leg, they settled down to eat and there wasnae a thing Cuchullain could do to get them parted frae their vittels.

In back o' the regular Clutches we had more of a mob than an army. Some o' the Castrati would hae burst into tears at a hard word let alone a blow and the freaks from the camp break-out were mostly too weak to do much more than spook the kwines who, for the most part, hadnae seen athing like them.

I did what I could to hold this clatter of humanity together, and McCann and One-Eye and the other Clutch Leaders who'd given their word to Colluden to back the Redeemer tore into the fighting like lilties. But I could feel the tide going against us and we were being forced back, slow but sure, when the sound of the Slug-horn broke over the valley.

I looked up and there was Rolande, standing on the battlements naked as a skinned jackrat, holding some kind of green stick up in the air. I didnae ken where to put my face wi the shame of it. Breasts and balls and white skin for all to see and that long, blonde hair blowing out behind like a banner in the wind.

*

And what a wind it was. Soughing down from the North East bringing on its breath the snowchill of early Winter. Morangy was right. It was freezing. I could hardly keep my teeth from chattering. And though going naked was a deliberate ploy on my part to exploit the shock value of my twin-sexed body, I could feel my balls retract and my penis wither in the icy blast to the point where I felt they might disappear up into my pubic hair and negate the entire exercise.

After the horn-blast the fighting halted down in the valley and all eyes turned to the battlements as I had intended. There is a picture in one of Euan-Noag's books which used to fascinate me when I was a bairn. It is by someone called Heironymous Bosch. The Garden of Delights I think it was called. Whatever . . . looking down on the scene below, evelings, women and Wildemen locked together in that dance of death which is so akin to copulation, I could not but help be reminded of that strange and powerful painting. Right in the centre of this cross-section of Albian society stood McCloed, claymore halted in mid-swing, white wolf-skin bloodied and sweatslicked as his matted hair. And suddenly I felt as though I ruled the world. McCloed was alive and I didn't feel cold any more. Hot blood sang through my veins. Flinging the slug-horn from me I raised the rifle over my head and shouted aloud over the silent valley.

'Fergeal is dead. The Maxwell is sorely wounded and no longer fit to rule. I call on all Clanswomen to put down their weapons and surrender. I claim Castle Ballater in the name of The Redeemer.'

It was an outrageous bluff of course. I was right in the middle of enemy territory with not a soul at my back. I had used the element of surprise to force my way out onto the battlements. Those women defending Ballater from within, Fergeal's few Priests and what remained of the depleted Palace Guard, had drawn back in awe and revulsion from the reality of my naked form.

But this was more than even they were willing to put up with. A buzz of dissent swept through the cluster of women, rising to a howl of anger. One of the company, and here I recognized Cameron's second-in-command – Fitzgerald – plucked up the courage to fling a challenge in my direction.

'Come on, freak,' she yelled, 'do your worst,' and she made a wild lunge at me, battle-axe raised to cleave me in twain.

I didn't want to kill her. I have always hated killing – even as a necessary means to an end – but I made a cold-blooded decision then.

The greatest good for the greatest number. I would make an example of this – the bravest and the best of the Clanswomen – to discourage the others. One death might save much bloodshed. It was worth a try. I lowered the M15 and shot the advancing soldier in the chest.

The bullets hit her at point blank range, tearing chunks from her body, splattering the women coming up behind with gobbets of gore and flesh.

As for the noise . . . it smote the eardrums like the death of an era, heralding the beginning of the end for the long reign of the Maxwells.

McCloed's Account of the Battle

I ken what they are now, these fire-weapons, but at the time I'd never seen the like. It was magick tae me . . . and tae those round me.

One moment Rolande was in danger of being torn apart by that band of harpies, and me thinking 'shite' for I couldnae get up there in time, and then – wallop – this great gobful of flames comes out of this stick-thing and the leading kwine just falls to bits in front of our eyes.

Then the rest of them started to greet and flee, flinging themselves off the battlements even to get away from the fire-thrower. And the panic spread to those kwine on the brae so that they lost all sense entirely. Some of them started to fight like mad-things to get themselves away frae The Redeemer while others scrabbled up the hill trying to batter their way into the Castle to get away frae us.

Our lot sensed victory then. A great cheer went up and we started to make mincemeat of the lot of them, hacking our way up the hill, squashing the kwine between us and the Castle walls.

The ones who reached the gates fared worst. We were

nearly upon them when the gates opened and it seemed like they'd escape after all. But it wasnae their salvation that came galloping out. It was their doom. Rolande on a white horse at the head of a clatter of loons. Big well-set up lads they were, well-fed and sleekit as mountain-cats. And they surged down the brae wi' a great roar, like a flood-tide that's broken through a dam, and we caught the women in the middle so they had nowhere left to run.

As Morangy said later . . . 'After that, it was all over bar the shouting.'

THE TRUE CHRONICLES OF THE REDEEMER

And the Maxwell became whole and challenged The Redeemer to the final conflict. And they fought from sun-down to sun-rise for three cycles of the moon. And great was the carnage.

Chapter
30

IT IS HARD TO CALL A HALT ONCE THE KILLING HAS BEGUN. EVEN yet my dreams are troubled by my remembrance of it. There must be those who can unleash the Morrigan of War and be untouched by the result. I am not one of them. Each individual death is on my conscience. Some more than others. The wifey from Carnoustie whose bread I had shared at the campfire, trampled under my horse's hooves. The young kwine, scarce past her first bleeding, torn limb from limb before me by a pack of vengeful evelings. The expression on her face as she disappeared under that mound of mishapen humanity will never leave me.

As a childe I had often wondered about the Maxwell's attacks, why, on her bad days, she locked herself away from the light and the entire court was forced go about on tippy-toes in order not to disturb her.

I wonder no more.

In my brief time in office I already have more lives on my hands than I dare to contemplate. And the Maxwell had lived many lives before I was born.

Once the wheels are set in motion then, it is almost impossible to halt the momentum. So I found that afternoon on the slopes of Ballater Brae. By the death of the day, scarcely a field surrounding the battleground that hadnae been washed in the blood of some poor spirit.

As I look out now over the same peaceful valley, with the same sun setting as it did then, painting the patchwork squares carmine, staining the rock-walls scarlet in reflection of the skies, I am reminded how they were streaked with real gore in the aftermath of that terrible battle.

We will have a fruitful harvest in this, the first year of the Redeemer's reign.

A powerful omen.

But then blood makes powerful fertiliser.

And out of death comes life . . . as I was to find most particularly during that crimson dusk. For the night was but a pup and I still had one more hurdle to cross.

It came in the form of the Lady Maxwell, Ruler of all the Territories and the Isles Beyond, Warlord of the Clans, High Queen of Alba. One moment the skyline was empty, nothing but a succession of inanimate castellations, etched on the wine-dark clouds. Next the Queen was there, stark against the sunset, calling a halt to the carnage, challenging The Redeemer to a final dual which would decide the Fate of the country once and for all.

In that instant I felt like a childe again, my future in this woman's hands. Never had she seemed more regal, bronze battle-armour glowing like liquid fire in the last arc of the dying sun, red-gold hair teased by the wind into molten wires about her face. A great swirl of the Maxwell plaid billowed back from her shoulders in eddies of scarlet and blue and she clutched in her hands the double-edged sword which she had so lately lent me to shield myself from the machinations of Fergael.

At her back and standing slightly to the left, Cameron kept watch on her mistress, mutilated stump bandaged flat to her chest so as not to impede the movement of her sword-arm.

But the Maxwell was without injury, no vestige remaining of the amputation that had disfigured her at our last meeting. This was the Maxwell as I had always known her. Tall, upright, her fine legs, bare under her short fighting-kilt, untouched by the knife.

A miracle.

Fergael's foul concoction had worked as she believed it would. Even in death the witch had had the last laugh.

I found out later that the Maxwell's plan had been to use the High Priest's blood, the last dark ingredient needed to make the spell work. The hag was there, already dead, in the Dark Tower. Waste not want not. But the two women together, hampered as they were by their lost limbs, could not move the huge bulk of the Source from off the witch's crushed body.

Cameron offered to fall on her sword, to sacrifice herself

so that the Queen might be made whole, but, to her eternal credit, the Maxwell would have none of it.

So it was Scawthatch's blood they used. Scawthatch, who had crept back to the Inner Sanctum to retrieve her lover's remains. Cameron slit her scrawny throat and tossed her in the vat and it was her life blood which washed the Maxwell's body, regenerating the stump of her leg so that it grew anew, like a docked lizard's tail or the ring which binds a worm's broken body after it has been stepped upon.

Whatever potions had been added to the vat – and the magick formula has been lost with Fergael's death – the Maxwell rose from the mixture whole, ready to defend her kingdom against the usurper that was me. In refusing 'the choice' I had made of her the bitterest enemy. In her eyes I was no more fit to rule Alba than the scurviest member of a death-camp and she roared her challenge down the valley daring me to prove her wrong in hand-to-hand combat.

McCloed wanted me to shoot her on the spot. 'Kill the bitch and be done with it' was the gist of his argument. But I knew that I had to live with myself afterwards and so I handed him the rifle with instructions that he wasnae to use it under any circumstances, and I called for a helmet and sword.

Enfidion and Susuki were brought from a farmcart at the edge of the killing-fields where they had been secreted, under the watchful eye of Sanke, ever since the Wildemen had arrived. In place of my bright armour, which was altogether too complicated to buckle on at this juncture, an ill-fitting goatskin was hastily stripped from a fallen comrade and wrapped round my waist. McCann handed me my shield and I was ready. Or as ready as I would ever be. I climbed to the battlements, with McCloed acting as my second and faced the Maxwell as I had done so many times in mock battles before.

This one began as they had always done, with the ritual salute, then I took a last look down into the valley, at the sea of upturned faces. And I thought of what most of their lives would be worth if I lost this, the ultimate fight, and I spat on my hands and resolved to sell my own life dear in defence of theirs.

Then the Maxwell was upon me and there was no more time for such esoteric niceties for I was fighting for my life in truth against an adversary with all the strength and cunning of many lifetimes behind her. She had the advantage of weight and height too, always had done in our play-battles of old. It was left to me to be the quicksilver one whole nimble toes could whisk my slighter body out of harm's way.

But today was a stag of a different colour. I had a long battle behind me. I was tired already, while the Maxwell was fresh, rested, fired with unnatural forces the like of which I had never before faced.

I could hear McCloed shouting for me to 'keep my guard up' and then the Queen was beating me back easily, forcing me across the ramparts with blows of such incredible intensity that, had one of them connected, I would have been cloven from stem to stern. An unnatural silence overhung Ballater so that our weapons, clashing one upon another, echoed and re-echoed around the upended bowl of the valley like the noise of two great dragons clashing their teeth at the sky.

I suddenly found myself with my back against the wall, unable to retreat further. The Queen made a great lunge at my throat which I managed to side-step just in time, arching away from the lethal blade-point which clanged against the granite sending a shower of mica glinting off in all directions.

The Queen recovered almost instantly, turning to face me so that we resumed our pattern of thrust, parry and thrust, retracing our steps back along the long length of the parapet.

The sky was almost dark now. A crescent moon had risen but it shed little light and, as the shadows lengthened, I heard Cameron call out for torches to be brought so that we could 'see our hands in front of us'. The wind had died somewhat but it still sang sadly through the stone, punctuating our rasping breaths like a woman greeting for a dead childe. And time and space merged into one so that it seemed the Queen, my mother, and I fought alone on a high mountain that stood at the top of the world and nothing existed but the blur of the flickering torches and the wind's keening and our grunts of effort as we gave or parried blows.

So we fought and after a while I began to get the measure of her, to pace myself, so that the pain in my arms and across the back of my shoulders settled into a dull ache. On and on we continued, while the stars came and went and until the pale duck-egg streaks of the morning began to lighten the sky.

The sunrise found us weak-kneed and light-headed, still clashing away at each other, although by now only one blow in ten was connecting.

Down below many of the watchers had fallen asleep where

they stood, dead and living huddled together, too tired to know, or care, what their future fate might be.

The sun rose hot on my head so that, inside Susuki I found it more and more difficult to breathe. Transferring Enfidion to my right hand (I am what Cameron calls a Southpaw), I tore the helmet from me and flung it aside. From the corner of my eye I saw McCloed retrieve it. He and Cameron were standing side by side now, like old comrades after a night's drinking, senses dulled by the seemingly never-ending succession of blows and counter-blows as first the Queen, then myself, gained the advantage. We were too well matched altogether and the fight might have gone on til Doomsday, but as I took my helmet off, my long hair fell across my shoulders and I noticed the Queen's expression change. Her face took on a pinched quality and it seemed as though she was trying to fight without actually looking me in the eye, concentrating instead on an area somewhere in the region of my Adam's apple. And it came to me quite suddenly that every time she aimed a blow at my head, she was seeing in me my mother, the one person that she had ever truly loved.

I grasped the psychological advantage for the straw that it was, playing it for all that it was worth. I knew that I could not last much longer before, like the sleepers in the valley, I dropped in my tracks from sheer fatigue. So I began to dip and weave, making her look at me, forcing her to focus on my face, crooning to her as my mother would have crooned, as Ymer had done in her impersonations of me, speaking to her words of love rather than hate.

Her eyes began to waver, at one point tears began to well in them and I saw, struggling to get out, that echo of uncertainty that heralded the black moods which could tip her so easily into the depths of despair.

I began to push home my advantage, driving her backwards. I would have had her too but Cameron put her spoke in reminding the Queen that I was a renegade traitor. And the Maxwell rallied, shaking the mood away, dredging a last burst of determination from somewhere in the centre of herself. With a final desperate effort she drove me to the edge of the battlements, up the short flight of stairs to the watchtower, the highest point on that great high bulk overlooking not only the steep slope of Ballater to the North but also the sheer South-facing drop down walls and cliff-face to a gorge bottomed by a tumble of jagged rocks.

It wasn't until I felt the draught on my back that I realised that she had led me, like a lamb to the slaughter, to the gap in the tower where defenders were wont to pour molten tar onto the heads of adversaries foolish enough to try to scale the walls. Behind me was empty air, before me death in bronze armour.

I have never been good with heights. The moment I glanced over my shoulder I realised I'd made a mistake. My head began to swim and I reached out to steady myself, dropping my shield. The Queen seized the moment, bringing her sword down in a mighty side-sweep which chopped Enfidion from my grasp. The weapon fell, end over end, sparkling in the sunlight and landed with a hollow clang on the rocks beneath.

The Lady Maxwell knew she had me. She savoured the moment, taking her time.

'You have been a noble adversary, Rolande,' she said. 'And you have taught me a lesson that I shall not long forget. Never trust anyone.'

She placed her sword-point against my throat and forced me backwards until my back felt taut as a bowstring ready to snap. My eyes blurred and my vertigo returned spinning my senses so that I thought I was hallucinating when I saw Ymer appear at the Maxwell's back.

'Mother,' she screamed.

And the Queen straightened as though stung and half spun towards her daughter and I dived for the safety of the central ground away from that terrible drop, and in doing so I caught the Maxwell a blow in the shins with my shoulder so that she, already off balance, wavered and fell forward, over me and out through the cleft in the battlements.

Her body curved in an arc as Enfidion had done, turning over and over as her long scream filled the valley. Then she landed face down on the granite slabs with that sickening sound of bones breaking through skin the like of which there is no other. Then silence.

She was still alive when we reached her . . . but only just. Ymer and I raised her broken head and she smiled up as if to say she bore no grudge.

'The Maxwell is dead,' she said. 'Long live the Maxwell.'

Then she died. And Ymer began to wail. And Cameron lost her temper, beating back the awe-struck bystanders who were beginning to gather, telling them to 'get the blazes oot o' it and gi' the lassies room'.

And suddenly blood began to gush from between my legs and I leant across the body of the Queen and was violently sick, and just before I fainted, I felt McCloed scoop me up and carry me back to the sanctuary of the castle.

It was morning sickness – the first time I took it – though not the last. And exhuastion. And relief. For now it really was all over. And we had won . . . whatever that means.

Morangy managed to stop the bleeding – so the childe was saved – but we will not know until it is born whether it was damaged in the fight. I think not. Fanciful perhaps but I feel that the spirit of the Maxwell, loosed at the moment of her death, may have found refuge in the body of my unborn childe and that when I look into it's eyes, I may find some recognition there.

One interesting footnote. When Morangy stripped the Maxwell of her battle armour to prepare her body for the flames, he found that the leg was not the only thing that had regrown in Fergael's magickal vat.

And so the Maxwell died, as she had been born, a hermaphrodite – like me.

As for Fergael, her body disappeared that night, and there's never been hide nor hair of it found since.

The theory is that some of her Acolytes spirited it away, under cover of the battle, for burial in some sacred place.

But already the tales have started. Those old-wives tales the like of which I spoke right at the beginning of this overly protracted narrative. That the witch is not dead but risen and that when she returns it will be to give Alba back to it's rightful heirs – the women. Nonsense of course, as most such tales are, but I must stamp on them for they breed dissension and I am having enough trouble uniting the country as it is.

Nonsense.

And yet sometimes, when I wake in that bleak time before the dawn, with the night daemons on me and the childe stirring uneasily in my womb . . . I wonder.

THE TRUE CHRONICLES OF THE REDEEMER

And the Lovers were married. Rolande, McCloed and Ymer. These three. And the Greatest of these was The Redeemer. And intercourse was made good between the sexes and the name Eveling was stricken from the Book of Records to be replaced by the title Childe.

Epilogue

THE MAXWELL TOOK THE BLOOD-BATH BECAUSE I COULDN'T BE allowed to live. I knew about the Great Lie, didn't I? And she knew I would tell. She was right too. I have told, bellowing the knowledge the length and breadth of the land. Much good though it's done me.

Reactions were many and varied. Elation, and downright glee from the men. Horror, disbelief, distrust and despair from the women. Few took it calmly. Many refused to believe at all, counting it some kind of twisted propaganda conjured up from the lunatic mind of a pervert. That's what some of them are calling me now. The Pervert. Truly Fame is a double-edged sword.

It was when the suicides started, women burning themselves in the streets rather than face a world in which their dreams had been shattered, their God torn down and hurled in the mud, that I was forced to turn over this re-education process to Ymer. She and her Priests have had the unenviable task of making some sense of the remains of a shattered religion, while reconciling their sisters to the new realities. Because of the difficulty, I might say impossibility, of this task, I have allowed her to retain a purely female Priesthood. Alba is not yet ready for male priests and the last thing we need is a Holy war on our hands.

The thing that distresses me most is the people's attitude to me. I have always been popular with the masses – the Silver-tongued Childe, the Healer, the Queen's Favourite, The Redeemer. Now, in this position of supreme power, I am considered to be no more than a freak. I thought that, when my true sexuality was revealed, both sides would identify with me.

Instead, neither does. Just as well that in my growing years I did not have to deal with such an identity crisis. I was always, except in my bouts of love-play with Ymer, one thing at a time. No-one thought of me as a wierdo. Now, when apparently everyone does, I am forced to appear in public, my belly swollen as proof of my strangeness, and face a horde of gawpers the large majority of whom view me at best as an oddity, at worst, an excrescence. All this when my emotions are already imbalanced by the mothering hormones which flood my body. Is it any wonder I am aye bursting into tears? I doubt I'd hae survived this past trimester if it hadnae been for the stabilising influence of my husband – and my wife.

The three of us were wedded a decent period after the Maxwell's burning. We couldnae leave it too long because of the bairn. I was determined that the ceremony, coronation and triumverate nuptials combined, shouldn't deteriorate into some kind of three ring circus.

It was a decent day weatherwise, not great but without a wind to skin you at least. Watery sunlight picked out the first primroses among the heather as the three of us walked, link-armed, with me in the middle, through the arch of claymores formed by McCloed's Clutch and up into the Stone Circle. Ymer looked divine, McCloed magnificent. I struggled to look both and I fear, peaky from morning-sickness and bursting out of my battle armour, looked neither.

Luckily the vast congregation who had rolled up to see the event were too drunk or too far away to notice the difference. Assassination threats are a daily occurrence and the stone circle was ringed, for safety's sake, with a strong force made up of the newly formed Castle Guard. This polyglot mixture, consisting of the residue of the original Clanswomen supplemented by the breed-beasts and an occasional Wildeman, looked fearsome enough in their new dress uniforms of purple and plaid but they were an unruly bunch. Cameron commands them still and I do not envy her her job. She spends more time breaking up fights than anything else. In barracks the kwines and loons keep very much to their own territory so that one couple, who broke the unwritten rules and were caught fraternising after a drinking bout, were ostracised by both elements and had to be removed to one of the outposts to restore peace.

It is very much the same all over the country. Women are still suspicious of the thought, never mind the deed, of co-habiting with a member of the opposite sex while the men, revelling in their new-found freedom, tend to push their luck and end up alienating those who might, with a bit of coaxing, be persuaded to get used to the idea.

I have passed a law making intercourse among the sexes acceptable practice. But law and actuality are two different things. It is the children, those between birth and seven (or those like my own child, not yet born) who are Alba's hope now. We must trust that they find the 'new' way acceptable, enjoyable even. Otherwise the human race, as we know it, may die out altogether.

Meanwhile, we struggle on, Ymer directing the church, McCloed organising the army and me trying to make some sense of the overall picture.

McCloed has done a superb job. He is a born Leader as his father was before him, inspiring loyalty from both sides. There was a point when we thought we would have the same problem with the forces as with the Castle Guard. On my suggestion we have gone back to the Clan system and touch wood, so far, it is working remarkably well. At least men and women of the Gordon Highlanders have something in common. One of my better ideas, I think, but I doubt that I'll get any credit for it.

Heaven's defend us, that was a sharp one. Ever since I got out of bed this morning I've been getting these stabs in the back. It wouldnae surprise me if this time tomorrow, Alba has an heir, of whatever declension. Fingers, toes and eyes crossed that McCloed gets back in time for the birthing. He's on manoeuvres down near Dundee and is due home afore dark. He's been away a moon's-phase and I miss him. Bollocks to all this blabber about the birthing room being sacred to the mother. I've assisted enough birthings in my time to know it won't be an easy process. I reckon I'll be glad of all the help I can get. Just his hand to hold would be something. He's such an uncomplicated soul. So dependable, so sure of himself and the future.

Me? I'm no longer sure of athing. Not even that I'll live through the whole blasted experience. It's a barbarous carry-on really. Somebody should have invented a way round it by now. I just wish I might be left in peace to spawn in some quiet location then it wouldnae matter if the bairn turned out to be man, woman or childe. Instead the whole nation awaits the outcome of this lying in. Bets are being laid as far afield as John O'Groats and Edinburr as to the sex of the infant. I understand it's ten to one on a kwine, a score to one on a loon and fifty to one, if you please that it'll be something in between. So for the first time in living memory someone stands to gain something from the birth of a freak.

Not that there's such a thing any more – in theory. I've had both the words freak and eveling stricken from the Book of Records and replaced by Childe, which, in The Maxwell's reign used to denote anyone of Royal Blood. Neat, eh?

So I'm Childe Rolande. And Blossom and Isla and Sanke and Cilla and even Morangy are all my Children. I, who was reared by them, am now the Universal Mother and Father.

What a responsibility.

Is it any wonder I look back with nostalgia to the days of Euan-Noag and his travelling show before this all began?

Incidentally, I have created a Royal Troupe of Players, who entertain at banquets. It's an excuse to have my friends around me to tell the truth. Blossom is in charge. Not a very dignified position for Queen Mother, for such is her official title, but she's happy. I've promised her a dancing school, all of her own, when she becomes too old to perform, which may not be long now. Silver lights have begun to dapple her golden hair and only last evening, when she came to show me her latest prodigy, a three year old from one of the open camps in Stirling, she was complaining of pains in her joints.

Cilla and Sanke still have itchy feet. They have asked whether they might set up a travelling show for the Summer Seasons and I have given my permission and set aside a sum from the Royal coffers to facilitate them. They hae been holding auditions ever since McCloed went away (he thinks it's a load of nonsense) and the Castle has resounded with singing (some good, some not so good) and the lilt of music and laughter.

I'm cranky these days so I stay well out of it. I feel grotesque and find it wellnigh impossible to sleep. I've delegated the task of overseeing the final yea or nay to Ymer – as if she hadn't enough to do – and she seems to enjoy it fine. She tried to drag me into the Great Hall once or twice but I was too fatigued to take a deal of notice. Anyway, I make the applicants so nervous, they drop their balls or miss their notes or suddenly develop two left feet in my presence. That's another drawback to being "The Redeemer". Except for my immediate circle, and those Wildemen who have had me on my back in wrestling matches during Cullodan's days, everyone holds me in such awe.

285

It's nae natural.

And I canna believe a word most folk say. They tell me what they think I want to hear, not what's true. I have to rely on McCloed and Ymer to translate for me. Thank the Source for Morangy. He, at least, takes it upon himself to "Keep me in my place" and brings me the latest gossip – the more scurrilous the better – going the rounds about me. He's even making a collection of the scatalogical verses which are rife, concerning my sexual proclivities and how we three prongs of the triumverate marriage spend our free time. Most of it is pornographic, a lot of it hilariously so. The majority of it is physically impossible – especially in the shape I'm in now. Ymer howls with laughter at it. McCloed gets furious. Some of it makes me cross but Morangy says it's good for me, I'm trying to create a Democracy where everyone can speak freely am I not, and isn't it better to let folk blow off steam in so harmless a fashion than have them thinking it but saying naething (afraid to lose their tongues as they used to be in Fergael's time)?

Morangy is very chirpy altogether at the moment. He and Isla were wed last New Moon. Ymer performed the ceremony and Isla is to be our bairn's wet-nurse, since I doubt I'll hae time for such fashing, when the time comes. She's well suited to it wi' her three breasts. The more bizarre predictions say that my offspring may turn out to be the eagle, which is my supposed alter-ego. This has given rise to a family joke that the wain could be a gannet if it likes, it willnae go hungry with Isla suckling it.

It was the first time a pair of freaks – sorry, Children – have been joined in the Sacred Circle. Not counting us, of course. We three started what I hope will be a long tradition, with the triumverate marriage.

Ymer couldnae officiate at that one so Aillil was hastily made up to Deputy High Priest and Enroller of the Sacred Scrolls. It took her mind off Scawthatch, who was her natural sister, poor benighted kwine.

Just as well we had a good day for it. All the big Ceremonies, the Namings, the Couplings, the Burnings and the Celebration of the Four Quarters, have aye been held outside. Why, with a climate like Alba's I'll never know. I must speak to Ymer about translating some of them – particularly those held at Midwinter – to the Dark Tower. Since we don't seem to be able to demolish the damn place we may as well try to alter it's awesome reputation. Let in a bit of fresh air. Lay Fergael's ghost once and for all.

Another pain. Fergael's cold hand clutching me from her unknown grave?

I'd better stop. I'm becoming fanciful and that's only a step away from maudlin. Ymer will be here soon to rub my back with juniper oil. That should help some.

How beautiful she looked at the ceremony. White linen and black hair and red lips and green eyes. When they crowned her in mistletoe I could hardly keep my hands off her. McCloed either. Blossom had designed the costumes and she'd chosen to dress her son as a magnificent barbarian in a philibeg woven from the heather colours of his father's native Isle of Skye. His jacked was Harris tweed, blue as the distant hills and his cloak the full skin of a Sno-bear, its snarling mask curled over one shoulder like a warning and one large paw was fashioned into the sporran from which he produced the three rings of beaten gold that were to join us in unholy matrimony. His auburn hair had been washed and curled (much to his disgust), his beard had been trimmed and, instead of mistletoe, they crowned him with laurel, fitting for a general of such strength and reputation.

I, of course, wore the golden battle armour of 'The Redeemer', codpiece, breastplate and all. But when I removed Susuki, it was the antlered crown of the Maxwells, studded with topaz and cairngorms, which they placed on my braided hair. The old and the new combined. I hope the significance of it was not lost on the audience. We raised a round of applause at least.

People love a good ceremony – even one as bizarre as this one undoubtedly was – and the Wildemen, mostly half-cut on homebrew, started the chant which followed us out of the Circle and all the way back to Ballater.

'Long live the Redeemer. Long live the Three in One.'

Seven nights feasting followed. No work was done, except the feeding of livestock, the length and breadth of Alba. The Maxwells grainhouses were flung wide and Royal Beeves and Venison and poultry and rabbit filled every belly to bursting point.

People still talk about it – will continue to talk – until I give them something else to talk about – which, if these pains in my back are athing to go by – won't be long now.

Great Godmother, that one was more like a sword-thrust. I maun lay down my quill now and put my mind, and my body, to more pressing matters. The tale is all told anyway, though so far we havenae actually lived happily every after. That only happens in faerie-stories.

Here comes another contraction.

Breathe. Breathe. Breathe through the wave of pain.

Where in the Mother's name is the damn bell? Ymerrrrr. Breathe, breathe.

Where is everybody? Shit. Here I am, the Redeemer, and I could die here and no-body to attend me.

Breathe, breathe.

Steady. Nobody's going to die. It's the contraction that's dying. Good.

Come on now. Get a grip of yourself. Women have been doing this since time began. Maybe if I get down on my hands and knees it'll be easier?

Her comes another one. My sacrificial aunt. I take it all back about the kick in the balls. It was naething compared wi this. This is tearing me apart. Damnation, now the waters have burst. I've soaked my best lying-in gown. What a mess.

Is everybody deaf in this damn place? If I scream any louder I'll bring the house down. McCloed. Where are you? McCloed you sonofabitch. You did this to me.

Mother protect me. This isnae what I anticipated.

It's so . . . undignified.

And it HURTSSSSS.

When I recover I must set Morangy to inventing something to ease this pain.

Morangyyyyyy.